thinks, but she's compassionate and thoughtful. . . . In a lot of ways, the most interesting female protagonist I've read in a long time."

—*That's Normal*

"Once again Christina Lauren have created a book boyfriend that will probably end up on every blogger's top ten."

—*The Sub Club*

"[A] smoking-hot story. I particularly appreciated . . . the modern tone. It felt *of the moment*."

—*Dear Author*

The Beautiful Bastard series

"Hot . . . if you like your hookups early and plentiful. . . ."

—*EW* on *Beautiful Stranger*

"A devilishly depraved cross between a hardcore porn and a very special episode of *The Office*."

—*Perez Hilton* on *Beautiful Bastard*

"A beautiful read, an astonishing love story, a couple whose journey I understood and felt from beginning to end—this is a book I would recommend with all my heart."

—*Natasha Is a Book Junkie* on *Beautiful Secret*

"This book, like the others in this series, sucked me in right away, and I couldn't get enough."

—*The Autumn Review* on *Beautiful Player*

"The perfect blend of sex, sass, and heart, *Beautiful Bastard* is a steamy battle of wills that will get your blood pumping!"

—S. C. Stephens, #1 *New York Times* bestselling author of *Thoughtless*

Books by CHRISTINA LAUREN

WILD SEASONS

Sweet Filthy Boy

Dirty Rowdy Thing

Dark Wild Night

Wicked Sexy Liar

THE BEAUTIFUL SERIES

Beautiful Bastard

Beautiful Stranger

Beautiful Bitch

Beautiful Bombshell

Beautiful Player

Beautiful Beginning

Beautiful Beloved

Beautiful Secret

Praise for *New York Times* and #1 international bestselling author Christina Lauren

"Full of expertly drawn characters who will grab your heart and never let go, humor that will have you howling, and off-the-charts, toe-curling chemistry, *Dark Wild Night* is absolutely unforgettable. This is contemporary romance at its best! Beautifully written and remarkably compelling—it reminded me why Christina Lauren's books have a place of honor on my bookshelf."

—Sarah J. Maas

Sweet FILTHY BOY
THE *ROMANTIC TIMES* 2014 BOOK OF THE YEAR

"A sexy, sweet treasure of a story. I loved every word."

—Sylvia Day, #1 *New York Times* bestselling author of the Crossfire series

"A crazy, hilarious, and surprisingly realistic and touching adventure. . . . One of the freshest, funniest, and most emotionally authentic erotic romances."

—*Romantic Times Book Reviews*

"No one is doing hot contemporary romance like Christina Lauren. *Sweet Filthy Boy* is beyond swoon-worthy."

—*Bookalicious*

"Funny and adorably charming. . . . Tender, hot, and even heartbreaking at times, but so worth it."

—*Heroes and Heartbreakers*

"Had my heart pounding from cover to cover. . . . A must-read!"

—Fangirlish

"A deliciously filthy romp that you're going to love!"

—*Martini Times Romance*

"*Sweet Filthy Boy* has everything necessary for a great romance read. Love, passion, heat, turmoil, and humor are all perfectly combined. Add in the stellar writing and there is nothing more I could ask for."

—*Bookish Temptations*

"Christina Lauren are my go-to gals for when I'm in the mood for a laugh-out-loud, sizzling, sexy romance."

—*Flirty and Dirty Book Blog*

 **ROWDY THING**

"Lauren has mastered writing delectable heroes and strong-willed heroines to match, and the contrast between rough-edged Finn and polished Harlow makes for a passionate romance."

—*Romantic Times Book Reviews*

"Most of the time when I read contemporary romance, I find myself suffering the lead girl for the sake of the story. Maybe I just don't identify with her, or I can't imagine myself being friends with her. With Harlow, I don't find myself just wanting to know her, I want to *be* her. She's not afraid to say what she

Dark WILD NIGHT

BOOK THREE OF WILD SEASONS

CHRISTINA LAUREN

G
GALLERY BOOKS
NEW YORK   LONDON   TORONTO   SYDNEY   NEW DELHI

G

Gallery Books
An Imprint of Simon & Schuster, Inc.
1230 Avenue of the Americas
New York, NY 10020

First Gallery Books trade paperback edition September 2015

GALLERY BOOKS and colophon are registered trademarks of Simon & Schuster, Inc.

For information about special discounts for bulk purchases, please contact Simon & Schuster Special Sales at 1-866-506-1949 or business@simonandschuster.com.

The Simon & Schuster Speakers Bureau can bring authors to your live event. For more information or to book an event, contact the Simon & Schuster Speakers Bureau at 1-866-248-3049 or visit our website at www.simonspeakers.com.

Cover photograph by © Stefano Cavoretto/Shutterstock

Razor Fish logo design by Heather Carrier

Manufactured in the United States of America

10 9 8 7 6 5

Library of Congress Cataloging-in-Publication Data is on file.

ISBN 978-1-4767-7794-8
ISBN 978-1-4767-7795-5 (ebook)

For Eddie, our Superman

Chapter ONE

Lola

I MENTALLY DRAW THE panels of the scene before me as we follow the receptionist down the marble hallway: *the woman wears six-inch black heels, her legs go on forever, her hips shift with each step.*

Her hips shift left.

Her hips shift right.

Her hips shift left.

My agent, Benny, leans in. "Don't be nervous," he whispers.

"I'm fine," I lie, but he just snorts in response, straightening.

"The deal is all drafted, Lola. You're here to *sign*, not to impress anyone. Smile! Today is the fun part."

I nod, trying to trick my thoughts into agreement—*Look at this office! Look at these people! Bright lights! Big city!*—but it's a wasted effort. I've been writing and drawing *Razor Fish* since I was twelve, and every single second of the fun part, to me, has been creating it. The *terrifying* part is walking down a sterile hallway lined with glass-front cubicles and glossy framed movie posters to sign a seven-figure contract for the film translation.

My stomach seems lodged somewhere in my windpipe and I go back to my safe place.

Her hips shift right.

Her hips shift left.

Her long legs span from the earth up to the clouds.

The receptionist stops at a door and opens it. "Here we are."

The studio offices are almost obscenely fancy; the entire building feels like the modern equivalent of a castle. Every wall is brushed aluminum and marble; every door is glass. Each piece of furniture is either marble or black leather. Benny leads us in with confidence, crossing the room to shake hands with the executives on the other side of the table. I follow him in, but when I release the glass door it swings closed heavily, and the jarring *gong* of glass abruptly meeting metal echoes through the room—a sound broken only by two startled gasps coming from across the table.

Fuck.

I've seen enough photos of myself in stressful public situations in the past three months to know that, right now, I don't *look* ruffled. I don't duck my head and apologize; I don't slouch or wince even though, as soon as the door slams dissonantly shut, I'm tied into a hundred thousand knots inside. Apparently, I'm just good at hiding it.

The *New York Times* gave *Razor Fish* a brilliant review, but found me "aloof" during an interview that I'd believed to be spirited and engaging. The *Los Angeles Times* described our phone call as "a series of long, thoughtful pauses followed by single-word answers" whereas I had told my friend Oliver that I was worried I'd talked their ear off.

When I turn to face the executives, I'm unsurprised to find they both look as polished as the architecture. Neither woman across the table says anything about my less-than-subtle entrance, but I swear the slamming echo reverberates throughout the room the entire time I walk from the door to the table.

Benny winks and gestures for me to sit down. I find a soft leather chair, smooth my dress over my thighs, and carefully take a seat.

My hands are clammy, my heart thundering. I'm counting to twenty over and over to keep from panicking.

The panel shows the girl, chin up, with a ball of fire in her lungs.

"Lorelei, it's wonderful to meet you face-to-face."

I look to the woman who's spoken and take her offered hand to shake. Her hair is blond and glossy, perfect makeup, perfect clothes, perfectly expressionless. From my early-morning creeping on IMDb, I'm fairly sure she's Angela Marshall, the executive producer who, with her frequent collaborator Austin Adams, fought to win the rights to *Razor Fish* in the bidding war I didn't even know was happening last week.

But her hair in the picture was red. My eyes shoot to the woman on her left, but she has soft brown skin, black hair, and enormous brown eyes. Definitely not Angela Marshall. The only person I've seen frequently in magazines and photos is Austin, but there isn't another man besides Benny in the room.

"Please, call me Lola. It's nice to meet you . . . ?" I let the question hang, because in normal situations I think this is where the names are exchanged. Instead, the handshake goes on forever, and now I don't know where to direct my effusive gratitude. Why isn't anyone introducing themselves? Am I expected to know every name here?

Releasing my hand, the woman finally says, "Angela Marshall."

I sense that it was some sort of test.

"So good to meet you," I say again. "I can't believe . . ."

My thought ends there and they all watch me, waiting to hear what I'm going to say. Truthfully, I could go on for days about all the things I can't believe.

I can't believe *Razor Fish* is out in the world.

I can't believe people are buying it.

And I *really* can't believe fancy people working at this enormous movie studio are making my graphic novel into a movie.

"We can't believe any of it." Benny comes to my rescue, but laughs awkwardly. "We're just thrilled about how this all went down. *Thrilled.*"

The woman next to Angela gives him the *Oh, I'm sure you are* face, because we all know Benny made out pretty great in the deal: twenty percent of a lot of money. But that realization pulls the other one with it: I made out even better than he did. My life is forever changed with this single transaction.

We're here to sign a contract, to discuss casting, to lay out the schedule.

The panel shows the girl, waking up with a start as a steel rod is shoved into her backbone.

I hold my hand out to the other woman. "Hi, sorry I didn't get your name. I'm Lola Castle."

She introduces herself as Roya Lajani, and then looks down at some pages in front of her as she takes a breath to start whatever conversation happens in these moments. But before she can speak, the door swings open and the man I recognize as Austin Adams breezes in, letting in a blast of ringing phones, heels clicking down the hall, and voices booming from adjacent rooms.

"Lola!" he says to me in a warm, cheerful voice and then winces as the door crashes shut behind him. Looking to Angela, he says, "I hate that fucking door. When the hell is Julie getting it fixed?"

Angela waves her hand in a *Don't worry about it* gesture and watches as Austin ignores the seat next to her and pulls out the chair on my right. Sitting down, he studies my face, smiling widely at me.

"I'm a huge fan," he says without further preamble, without even introducing himself. "Honestly. I'm just in awe of you."

"I . . . wow," I say, laughing awkwardly. "Thanks."

"Please tell me you're working on something new. I'm addicted to your art, your stories, everything."

"My next graphic novel is out this fall. It's called

Junebug." I sense Austin leaning in excitedly and instinctively add, "I'm still working on it." When I look back up at him, he's just shaking his head at me in wonder.

"Is this surreal?" His eyes turn up warmly as his smile softens. "Has it sunk in yet that you're the mastermind behind the next huge action movie?"

This line, in this situation—where I worry I'm going to hear a lot of empty praise—would normally make me hold my breath in order to tamp down a skeptical reaction, but despite being a big-shot producer and director, Austin already seems so *genuine.* He's good-looking but totally disheveled: his reddish blond hair looks finger combed, he's unshaven, in jeans and wearing a button-down shirt that he's misaligned, leaving it longer at the hem on the right side than the left. The starched collar is tucked in on one side, too. He's a very expensive mess.

"Thanks," I say, balling my hands together so I don't start to fidget with my earlobe or my hair.

"I mean it," he adds, leaning both elbows on his thighs, still focusing only on me. I'm not sure he's even acknowledged Benny yet. My knuckles have gone white. "I know we're supposed to say that, but in this case it's *really* true. I was obsessed from the very first page, and told Angela and Roya we had to have it."

"We agreed," Roya chimes in, unnecessarily.

"Well," I say, struggling to find something other to say than another thank you. "That's great. I'm glad that it seems to have grabbed a little audience."

"Little?" he scoffs, leaning back in his chair and glancing down at his shirt before doing a double take. "Motherfuck. I can't even dress myself."

I pull my lower lip into my mouth to crush the laugh that is threatening to burst from my throat. This entire situation was sending me into mute-panic territory until he walked in. I grew up shopping at Goodwill, we were on food stamps for a few years, and I still drive a 1989 Chevy. I can't even process how this is going to change my life, and the sterile Stepford Sisters across the table only add to the foreign atmosphere of the room. But Austin seems like someone I can imagine working with.

"I know you've been asked this before," he says, "because I've read the interviews. But I want to hear it from you, the true inside scoop. What made you start writing this book? What *really* inspired you?"

I have indeed been asked this before—so many times, in fact, that I have a standard, canned answer: *I love the everyday female superhero because she gives us an opportunity to handle complicated social and political imbalances head-on, in popular culture and art. I wrote Quinn Stone as the everygirl, in the spirit of Clarisse Starling or Sarah Connor: she becomes a hero via her own bootstraps. Quinn is found by a strange, fish-like man from another time dimension. This creature, Razor, helps Quinn find the courage to fight for herself and her community, and in so doing, he realizes he doesn't want to leave her to go home, even when he eventually can. The idea came to me from a dream where a big, muscular man covered in scales was in my room, telling me to clean up my closet. The rest of the day I won-*

*dered what it would be like if he really did show up in my bed-
room. I named him Razor Fish. I imagined my Razor wouldn't
give a crap about my messy closet; he'd tell me to get the hell up
and fight for something.*

But that isn't the answer that bubbles up today.

"I was pissed-off," I admit. "I thought grown-ups were
either assholes or fuckups." I watch Austin's green eyes go a
little wide before he exhales, nodding subtly in understanding. "I was angry with my dad for being a mess, and my mom
for being such a coward. I'm sure it's why I dreamt of Razor
Fish in the first place: he's abrasive and doesn't always understand Quinn, but deep down he loves her and wants her to be
looked after. Drawing him and how he initially doesn't understand her humanity but then trains her to fight, and eventually
defers to her . . . getting lost in their little story was the treat
I gave myself when I finished dishes and homework and was
alone at night."

The room is quiet and I feel an unfamiliar need to fill
the space. "I liked seeing Razor start to appreciate the ways
Quinn is strong that aren't classic. She's scrawny, she's quiet.
She's not built like an amazon. Her strengths are more subtle:
she's observant. She trusts herself without question. I want to
make sure that's captured. There is a lot of violence and action
there, but Razor doesn't have a revelation about her when she
learns to throw a punch. He has a revelation about her when
she figures out how to stand up to him."

I glance at Benny—this is the most open I've ever been
about my life and my book, and surprise is clear on his face.

"How old were you when your mom left?" Austin guesses. He's acting like there isn't anyone else in the room with us, and it's easy to pretend there isn't, the way everyone has grown so still.

"Twelve. Right after my dad got back from Afghanistan."

The room seems to be swallowed by silence after I say this, and Austin finally heaves out a sigh. "Well, that's *shit*."

Finally, I laugh.

He leans in again, eyes insistent when he says, "I *love* this story, Lola. I love these characters. We've got a screenwriter who will knock this out of the park. Do you know Langdon McAfee?"

I shake my head, embarrassed because the way he says it makes me feel like I should, but Austin waves away the question. "He's great. Laid-back, smart, organized. He wants to cowrite this with you."

I open my mouth at this unexpected revelation—*me*, cowriting a *screenplay*—and nothing but a choking noise comes out.

Austin keeps talking through my stunned reaction: "I want to talk a lot, okay?" He's already nodding as if prompting me. "I want this to be everything you want it to be." Leaning in, he smiles and says, "I want you to see your dream come to life."

"TELL ME THE details again," Oliver says. "I'm not sure you were speaking English the first time."

He's right. I've barely caught my breath—let alone remembered how to make words—since I tripped into his comic book store, Downtown Graffick, already babbling. Oliver looked up when I burst in, his sweet smile slowly dissolving into confusion as I spilled a thousand incoherent words and my emotions all over the floor. I spent two hours on the drive back from L.A. on the phone with my dad, struggling to process the rest of the meeting. Not that it really helped because, here, saying it out loud in front of one of my favorite people makes it surreal all over again.

In the eight months we've been friends, I don't think Oliver has ever seen me like this: stuttering and breathless and near tears because I'm so overwhelmed. I pride myself on being steady and unruffled even with my friends, and so I'm trying to get myself together, but goddamn, it is *hard*.

They're

> *making*

> > *a movie*

> > > *out of my childhood ideas.*

"Okay," I start again, taking a huge breath and blowing it out slowly. "Last week, Benny called and said something was going on with the film option."

"I thought he sent it out—"

"Months ago," I interrupt. "Right. It's always silence before the explosion, I guess? Because on the drive from his office to their office this morning, he told me it sold in this insane bidding war. . . ." I press my palm to my forehead. "I'm sweating. Look at me, I'm sweating."

He does look, eyes softening as he laughs, then shakes his head a little before he blinks back down at the box he's cutting open. "This is unbelievable, Lola. Keep talking."

"Columbia and Touchstone won," I tell him. "We drove to the offices and I met some people today."

"And?" He looks back up at me as he pulls a stack of books out of the box. "Did they impress?"

"I mean . . ." I flounder, remembering how it felt when Austin turned his attention to everyone else in the room, and the meeting dissolved into a blur of acronyms and under-the-breath instructions to *make note of Langdon's schedule for the script kickoff* and *see if we can get the P&L to Mitchell by noon.* "Yes? There were a couple people there who were sort of quiet and stiff, but the executive producer—Austin Adams—is so genuinely nice. I was so overwhelmed that I don't know how much I was processing." I run both hands into my hair and tilt my head up to the ceiling. "This is all so insane. A *movie.*"

"A movie," Oliver repeats, and when I look back at him, I see him watching me with his mysterious, warm blue eyes.

He licks his lips and I have to look away. Oliver is both my former husband and my current crush, but it will forever remain unrequited: our marriage was never really a marriage. It was that-thing-we-did-in-Vegas.

Of course, the other two couples who hooked up in Vegas—our friends Mia and Ansel, and Harlow and Finn—are happily married. But Oliver and I occasionally (especially when drunk) like to commend ourselves for being the only ones who did the shotgun Vegas wedding thing like normal people: with nothing but regret, an annulment, and a hangover. Given the emotional distance he's always kept, I'm pretty sure he's the one out of the two of us who really means it when he praises our choice.

"And it isn't just oh, we like the idea, let's buy this option and sit on it," I say. "They bought it and already have a director in mind. We talked about possible *casting choices* today. They have a big effects guy asking to be involved."

"Unreal," he murmurs, leaning forward to give me his undivided attention. And if I didn't know Oliver better, I would think he just glanced at my mouth. But I do know him better: he just looks at every part of my face when I'm speaking. He is the *best* listener.

"*And* . . . I'm going to cowrite the script," I tell him, a little breathless, and his eyes widen.

"Lola. Lola, holy *hell.*"

While I launch into a replay of the entire meeting this morning, Oliver goes back to unpacking the newest shipment of comics, looking up at me occasionally wearing his absorbed, little smile. I thought that over time I might figure out what he's thinking, how he's reacting to something. But he's still largely unreadable to me. The loft apartment I share with my friend London is only two blocks away from Oliver's comic store, and even though I see him nearly every day, I still feel like I spend half the time we're together trying to work through what he might have meant by this or that single-syllable answer or lingering smile. If I were more like Harlow, I would simply *ask*.

"So you're looking forward to seeing it on the screen?" he asks. "We haven't talked about this because it all happened so fast. I know some artists aren't wild about the idea of an adaptation."

"Are you kidding?" I ask. How can he be serious with that question? The only thing I love more than comics is movies based on comics. "It's overwhelming but amazing."

And then I remember that there is an email with seventeen scripts attached in my inbox, for me to read "as reference," and a wave of nausea sweeps through my torso. "It's a little like building a house, though," I tell him. "I just want to be at the part where I can go live in it, and skip all the parts where I have to pick out fixtures and knobs."

"Let's just hope they don't George Clooney your Batman," he says.

I give him my best eyebrow wiggle. "They can George Clooney anything of mine they want, sir."

Not-Joe, Oliver's sole employee and a mohawked stoner we all feel a certain pet-owner level of fondness for, steps into view from behind some shelves. "Clooney is gay. You know that, right?"

Oliver and I both ignore this.

"In fact," I add, "if *George Clooney* is ever accepted into the *Oxford English Dictionary* as a verb, that activity is immediately getting added to my bucket list."

"As in, 'Have you ever been George Clooneyed?'" Oliver asks.

"Exactly. 'We went for a walk, and then George Clooneyed until around two. Good night.'"

Oliver nods, putting some pens away in a drawer. "I'd probably have to add that to my bucket list, too."

"See, this is why we're friends," I tell him. Being near him is like a dose of Xanax. I can't help but be calmed. "You would get that *George Clooney* as a verb would be such a monumental thing that, gay or straight, you'd want a piece of it."

"He's totally gay," Not-Joe says, louder this time.

Oliver makes a skeptical noise, finally looking over at him. "I don't reckon he is, though. He got married."

"Really?" Not-Joe asks, coming to rest his elbows on the counter. "But if he was, would you do him?"

I raise my hand. "Yes. Absolutely."

"I wasn't asking you," Not-Joe says, waving me away.

"Who's the front and who's the back?" Oliver asks. "Like, am I getting George Clooneyed by George Clooney, or am I doing the Clooneying?"

"Oliver," Not-Joe says. "He's George *Fucking* Clooney. He doesn't *get* Clooneyed!"

"We're turning into idiots," I mumble.

They both ignore me and Oliver finally shrugs. "Yeah, okay. Why not?"

"Like, actually losing IQ points," I interject again.

Not-Joe pretends to grab a pair of hips and thrusts back and forth. "This. You'd let him?"

Shrugging defensively, Oliver says, "Joe, I get what we're talking about here. I also get what the man-on-man sex would look like. What I'm saying is if I'm going to be with a guy, why not Bad Batman?"

I wave a hand in front of his face. "We should get back to the part where my comic is going to be a movie, though."

Oliver turns to me and relaxes and his smile is so sweet, it makes everything inside me melt. "We absolutely should. That's bloody brilliant, Lola." He tilts his head, his blue eyes holding mine. "I'm really fucking proud for you right now."

I smile, and then suck my bottom lip into my mouth because when Oliver looks at me like that, I can't even be a little cool. But it would terrify him to see me swoon over him; it's just not what we do.

"So how are you going to celebrate?" he asks.

I look around the store as if the answer is right in front of me. "Hang out here? I don't know. Maybe I should do some work."

"Nah, you've been traveling constantly, and even when you are home, you're always working," he says.

Snorting, I tell him, "Says the guy who is in his store every waking hour."

Oliver considers me. "They're making your *movie*, Lola Love." *And the nickname makes my heart spin in my chest.* "You need to do something big tonight."

"So, like, Fred's?" I say. This is our usual routine. "Why pretend we're fancy?"

Oliver shakes his head. "Let's go somewhere downtown so you don't have to worry about driving."

"But then *you* have to drive back to Pacific Beach," I argue.

Not-Joe pretends to play the violin behind us.

"I don't mind," Oliver says. "I don't think Finn and Ansel are around, but I'll round up the girls." He scratches his stubbly jaw. "I do wish I could take you to dinner or something, but I—"

"Oh, God, don't worry." The idea of Oliver leaving his store to take me out to dinner makes me both giddy and totally panicky. It's not like the building would catch fire if he left here before dark, but it doesn't mean my body doesn't feel that instinctive panic. "I'll just head home and freak out alone in my room for a bit, and then get exceedingly drunk later."

His smile melts me. "Sounds good."

"I thought you had a date tonight," Not-Joe says to Oliver, coming up behind him with a giant stack of books.

Oliver blanches. "No. It wasn't—I mean, it's not. We aren't."

"A date?" I feel my eyebrows inch up as I try to ignore the growing knot in my stomach.

"No, it's not like that," he insists. "Just the chick across the street who works—"

"Hard Rock Allison," Not-Joe sings.

My heart drops—this isn't "just the chick across the street" but someone we've all remarked upon once or twice for her keen interest in Oliver—but I work to give an out-wardly positive reaction.

"Shut up!" I yell, smacking Oliver's shoulder, and adding in a dramatic French accent, "A *very* hot date."

Oliver growls at me, rubbing the spot and pretending it hurt more than it did. He nods to Not-Joe. "She wanted to bring us *both* dinner, here in the store—"

"Yeah, so she could bang you," Not-Joe cuts in.

"Or maybe because she's *nice,*" Oliver says, a playful challenge in his voice. "Anyway, I'd rather go out and celebrate Lola's movie. I'll text Allison and let her know."

I'm sure Hard Rock Allison is a nice woman, but right now—knowing Oliver has her cell number, knowing he can just casually text her to change some plans they made—I sort of want her to get hit by a train in the blackened-soul way that you want horrible things to happen to the new girlfriend. Allison is pretty, and outgoing, and so tiny she could fit in my messenger bag. This is the first time I've been faced with the prospect of Oliver dating, the first time our friendship has been faced with this, at least as far as I know. We got married and divorced in less than a day and it's clear he was never really into me, but we've never discussed dates with other people before.

How should I react here?

Cool, I decide after checking myself. *Happy for him.*

"Definitely reschedule," I say, giving him the most genuine smile I can manage. "She's cute. Take her to Bali Hai, it's so pretty there."

He looks up at me. "I've been meaning to go there for ages; you love that place. You should come along."

"Oliver, you can't bring me along on a *date*."

His eyes go wide behind his glasses. "It's not. I don't—I *wouldn't*," he says, adding quickly, "Lola. It wouldn't be a bloody *date*."

Okay, so he's clearly not into Allison. The knot in my stomach uncoils, and I have to stare at the countertop with mighty concentration to keep from smiling.

After a few deep breaths, I succeed.

I look back up at him and he's still watching me, expression as calm as the surface of a lake in a canyon.

What are you thinking? I want to ask.

But definitely don't.

"Lola," he starts.

I swallow, unable to keep from blinking—for just a second—down to his mouth. I *love* his mouth. It's wide; his bottom lip and top lip are the same size. Full, but not feminine. I've drawn it a hundred times: with lips barely parted, lips pressed closed. With lips curved in his tiny smile or arced in his thoughtful frown. Lips with teeth sharply sawing across or, once, his mouth soft and open in an obscene gasp.

The count of two is all I get before I look back up at his eyes. "Yeah?"

It's a year before he answers and by the time he does, I've gone through a million possibilities for what he'll say next.

Have you ever thought about kissing me?

Reckon we could go shag in the back room?

Would you ever cosplay Zatanna?

But he simply asks, "What did Harlow say when you told her about the movie?"

I take a deep breath, shutting down the image of him leaning forward and putting his mouth right up against mine. "Oh, I was going to call her next."

And then what I've just said sinks in.

Oliver's eyebrows go to his hairline, and beside him, Not-Joe makes a high-pitched noise of panic that tells me either the cops are at the door or we're all going to be murdered by Harlow and it's my fault.

"Oh, *shiiiiiit*, why did I do that?" I ask, covering my mouth. Harlow is always the one I tell after Dad. She would kill me if she knew I came here. "What was I thinking telling you first?" I take a step closer and give them both my most threatening face. "You *cannot* tell her you knew before she did and that I've been here for—"

"A half an hour," Not-Joe interrupts helpfully.

"A half hour!" I cry. "She will cut us into tiny pieces and bury us in the desert!"

"Call her right the fuck now, then," Oliver says, pointing a finger at me. "I am not prepared to face Harlow with an ax."

Chapter TWO

"*W*HEN DID *YOU* know, Oliver?"

I look up across the table and grin. "Know what, Harlow?"

"Don't be cute." She glances to the side to make sure Lola is still at the bar. "When did you know that the movie was optioned *and* green-lit in one swoop?"

She looks back and forth between Joe and me, waiting, but Joe bends to take an enormous bite of his burger, leaving me to answer.

"Today," I hedge. It's a bullshit answer because even Lola only found out this morning. Harlow wants me to report down to the hour.

Harlow narrows her eyes at me but tucks her smart reply away when Lola returns, carrying a tray of shots. She glances over at me and gives me her secret little grin. I'm not even sure she knows she does it. It starts with her lips turning up at the corners, eyes turning down just slightly, and then she blinks slowly, like she's just captured me in a photograph. And if she had, the image would show a man who is deeply, bloody lovesick.

There's a scene in *Amazing Spider-Man* 25, when Mary Jane Watson is first introduced. Her face is obscured from both the reader and Peter Parker, and up until this point, Peter has only known her as the girl his aunt wants him to ask out on a date, "that nice Watson girl next door."

Peter isn't interested. If his aunt likes her, Mary Jane is *not* his type.

Then in issue 42 her face is revealed and Peter realizes just how amazing she is. It's a gut-punch moment: Peter's been an idiot.

This is as good an analogy as any to describe my relationship with Lorelei Castle. I was married to Lola for exactly thirteen and a half hours, and if I were a smarter man, maybe I would have taken the chance while I had it, instead of assuming—just because she was wearing a short dress and getting drunk in Vegas—that she wasn't my type.

But a few hours later, we were *all* drunk . . . and impulsively all married. While our friends defiled hotel rooms—and each other—Lola and I walked for miles, talking about everything.

It's easy to share confidences with strangers, and even easier when drunk, so by the middle of the night I felt quite intimate with her. Somewhere the Strip turned dark, hinting at the seedy underbelly the city has to offer, and Lola stopped to look up at me. The tiny diamond Marilyn piercing in her lip caught the light, and I grew mesmerized by the soft pink of her mouth, long since rubbed free of lipstick. I'd lost my buzz, was already thinking about how we'd deal with the annulments the next day, and she quietly asked if I wanted to get a room somewhere. Together.

But . . . I didn't. I didn't, because by the time she made it an option, I knew she wasn't one-night-stand material. Lola was the kind of girl I could lose my mind for.

Only, as soon as she returned to San Diego her life exploded in a hurricane. First, her graphic novel *Razor Fish* was published and quickly stampeded onto every top-ten list on the comic scene. And then it went mainstream, showing up in major retailers, with the *New York Times* calling it "the next major action franchise." The rights to her book have just sold to a major motion picture studio, and today she met the executives putting millions into the project.

I'm not sure she even has a millisecond of time to think about romance, but it's fine; I think about it enough for the both of us.

"I don't know who started the tradition that the birthday girl cuts her own cake," Lola says, sliding a shot glass of questionably green alcohol in front of me, "or this new version where the girl whose movie is being made buys the shots. But I'm not a fan."

"No," Mia objects, "it's that the girl who is about to run off to Hollywood buys the shots."

"As penance," Harlow says. "In advance."

Everyone turns to give their best skeptical look to Harlow. Compared to the rest of us, Harlow's entire existence is rooted in Hollywood. Raised by an actress mother and Oscar-winning cinematographer father, and married to a man who is about to be a break-out Adventure Channel star, I'm pretty sure we're all thinking the same thing: if Hollywood entrenchment determines who is footing the bill, Harlow should be buying the shots.

As if sensing this, she waves her hand saying, "Shut up. I'll buy the next round."

Everyone raises their shot glass to the middle, and Harlow delivers the toast: "To the baddest badass that ever lived: Lorelei Louise Castle. Go fucking conquer, girl."

"Hear, hear," I say, and Lola catches my eye, giving me her secret grin one more time.

We clink our glasses—Harlow, Mia, Joe, Lola, London, and I—and tilt back our shots before giving in to an oddly synchronized shudder.

Lola's roommate, London, gags. "Green chartreuse." She coughs, and her blond hair is piled in a messy bun on top of her head; it bobs precariously as she shakes her head. "Should be outlawed."

"It's God *awful*," I agree.

"I had the bartender make up something called Celebration," Lola says with a grimace, wiping her mouth with the back of her hand. "Sorry. I feel like I need a shower now."

Mia coughs. "That guy must equate celebration with pain." She steals my beer and takes a swig before turning back to Lola. I so rarely get to hang out with Mia without Ansel attached to some part of her; it's actually quite nice to get her alone and excited to socialize. She's sweetly delicate, in the way a little sister might be. "So let's hear it, Miss Fancy. Tell us about this morning."

Lola sighs, sipping her water before giving a wide-eyed, awestruck shrug. "Honestly, what is this life, you guys?"

I lean back against the booth and listen fondly as Lola recounts much of what I've already heard. In truth, I imagine I could hear it a hundred times and it would never really sink in; I can't imagine how it must feel for *her*.

Lola, who by her own admission spends more time talking to the people in her head than to the people all around her, is truly brilliant. As much as possible, I try to temper my reactions to her work, because I know in part it's carried by my affection for her. And anyway, it's not like I can blab on to her constantly about how the creator is a fucking genius, and one of the smartest, sexiest people I know. But I do emphasize however often I can to customers that the book itself is fresh and unlike anything I've ever read before, and yet it *feels* familiar.

Razor Fish makes me feel that same buzz I felt as a kid picking up my first comic from the local newsagent. I'd been obsessed with the strength, the battles, the power of a story told in words and color. At age eleven, I was the tallest, skinniest kid in Year Seven—our first year of high school—and aptly nicknamed Stickboy by the class bullies. Even when my mates caught up by Year Eleven, the name still stuck. But by then, I'd towered over the other boys for so long and had begun cycling everywhere. I wasn't skinny anymore—I was strong, and dominating in school sports. Stickboy was the name of a superhero, not a coward.

I look at Lola and marvel over how similar we are—lonely childhoods turning us into introverted yet ambitious adults—and how central comics have been to both our lives.

But while she's still floating on the cloud of her new venture, reeling about the surreal offices, laughing about the stiff beginning to the meeting and the explosion of Austin into the room, I need the edge rubbed off a bit, and pick up my beer, taking a sip. I need to file down my senses enough to let some of this process. Truly, Lola's life is about to change. What has up to this point been mostly a passion for her is quickly becoming a business—which will bring tensions and problems that I can relate to perhaps more than she realizes. Besides, Lola is wildly talented, but she's still sheltered: Hollywood can make dreams happen, but it can also be harsh and ruthless. I want to push back the uneasy reflex that wants to fuss a bit over her, that *worries,* that thinks this is going to break her or, at the very least, dull a brilliantly creative piece of her—the part that created all of this in the first place—and I'm not sure it's worth sacrificing for a slice of the life-dream real estate.

It makes me want to protect her, to tell her to listen to those voices inside her head, because to Lola those voices are more real to her than the majority of those in her life, and have been for much of her life since childhood. It was the same way with me. I grew up with no siblings, and absentee parents. My grandparents took custody of me when I was a kid, but I was eight and more interested in Superman and Batman than I was in what Gran had watched on tele that day or the people who came through my granddad's shop.

Just as she's getting to the end—to where the logistical details started to feel as though they were raining down, and it all became more blurry and jargon-filled—her phone lights up on the table and she glances down and then shoves back in the booth, eyes bolting to mine. "It's *Austin*."

That she looks to me right now—not Harlow, London, or Mia—makes my heart light up; a sparking flare thrown into the cavern of my chest.

"Answer it," I urge, nodding to the phone.

She fumbles, nearly knocking it off the table, before answering at the last minute with a rushed "Hello?"

I don't have the benefit of hearing the other side of the conversation so I'm not sure what makes her blush and smile before saying, "Hi, Austin. Sorry, no. I just almost didn't get to the phone on time."

She listens intently, and we all *stare* intently, getting only one side of the exchange: "I'm still a little shell-shocked," she tells him, "but I am okay . . ." She lifts her eyes to scan the table, saying, "Yes, out with some friends . . . just a neighborhood bar . . . in San Diego!" She laughs. "That's a crazy long drive, Austin!"

The fuck?

I look up at Harlow, who turns to me at the same time, seems to be thinking the same thing. He's not driving down here, is he? I glance at my watch; it's nearly ten, and would take two hours.

"I'm excited, too," she's saying, and reaches up to play with her earring. "Well, I've never written a script before so my goal here is just to be useful. . . ." She giggles at his reply.

Giggles.

My eyes snap to Harlow's again.

Lola giggles with *us*. She does not giggle with people she met only hours ago. Unless that person is me, in Vegas—and I fucking prefer to think that situation is unique.

"I can't wait to hear them . . . no I won't, opinions are good . . . I know, sorry. It's loud here. . . . Okay, I will." She nods. "I will! I promise!" Another fucking giggle. "Okay . . . Okay. Bye."

She hits end on the call and exhales, before sliding her eyes up to me. "That was Austin."

I laugh, saying, "So I heard." Even with an awkward, foreign object suddenly lodged in my chest I can appreciate how exciting this must be, to be so immediately comfortable with the person at the helm of the most important creative work in her life so far.

"He's not driving down from L.A., is he?" London asks with—if I'm not mistaken—a hint of suspicion in her voice.

I have always liked London.

"No, no," Lola says, grinning down at the table. "He just joked about it."

For a few moments we all just sit there, staring at her.

Harlow is the first to break. "Well, why the fuck *did* he call?"

Lola looks up, surprised. "Oh. Um, he just wanted to

know that I was okay after the meeting . . . and that he was putting together some thoughts on translating the first bit into a film."

" 'The first bit'?" I repeat.

She shakes her head in a staccato, overwhelmed gesture and a strand of her long, straight hair catches against her lipstick. I can't help it; I reach forward to pull it away. But she does, too, and her fingers get there before mine.

I quickly drop my hand and feel the way Harlow turns to me, but I can't look away from Lola, who is staring up at me, eyes full of silent frenzy.

"Holy shit, Oliver."

Beside us, London picks up her phone. "I'm going to google this Austin Adams character."

I've always *really* liked her.

" 'The first bit'?" I repeat to Lola, more gently.

"He was saying the studio sees *three* films," she practically squeaks. "And he has some ideas he wants to talk to me about."

Harlow swears, Mia squeals, Joe grins widely at her, but Lola covers her face with a tiny shriek of panic.

"Holy shit!" London yells. "This guy is *hot*!" She turns her phone out for us to see.

Okay, maybe I don't like London as much as I thought I did.

Ignoring her, I remind Lola, "This is good," as I gently coax her arms down. Unable to help it, I add, "He wants to talk to you about it now? Do you have to go to L.A. again tomorrow?"

She shakes her head. "I think by phone at some point?

I mean, I can barely imagine cowriting one script, let alone three," she says, and then presses her fingertips to her lips.

"Collaboration is what this one is all about," I remind her. "Isn't that what Austin told you earlier today?" Seeing her grow more worried helps me keep my own trepidation at bay. "Maybe in the second and third films you can drive even more of the process, but this is great, right?"

She nods urgently, soaking up my confidence, but then her shoulders slump and she gives a small, self-deprecating laugh. "I don't know how to do this."

I feel her hand come over mine, shaking and clammy.

"This requires more alcohol!" Harlow says, triumphantly unfazed, and in my peripheral vision I see her getting up for more shots.

Joe reaches over, rubbing the back of Lola's neck. "Lola, you're a star in the middle of a pile of gravel. You're going to reign."

I nod, agreeing with him. "You've got this. No one knows this story better than you. You're there to guide it. They are the experts on the film side."

She exhales, forming her soft lips into a sweet O and holding on to my gaze like it's keeping her from melting down. Does she know how I want to be her courage?

"Okay," she says, repeating, "Okay."

EVENTUALLY WE MANAGE to polish off five shots each and have moved on from the insanity of Lola's day to a raucous debate over how the world is going to end. As usual, we have Joe to thank for it, but Lola is rosy and dissolving into her adorable snickery giggles with every impassioned suggestion—zombies, electromagnetic pulse, alien invasions—and at least seems completely, *happily* distracted.

"I'm telling you, it's going to be the fucking livestock," Joe tells us, barely missing Harlow's wineglass when he sweeps his hand in a total-destruction gesture. "Some sort of cow or swine flu. Maybe some bird thing."

"Rabies," Mia says, nodding in drunken slowness.

"No, not *rabies*," he says, shaking his head. "Something we don't even know yet."

"You're a ray of sunshine." London pokes him in the shoulder and he turns to look at her.

"It's a matter of fact," he says. "Fucking chickens are going to be our ruination."

Lola finger-shoots herself in the head and pretends to collapse onto me, convulsing in fake death. Her hair sweeps across my arm, my skin bare beyond the short sleeve of my T-shirt, and for the first time I don't fight the urge to touch it. I cup my hand over her scalp and slide it down, dragging my fingers through her hair.

She tilts her head and looks up at me. "Oliver *must* be drunk," she announces in a slur, though it seems I'm the only one who hears her.

"Why's that?" I ask. My smile down at her is a subconscious thing; instinct in response to her proximity.

"Because you're touching me," she says a little more quietly.

I lean back a little to see her face better. "I touch you plenty."

She shakes her head and it's slow and lolling against my arm, finally thumping back against the booth. "Like a buddy. That was like a lover."

My blood turns to mercury. If only she knew. "Was it?"

"Mm-hmm." She looks tired, eyelids heavily demanding rest.

"Sorry then, Lola Love," I say, brushing her bangs to the side of her forehead.

She shakes her head dramatically, one side completely to the other. "Don't be. You're my hero."

I laugh, but she sits up in a surprising burst of movement and says, "I'm serious. What would I do without you right now?" She points to Harlow. "*She's* married." She points to Mia. "*She's* married, too."

Apparently having tuned in, London leans forward. "*I'm* not married."

"No," Lola says, giving her an enormous, drunken grin. "But you're always surfing. Or bartending. Or busy rejecting men."

Joe nods, and London slaps his chest playfully.

"So, Oliver is my hero," she says, turning back to me. "My rock. My sounding rod." Her eyebrows come together. "Lightning rod?"

"Sounding board," I whisper.

"Right." She snaps. *"That."* Lola lowers her voice and leans in close. So close my heart is a stuttering, wild thing in my throat. "Don't you ever leave me."

"I won't," I tell her. Fuck. I couldn't. I want to wrap her up and carry her around, protecting her from all of the insincere, greedy people she's destined to meet.

"Don't," she says, holding a weaving, threatening, drunken finger in my face.

I lean in, biting the tip, and her eyes go wide. "I *won't,"* I say around it, and fuck if I don't want to lean in farther and nip her lips, too.

Chapter THREE

Lola

I'M A ZOMBIE before coffee, especially after a night of shots and celebration and who knows what else. I don't even remember walking home from the bar, so I don't fully believe my eyes when I find Oliver asleep on my couch at 7 a.m.

He's sprawled awkwardly, so long and angled. One of his feet is flat on the floor; the other hangs over the end of the couch. His shirt rides up to his ribs, exposing a flat stomach cut down the middle with a dark line of hair. Limp-legged, arms askew, and with his neck at an angle that will be sore when he wakes . . .

He's really here, and he looks amazing.

It isn't the first time he's crashed at my place; the loft is only a few blocks from the store so we gave Oliver a key in case he ever needed to let one of us in, fix a leaky faucet, or make a quick sandwich on a break. In the eight months I've known him, he's slept here twice: One night he worked so late before the store's grand opening he could barely walk to our place, let alone drive home. He was gone before I was awake. Another night we'd gone out after the store closed, and had too many drinks for any of us to operate a moving vehicle. But that time, it had been the whole tangle of us, with random bodies crashing on any available soft surface.

London is already up and gone—surfing, most likely—and I've never had the joy of waking up and finding him here, alone. Admittedly, I'm being supercreepy, staring at him while he's still asleep—and I'll make every effort to feel bad about it later—but right now I just love seeing him first thing in the morning. Absolutely relish it.

I know it's only a matter of time before Oliver's stress about opening the store lessens and he can focus on other areas of his life . . . like dating. Like Hard Rock Allison. Heaven knows he has enough girls hanging out at the store hoping the hot owner will notice them. I don't like the idea, but I know eventually it's going to happen. The obliterating distraction of career has been true for me, too, and all of the travel recently has allowed me to keep my head in the sand about how much I genuinely like him. It's allowed me to be happy taking whatever I can get.

But in the past few weeks, even with things feeling more insane than ever, I've emerged from the fog. I've had to admit to myself that I want him. And last night we were more flirtatious than we've ever been. The memory trips a fluttery, anxious beat in my chest.

When we met in Vegas, he was good-looking and interesting and had the sexiest accent I'd ever heard, but I didn't *know* him. He didn't want me? No big deal. But spending time with him—nearly all of my free time, if I'm being honest—and having him be such a fixture in my life has made the minor gnaw of desire grow into this painful kind of ache. Now, I know him, but I don't know his heart. Not that way. And lately . . . I want to. I want to tell him, *Just give me a week. A week of you, and your lips and your laugh in my bed. Just one week and then I think I'll be okay.*

It's a lie, of course. Even having never kissed him—beyond the quick, soft kiss at our sham-of-a-wedding—I know I would be worse off if I had him for a week and then lost him. My heart would be warped afterward, like a wool sweater loaned to a body too big and growing misshapen until it doesn't fit quite right anymore. Who knows, maybe I came to Oliver misshapen to begin with. But unlike every boyfriend I've had—a couple of weeks here, a month there—Oliver never seems to poke at the tender spots, needing to know every detail. Instead he's collected my details as they've been offered.

Maybe it's why he's still so close to me; I haven't yet had the chance to ruin it by clamming up exactly when intimacy is needed.

Our first night, while our best friends were breaking headboards in Vegas hotel rooms with their libidos, Oliver and I walked up and down the Strip talking about work. About writing and illustrating, about the portrayal of women in comics, about the books we were currently reading. We talked about *Razor Fish,* and about his store—vaguely; I didn't even know early on that he would be moving to San Diego.

It was so easy being with him, like a tiny taste of something delicious I want to keep eating until I explode. Somewhere at the tail end of the chaos on the Strip, I'd grown brave enough to stop him mid-step, and, with a tentative hand on his arm, turn him to face me.

"Our rooms are probably being used," I started, staring at his chin, before forcing my eyes to his.

He smiled, and it was the first time I realized how perfect his teeth are—white and even, with uniquely sharp canines that made him nearly wolfish—how smooth his lips are, how blue his eyes are behind his glasses. "Probably."

"But we could . . ." I trailed off, blinking to the side.

He waited, watching me, eyes never betraying that he knew exactly what I was going to say.

I looked back up at his face, finding my bravery: "We could get a room for the night, if you wanted. Together."

His expression remained exactly the same—Oliver's amazing poker face held that gentle smile, that nonjudgmental, soft gaze—and he very politely declined.

I was mortified, but eventually got over it, and we've never spoken about it since.

Later, when I discovered he'd moved here and we had these people in common, and this passion for comics in common, too, we saw each other all the time and the awkwardness of that rejection dissolved. In its place came sort of a perfect friendship. Oliver doesn't judge, he doesn't mock, he doesn't push. He doesn't mind my quiet moods, where all I want to do is bend over a scrap of paper and draw. He doesn't mind when I get worked up over something and babble for an entire hour. He's honest in this completely easy way when I show him new story ideas. He plays weird music for me and makes me sit and listen because, even if I hate it, he wants me to understand why he likes it. He can talk about everything from *Veronica Mars* to *Gen[13]* to NPR to car repair, or he can just as easily not talk at all, which I sort of love, too. He listens, he's funny, he's kind. He's entirely his own self, and that easy confidence is only part of what makes him nearly irresistible. The fact that he's tall, gorgeous, and has the most perfect smile doesn't hurt, either.

Two months after our marriage and annulment, I brought him over to meet my dad, Greg. That night, sometime over barbecued chicken and a bag of chips with salsa—and while I was off in the backyard trying to capture the sunset with oils—Oliver heard the rest of my story.

Dad came home from his third tour in Afghanistan when I was twelve, and he was a complete mess: he went from being a celebrated triage nurse to being an honorably discharged veteran, unable to sleep and hiding OxyContin in the kitchen. Mom couldn't even take a month of it before she left in the middle of the night without anything as formal as a goodbye. To either of us.

I tried to pick up Dad's pieces, Dad tried to pick up my pieces, and we muddled through for a few years until we realized we each had to carry *our own* pieces. It wasn't good, but it got better, and my relationship with my father is one of the most cherished things I'll ever have. I tell him nearly every thought I have, no matter how small. It's what allows me to keep them mostly inside the rest of the time. I'd rather lose the sun than him.

I never knew exactly what Dad said to Oliver, but after that night, instead of ever asking about it, Oliver just folded it into the Lola Canon and let it be. Little details would come out in conversation—the shorthand that so far I've only ever had with Harlow and Mia—showing me that he knew more than I'd ever told him.

Mia and Harlow had been in my life when it all happened, so I'd never had to download it all in one sitting. But if there was ever anyone else I wanted to know me that well, it was Oliver. After a few beers almost a month ago, I'd finally asked him, "So how much of my origin story did my dad tell you?"

He'd stilled mid-sip with his beer bottle touching his lips, and then slowly set it down. "He told me his version. From when you were small, until now."

"Do you want to hear mine?"

Oliver turned to me, and he nodded. "'Course I do. Someday. Whenever and however it comes out."

I'd almost kissed him that night, nearly been brave enough. Because when I told him that I wanted to hear his story, too, he'd looked so grateful, so full of what on my face would mean love, that it was the first and only time I'd thought maybe he was in just as deep as I was. And I had to ruin it by looking back down at the table.

When I looked up again, the poker face was firmly in place and he'd changed the subject.

I'm thinking about all of this now, watching him sleep. I'm also wishing he would wake up so I can grind some coffee beans. But my phone does the job as it starts barking at top volume on the counter: Benny's trademark ring.

"Hello?" I answer as fast as I can, nearly dropping my phone.

Oliver bolts upright at the sound, looking around wildly. I wave my hand from the kitchen until he sees me and then relaxes. He wipes his face and looks at me in this bare, tender way.

It's the same way he looked at me that night a month ago in the bar. His lips part a little, eyes narrowed so he can see me without the benefit of his glasses. His smile is the sun coming out from behind a cloud. "Hey," he says, voice raspy and broken a little from sleep.

"Lola, it's Benny." Benny's voice rips through the phone. "I've got Angela on the line."

"Oh?" I murmur, stuck on Oliver's face. As I watch, it transitions from relieved and happy to a little confused as he looks around the room.

He sits up and props his elbows on his thighs, putting his head in his hands, groaning, "*Fuck*. My head."

Harlow once said the way someone looks at you when you're the first person they see in the morning is the best way to gauge how they feel. I blink down to the counter and drag my nail between two tiles to keep from trying to interpret Oliver's early morning expressions.

"It's early, sorry for that," Angela says. "You okay?"

"I'm pre-coffee," I admit. "I'm not much of anything yet."

Oliver looks up and laughs from the couch and Angela laughs less genuinely across the line. I put it on speakerphone so he can hear.

"Well," Angela continues, "yesterday was a big day, and the press release goes out today."

"Do you need anything from me?" I ask.

"Nothing, except for you to be prepared," she says. "I don't need you to answer any questions today. That's our job. We can send over some social media copy to use for later. We'll set up some interviews. What I need from you now is to be aware of what this means."

Oliver watches me from the living room, eyes theatrically wide.

"Okay . . . ?" I say, smiling only because I'm so grateful he's here and getting this all firsthand. Angela sounds pretty fucking serious right now. I feel like I need a witness.

"It means you'll be recognized."

Oliver looks playfully scandalized and I stifle a giggle. The book has already been in the top three for graphic novels on the *New York Times* list for the past ten weeks and my life hasn't changed much at all, save more travel for signings and a few conventions. Clearly we both seriously doubt our neighborhood is going to become paparazzi ground zero.

"Maybe photographed and followed," Angela continues. "It means you'll be asked the same question a hundred times and will need to seem to answer it for the first time every single time it's asked. It means you can't control what's written about you. Is this all clear?"

I nod, still holding on to Oliver's amused gaze, but they can't see it so I manage a "Yes."

"You'll be great," Benny says in his reassuring voice. "This is fantastic, Lola."

"It is," I agree in a squeak. I know Harlow would never understand this inclination of mine, but I really just want to hide in my writing cave until it's all done and I can go see the film in a wig and sunglasses.

It's fine. I'm fine.

"Good," Angela says. "It should be up on *Variety* within the hour. Enjoy the moment, Lola. This one is all yours."

I can tell the call is about to end but there is the loud familiar clang of the dreaded glass door in in the background and a muffled male voice saying, "*Fuck.*"

Angela clears her throat. "Ah, it appears Austin would like a word."

"Okay," I say. Oliver has gotten up from the couch and steps into the kitchen.

"Lola!" Austin booms, and I'm glad I have it on speaker because against my ear it would have been deafening.

"Good morning," I say, and reach up to playfully tap Oliver's nose to draw his attention away from where he's sternly staring at the phone.

"Look, I have a meeting in five," Austin says, "so I just wanted to pop in, but I was thinking last night: what if Razor wasn't from a parallel time loop, but actually from another planet?"

I blink, and my brain seems to stall out.

Oliver's eyes widen, and he mouths, "What the hell?"

"Sorry," I say, and shake my head to clear it. I thought Austin really connected to the book. "An alien? Like from Mars?"

"Well, the specifics could be decided down the road," Austin says casually. "I'm just thinking that for the American public, an alien would be easier to understand than the idea of various parallel time loops."

"But Doctor Who is a thing" is all I can think to say.

"That's BBC."

"So the Brits are smarter?"

He laughs, thinking I'm being rhetorical. "Right? Well, just think on it. I think it could be a really easy change for us to make that wouldn't influence the story much at all—just make it more accessible."

I nod, and then realize again they can't see me. "Okay, I'll think about it."

"Great!" he crows. "Talk to you later, Loles."

My phone gives out three beeps, indicating the call has ended, and I carefully slide it onto the counter.

Oliver crosses his arms over his chest and leans back against the sink. " 'Loles'?"

My eyebrows inch up to the roof. "We're starting with that?"

He laughs, shaking his head slowly. "I'm not sure either of us wants to start with Mars."

I walk over to the fridge and pull out the bag of coffee beans. "I . . ." I turn, pouring the beans into the grinder, and look up at him helplessly as it loudly pulverizes my coffee. My brain is mush, my heart sags, my lungs seem to have given up and simply shut down.

Turning off the grinder, I say, "I don't even know what to say. A Martian. An actual Martian. That's not even a real suggestion, is it? I mean, Razor and all other Bichir evolved in Loop Four from the same earthly material we did, just . . . differently. In an alternate time, under alternate conditions." I rest both hands on my head, trying not to panic. "The whole *point* of him, and who he is, is alternate evolution." I look up into his deep blue eyes. "Here. On *Earth*. The only reason he cares about Quinn initially and what she's doing is because Earth is his planet, too. It's just a different version of it."

I know Oliver already knows this, but talking it out will unknot something in me.

Either that or completely send me into a spiral.

"You can push back, Lola," he says. "For what it's worth, I don't agree at all with Austin that it's too complicated a story line."

"I thought we might be discussing more nuanced changes," I say, "like having Quinn fight only one attacker in her first fight, or having Razor come to her rescue a little sooner with the Andemys."

Oliver shrugs, spinning a spoon on the tile countertop. "Yeah, me, too."

"And a press release?" I shake my head, dumping the grinds into the coffeemaker. "I'm going to hide in the shop today, if that's okay."

"I think the shop may be the least hidey place you could find, Lola Love."

I nod, loving the way he says my name. His *o*'s are always so wiggly, nothing makes my spirits lift like listening to his voice. "Are you hungry?"

He reaches beneath his shirt to scratch his stomach, and my heart dive-bombs into my feet. "Starving," he says, shrugging.

I point to a pile of fruit on a platter and reach above the fridge for the cereal, grabbing the Rice Krispies because I know it's what he wants. He's already beside me at the fridge getting out the milk.

"I'm in a world where someone sends over *social media copy*," I say. "I guess I should start some social media, huh?"

He laughs, peeling a banana. "Let Joe run your Twitter. He'd be good."

I gape at him. "He'd post dick pics."

Oliver shrugs as if to say, *Like I said*, and then pauses, staring back at me.

"What?" I say.

"Nothing." He nods to the fruit in his hand. "I'm just honestly not sure where I'm supposed to look when I eat a banana. It was a little eye-contacty there for a second. I didn't want to be suggestive."

"Especially not after discussing Not-Joe's dick pics."

With a grimace, Oliver puts the banana down and pours his cereal. "Hand me a knife?"

I giggle as I grab one, and he rolls his eyes. Every time he says "knife" I can't help it. It's one of the only times he's ever full-on Paul Hogan.

"Do you really think people will recognize me?" I ask, chewing my thumbnail. I can't even face the idea of Razor as an alien from Mars right now; it's oddly easier to focus on the publicity side of all this.

Oliver looks up at me, studies my face. I know what he's thinking when his eyes land on my diamond Marilyn piercing: I'm not very incognito. "Don't they already, sometimes?"

"Only geeks, and only *twice*."

"Well, now more people will." He says it with such easy calm. Sometimes I want to put him in a cage with a lion and measure his blood pressure.

"That makes me want to vomit, Oliver. Like, I should actually carry a bucket around with me."

He shakes his head, laughing. "Come on, Lola. You're being dramatic. You're so graceful all the time, why do you think it will be hard for you?"

"That's not true," I whisper.

He looks up at me, and shakes his head the tiniest bit.

"Sometimes I wish I could meet you all over again," he says, slicing his banana on top of his cereal. "And pay better attention."

My heart catapults into my throat. "What does that even mean?"

"It means exactly what I just said." He stirs the bananas into the bowl. "You're bloody amazing. I want to meet you for the first time again. And I want it to be different, and just us hanging out like this."

"Over Rice Krispies and coffee rather than on the Vegas Strip?"

He meets my eyes, and I know—I just *know*—he's remembering my stumbling proposition. I watch as he searches for the right words. "I'm just talking about a situation where no one feels pressured to—"

"I don't blame you for what you did that night," I say. I need to put this moment out of its misery. "It was the right call."

He holds my eyes for a breath longer before he smiles a little, digging into his food.

I lean against the counter and sip my nectar of the gods and watch him eat. In some ways, he's built like a stick figure: so long, so lean, loping stride and arms, nothing but sharp angles. But also, he's strong. Muscle ropes around his biceps, his shoulders. His chest is broad, tapering into a straight waist. *I could draw him,* I think. *I could draw him and I might even surprise myself with what I see.*

"What are you thinking about?" he asks through a

mouthful of cereal. "You're staring at me as if you're surprised I have arms."

"I was thinking about what it would look like if I drew you."

I feel my eyes go wide. I definitely didn't mean to say this out loud, and we both know it. Oliver has gone so still, as still as the blood in my veins. He's looking at me as if he expects me to elaborate but I can't. Something shuts off in my brain when I'm nervous, some trapdoor closes.

Minutes pass and all I can hear is my own heartbeat, and the sound of Oliver eating. We're not strangers to silence, but this one feels pretty heavy.

"Well, do you want to?"

I blink up to his face. "Do I want to what?"

He takes a bite of Rice Krispies, chews, and swallows. "Draw me."

My heart inflates

inflates

inflates

explodes.

"It's no big deal, Lola. You're an artist. And I realize I'm a bit of a demigod." He winks and then ducks to take another milky bite of cereal.

Do I want to draw him? Hell yes, and real-talk time: I do it all the time. But usually from memory, or at the very least I do it when he doesn't know what I'm drawing. The idea of having unfettered visual access to that face, those hands, the ropey arms and broad shoulders . . .

"Okay," I squeak.

He stares at me, giving me a tiny lift of his brow that says, *Well?* and before I can overthink this, I'm off, running to my bedroom, and digging through my desk for my bigger sketchpad and charcoals. I can hear him in the kitchen, putting his bowl in the sink, running the water to wash it.

My mind is a blender, coherent thoughts are chopped and killed. I have no idea what I'm doing right now but if Oliver wants to be drawn . . . *well fuck*. I'm going to fill this goddamn book with sketches.

Sprinting back to the living room, I nearly wipe out on the wood floor in my socks and manage to grip the wall just in time to see Oliver with his back to me, looking out the enormous loft windows. He reaches behind his neck and pulls his shirt over his head and off.

Oh.

Oh.

"Oh," I groan.

He whips around and looks at me, mortification spreading over his face. "Were we not doing this? Oh, God, we weren't doing this. We were just doing face and stuff, weren't we?" Holding his shirt to his body, he says, "Fuck."

"It's fine," I manage, looking at a pencil in my hand as if inspecting the quality of the sharp peak. I'm staring so hard I could break it with the force of my eyes alone. Oliver is shirtless. In my living room. "This is totally fine, I mean it's really good to draw you without a shirt because I can focus more on muscle details and hair and nip—" I clear my throat. *"Things."*

He drops the shirt, eyes still searching mine to check that I'm sure. "Okay."

I sit on the couch, looking up at where he stands near the window. He looks out over the skyline, completely at ease. By contrast, my heart is tunneling a path out of my body through my throat. I spend more time than I should on his chest, the geometry of it: perfectly round, small nipples. A map of muscles, built of squares, rectangles, darting lines, and sharp angles. The triangular tilt where hipbone meets muscle. I feel him watch me as I draw the dark hair low on his navel.

"Do you want my pants off?"

"Yes," I answer before thinking and quickly shout, "No! No. God, oh my God, it's okay."

My heart could not possibly beat any harder.

His mouth is half unsure smile, half straight line. I want to spend a year drawing the exact shape of his lips in this moment. "I really don't mind," he says quietly.

The devil on my shoulder tells me, *Do it. Do it. Your geometric style never works with drawing legs. This would help.*

The angel just shrugs and looks away.

"If you're sure," I say, and then clear my throat, explaining: "You know I'm really bad at drawing legs and . . ."

He's already unbuttoning his pants, hands working the soft denim, unbuttoning the fly one tiny pop at a time.

It would be good for our friendship if I could look away, but I can't.

"Lola?"

With Herculean effort, I drag my eyes up to his face. "Yeah?"

He doesn't say anything more, but holds my eyes as he pushes his jeans down his hips and kicks them to the side.

"Yeah?" I repeat. I am breathing too hard for this. It has to be noticeable.

This is totally different. Something is happening this morning that is *not* canon Oliver + Lola. I feel like we're stepping through the doorway into Wonderland.

"Where do you want me?"

"*Want* you?"

"To stand?"

"Oh." I clear my throat. "Right there is good."

"I'm not backlit?"

He is, but I don't trust myself to direct him right now.

"I don't mind sitting—" he starts.

"Maybe just lie down or—" I stop abruptly as his words get processed. *Shit.* "Or sit. Sitting is fine. I mean, whichever."

He gives me his tiny mysterious smile and goes to the rug in the middle of the room and lays down in a giant sunbeam.

The panel shows the girl, staring at the boy, her skin covered in licking, blue flames.

Oliver tucks his hands behind his head, crosses his legs at the ankle, and closes his eyes.

Cock.

COCK.

It's all I can see.

It's there beneath his boxers, half-hard, obviously uncut, following the line of his hip. My God, it's thick. And if Oliver is a grow'er, he could knock a woman's teeth out when he fucks her.

I tilt my head, my hand hovering over the paper. Why is he half-hard? Is this a guy thing that happens when they're being drawn? Probably. Is that awesome or totally embarrassing?

Obviously for Oliver it's awesome because look at it. I mean *him.* Look at him.

"Lola? You okay?"

That's right. He can hear my lack of scribbling. I sit on the couch and begin furiously drawing every tiny detail of his body: the dark hair on his legs, the corded muscle of his thighs, deep grooves beside his hips, and yes, even the shape of him beneath his boxers.

I'm flipping through dozens of pages, determined to get every detail down and color it later. My hands are a mess of charcoal, my fingers cramping with the speed and intensity of my work.

"Roll to your stomach," I say.

He does, and I catch his hips flexing, pressing down once hard into the rug: an unconscious thrust.

Every muscle in my body clenches in response: a pleading wish thrown out to the Universe.

I catch sight of a long scar running up his left side, bisecting a few of his ribs.

"What's the scar?"

"Fall on the first bike trip," he murmurs, referring to his Bike and Build involvement, where he met Ansel and Finn and they biked across the U.S., building low-income housing on the way.

The scar is *big*—half an inch wide, maybe four inches long—and I wonder how long Oliver was off the bike after that.

"I never knew you crashed on that trip. What did you do about the biking and building part?"

He shrugs, readjusting his head on his arms, and I marvel over how easy he is in his skin. "Got stitches. I took maybe two days to recoup. Wasn't that big a deal, it just looks nasty."

I hum, listening to him talk about biking as I work to master the muscular curve of his calf, the arch of his foot, the protruding bone at his ankle. "Canberra is flat," he says. "We rode our bikes everywhere. It's a perfect city for it. Nice tracks. Good roads. Even though I rode all the time, my mates and I were idiots a lot, so of course I fell a lot, too." I love his voice, get lost in it as I count the vertebrae of his spine, the way his hair curls over his ear, the dark shadow of stubble cutting across his jaw. It's one thing to see all of this, and another thing entirely to imagine touching it, knowing it as well with my hands as I now do with my eyes.

I have a lifetime's worth of fantasies on these pages, and

I am convinced Oliver has just helped me create the sexiest thing comics will ever see.

I wipe the back of my hand across my forehead, sighing. "I think this is good."

Oliver rolls to his side, propping himself on one elbow. Seriously it's absurd. On the white rug in his blue boxer briefs he looks like he's posing for *Playgirl*.

"What time is it?" he asks.

I glance at the cock—*CLOCK* on the cable box. "Eight nineteen." I need to get out of here.

He stretches: muscles shaking, fists clenched, head thrown back in the relief of it. After an enormous happy groan, he asks, "You gonna show me what you did?"

"Not a chance."

"So it's quite pornographic, then?"

I laugh. "You're in your *boxers*."

"That's a yes? Now I really want to see what you drew."

"You will," I tell him. "Eventually. I want to go a little edgier with the next project." I duck my head, tuck my hair behind an ear. "You helped with some ideas for that. Thanks."

Is it awkward right now? It doesn't feel awkward but maybe I'm just terrible at reading these kinds of things. It felt really easy. It *feels* easy.

He stands, finds his jeans, and begins putting them back on. I bid farewell to the most perfect half-hard cock I've never seen. "Just helping a friend out," he murmurs. "As one does."

"Thanks," I say again.

"Hope it distracted you a little, at least."

I catch his eye as his head reappears from inside his shirt as he pulls it over his head. "Distracted me from what?"

Oliver laughs and comes close enough to reach out and muss my hair. "I'll see you later, Lola Love."

He's out of the apartment and heading down to his store before I remember the Martian Razor and that the *Variety* article has been posted sometime in the past hour.

———

HARLOW TOSSES HER purse onto the bench and slides into the booth across from me. "Sorry I'm late."

"No worries. I ordered you the salmon Caesar." I look back to the entrance to the restaurant. "No Finn? I thought he was flying in late last night?"

"He had to stay up for the week. Something about the fuse box or control panel and—" Harlow pretends to fall asleep on the table.

"I can never keep track of where he is," I mumble into my water glass.

"Here's a trick. When I look like this?" She gestures to her perfectly styled hair and makeup. "He's not here. If he was here this morning, I'd be too worn-out to—"

"Got it." I love my girl but she is Empress of the Overshare.

"So what happened to you guys after you stumbled out of Hennessey's last night? I couldn't tell who was propping up who."

I lean out of the way when the waitress drops off our

food, and thank her. "I don't remember how we got back to the loft, but Oliver slept over," I say once our waitress is gone.

I'm not looking at Harlow when I say this so it startles me when she slams her palms down on the tabletop, already halfway out of her seat. *"He what?"*

A few customers are looking over at us, and I hiss, "He slept on the goddamn *couch,* will you put your ass in your chair?"

Her face falls and she sits back down. "*God.* Don't do that to me."

"Do what?" I ask. "It's *Oliver.*"

She snorts. "Exactly."

I try to read her expression but she's gotten better at keeping her mouth shut since she's been with Finn, and even though I know she's thinking something, it isn't written all over her face.

"Well, okay, about that . . ." I start, and Harlow leans forward with her hands clasped together, forearms resting on the table, and two perfectly sculpted auburn eyebrows raised in interest.

I debate how much to tell her here. I have no idea what Oliver's dating life looks like and he may be perfectly busy without me, thank you very much. We hang out most days, but not most nights. By the number of stories Finn and Ansel have about Oliver *back in the day*—as well as Oliver's enviable poker face—I suspect he's getting a lot more action these days than I am, I just never hear about it. And, admittedly, with the book launch and travel and events, dating hasn't been at the forefront of my mind in months. Harlow's new marriage and Ansel's imminent stateside move have been the most common topics of conversation when the girls are together.

So . . . I haven't really mentioned my Oliver attraction to Harlow or Mia. Oliver has just been a nice, happy place for my thoughts to wander in times of stress—a relieving reminder to myself that I have someone I can talk to, that there is someone I can seek whose emotional beat mirrors my own when life gets crazy. Besides, Harlow, Mia, and I have known each other since elementary school, and I've learned over the years how quickly Harlow becomes *invested*. Oliver had a chance in Vegas, and didn't take it. I can't imagine he'd be interested in complicating our friendship now that it's obviously working well for both of us, and I don't want Harlow to feel resentful toward him for not reciprocating my feelings. Harlow's strength can also be her weakness: she is the most fiercely loyal person I know.

God, things get complicated when a group of friends is involved.

But with the books published, and travel getting lighter, and in the calm before the movie storm, I have more free time . . . which means Oliver-as-a-sexy-person is more and more on my mind

and this morning I saw him almost naked

and he's defined *everywhere*

and not circumcised

and uncut cocks are my kryptonite

and I've heard the stories about Oliver's oral skills amid Finn and Ansel's snickers

and *holy shit I am losing my mind.*

Across the table from me, Harlow clears her throat, setting her fork down with heavy intent. I look up from where I've been unconsciously doodling on a napkin.

"Testing my patience, friend," she says.

I clearly need to talk about it . . . and Harlow would understand my hesitation—wouldn't she?—because she's been around for every single one of my epic relationship failures.

"I mention that Oliver stayed over last night," I start again, "because, as it turns out . . . I find him to be rather attractive."

Harlow leans in even more, and I know her well enough to know that she's schooling her expression. "A fucking armadillo would find Oliver Lore to be *rather attractive,* Lola."

I shrug and she looks at me like she wishes she were a drill and could dig down into my thoughts. I get that look a lot, actually. In truth, she wouldn't have to go far; they're right there beneath the surface. It's just that the surface is pretty solid, like granite.

"Do you think Oliver might also find *you* attractive?" she asks evenly, sitting up and spearing a piece of lettuce.

I shrug. "I don't think so. I mean, he didn't seem all that interested in Vegas."

She mumbles something about *trying real hard not to meddle* and then shoves the bite in her mouth.

"There isn't any meddling to do," I tell her, but she stares up at the ceiling, avoiding my eyes. "Harlow, what the hell is wrong with you?" I reach across the table and poke her in the forehead. "I just need to talk this out a little," I tell her. "Because with you married and Mia married, Oliver is kind of my go-to buddy, and you know I have a really, really terrible track record with guys once they become . . ."

Harlow drops her eyes back to me, swallowing a bite of salad before saying, "Once they become more?"

"Yes," I say, and poke at a spear of asparagus. "Oliver and I see each other almost every day but we've never discussed dating or hookups. It's this odd conversation vacancy in our friendship, this topic we both seem to actively avoid. Maybe that's for a reason."

"Should I call Finn?" she says to herself. "I should call Finn. He'll remind me to keep my fucking mouth shut."

"But I don't want you to keep your mouth shut! My friendship with Oliver is probably the easiest of my life." She looks up at me, eyes flashing, and I laugh. "Other than you and Mia. I just . . ." I put my fork down. "Do you remember how much Brody hated me for like a year after we broke up?"

She nods, laughing. "And you were together for maybe two months? God, what a head case."

I shake my head. "I don't know . . . he was a nice guy and we'd been friends for so long. I still don't really get what happened, but it just . . . fizzled."

I feel Harlow's attention on me and then it diffuses when she looks down to her lunch.

"And Jack," I add. "I blew that one, too."

Harlow snorts.

"Harlow. Seriously?"

"Well, to be fair," she says, "you did *blow* him, right?"

"I mean blow *it*," I say and then groan when she giggles. "I blew *the situation*." Harlow chokes on a bite of lettuce. "Jesus Christ. I'm just trying to say I fucked it up. I always fuck it up. Either I say the wrong thing or don't say the right one, I'm too busy or too available—*whatever*, it's always something." She's got her head resting on her arms on the table, shoulders shaking in laughter. Sighing, I stab a bite of chicken, muttering, "God, you're a troll."

She pushes herself up, and wipes beneath her eye with a long, manicured finger. "I'm just saying, you're not the same person you were when you were eighteen or nineteen or twenty. You and Oliver are really good friends, and also really attractive people. That's all. I am shutting up now."

"I drew him this morning," I say. "Whorelow, he took his *shirt off*." Her eyes dart to mine, and I whisper, "He took his jeans off, too."

"He took his *clothes* off," she says, voice flat with disbelief. "Oliver did this. In your apartment."

"Yes! I saw him *nearly naked*," I tell her. There's really no point in telling her that he obviously did it to distract me, because then she would want to know why, and quite honestly Harlow doesn't really know a thing about my comics other than she likes Razor's muscles under the scales. "I want to say it was a little weird except it wasn't. He's . . . yeah. He's real fit, is all I'm saying."

Harlow presses her fist to her mouth in a dramatic gesture of restraint.

Leaning in, I whisper, "Can I tell you a secret?"

My best friend looks at me, and her eyes soften. Harlow pretends she's made of steel but she's not. She's all marshmallow. "You can tell me anything, Peach."

I take a deep breath, steadying myself for the admission. "I think I might really like Oliver."

She laughs, resting her forehead on her perched fingers. "Lola. Sometimes you're so clueless it's painful."

Chapter FOUR

Oliver

I LEAVE LOLA'S JUST after breakfast and our private little *art ses-sion*. Sliding the loft door closed behind me, it seems like my dick does a reflexive stretch in the fresh air. The memory of her in her pajamas, fuzzy socks, and of tiny smudges of charcoal on her forehead and cheeks from when she would absently sweep her hair out of her face . . . it warps my brain a bit, and I'm exhausted from focusing on not getting an erection for the past hour.

I'm not really sure what possessed me to pull that just now. I could see her working to stay calm after the call. Lola's ambition is mighty, and the only thing keeping her from taking over the entire fucking planet is how much she detests stepping out of her creative space and into the public eye. On top of that, she puts more thought into the mythology of *Razor Fish* than she puts into anything else in her life, so the idea of changing such a critical detail of her story . . . her meltdown was visible beneath the surface.

So, there I was, lying on the floor, bare except for my boxers, with her eyes moving over my body like tiny licks of heat. All I could do was think about riding a bike or counting out money in the register and definitely *not* how it would feel if Lola got up from the couch, walked over, and parted her long, slender legs, settling her weight over my hips.

Having her apartment so close to the shop has been a blessing and a curse. In the early days, I'd be in to work before dawn and there long after the streetlamps popped to life and all the other stores had closed up. At some point after the grand opening, Lola handed me a spare key and insisted I was welcome to use it. There have been loads of times it would have been easier to crash at her place for a bit, rather than drive all the way home to Pacific Beach. But with Lola, from day one it's always been a slippery slope. One little grin when she walks into the store leads to an uncontrollable, face-splitting smile when I find I'll see her again at the Regal Beagle later. A lingering glance leads to outright staring at her milky skin, shiny black hair, perfect curves. If I'm not careful, crashing at her place too regularly would make it a habit and I wouldn't be satisfied until I found my way curled around her, every night spent between her sheets, between her thighs.

I jog down the metal stairs that lead to E Street and burst out into the bright, January sunshine, tilting my face up. Oxygen, I need it. I stretch my back, taking several deep breaths.

I spend most of the day trying to stay busy enough that I don't replay what it was like to wake up and see her as she looked first thing in the morning: face soft and free of any makeup, tiny diamond glinting just above her full, cherry lips. Lola has perfect skin; I fantasize about searching for a single freckle or scar. Usually brushed to a shine, this morning her long black hair was mussed and tangled on the right side, telling me exactly how she slept. Her eyes were heavy with sleep and I wanted to turn back the clock, climb into her bed, and kiss the warm, swollen red of her mouth before she was fully awake, dig my fingers into her soft, thick hair and roll on top of her.

I've had the fantasy a million times, in a thousand different ways, but in every iteration, we always sleep naked. Sometimes I fall asleep on top of her; very often I'm still inside her. Sometimes we start moving again before we're fully awake, and what wakes me up is her quiet little noises right in my ear, carried by her warm exhales. Sometimes we make love when the sun is just up, because I love a good, slow fuck first thing in the morning.

Letting the daydream fill my thoughts, I pull a pile of books out of a box and find a razor to break down the cardboard for recycling. It's a quiet moment in the shop—Joe isn't in yet, the lunch rush hasn't been unleashed—and the image loops through my brain, like a skipping song: Lola's hips moving up as I move in, and she's so fucking warm. Her eyes are locked with mine—grateful for the way I make her feel, and a little cocky that I'm so obviously trying not to come before she does. When Lola loves me in my imagination, she's never shy, never closed off. I can see the intensity inside me matched in her expression.

It's always like this, every fantasy. I once wondered if it was bullshit that I bang her in my head more than we have imagined *conversations,* but when I drunkenly confessed this to Ansel, he just as drunkenly insisted it made perfect sense: "Well, first of all, I'd be fine living out my entire marriage in bed, naked with Mia. I don't have any qualms about admitting that."

"Fair enough," I said.

"But also," he continued, "you *talk* to Lola all the time. You two have become so close you almost have a secret language. Sex between you guys will be some sort of spiritual experience. All the things you want her to say to you, she'll say without words when you finally sleep with her."

When.

His confidence that it's only a matter of time is alternately reassuring and maddening. I want more than anything to believe him, but even with the jerking leaps forward in my friendship with Lola—this morning, particularly—I'm just not sure.

But . . . letting her draw me was one fantasy I'd never thought to have.

It felt more wide-open than even the most tender kiss, or the deepest kind of fucking. I had to just lie there and let her look at me. I itch to dig into those sketchbooks, to see how she isolated each part of me, what parts—if any—she drew again and again.

I knew she was drawing my legs when her charcoal would scratch heavily on the paper. It was quieter when she drew the details of my face, and that was when her breathing would break down into tiny, shallow bursts of air, in and out. And I knew she was drawing my half-hard cock when she stopped breathing—so nervous, but so eager to practice.

Was it only nerves, or was it more? With Lola I can't tell. She looks at me in a way she doesn't look at anyone else, but that could be meaningful only because I am her closest male friend, and have carefully, intentionally cultivated her trust. Trust is key with Lola. She closes down if she feels inspected, clams up if pushed.

But it's a delicate, slow process and unfortunately, I want *sex,* and—maybe more specifically—the intimacy that comes along with it. The truth is that if I can't have these things with Lola, I really should let myself find them with someone else. These are the moments that Finn and Ansel's lectures echo in my ears and I wonder if maybe I should take their advice: keep some of the numbers I'm given at the store—*fangirls,* as Lola calls them—or say yes when I'm asked out for coffee . . . or even flat-out propositioned for a quick fuck in the storeroom.

My phone buzzes with a familiar tone, and I reach for it across the counter.

It's a text from Lola. Dinner tonight?

Nothing out of the ordinary, but my heart trips into thunder. Sure, I type. Where?

I have a really long day ahead of me, can we just hang at your place?

I start to type a simple Sure, when more words from her pop up: My brain needs more Oliver time.

Lola's apartment is sometimes full of chaos. London blasts music when she's home, Harlow is over most of the time Finn is out of town, and she's more explosive weather event than she is woman. Add Ansel and Mia to the mix and I'm surprised the police have never been called. In addition to our more obvious similarities, Lola also needs a good deal of quiet time. Not just to work, but to *breathe*. It's one of the reasons we got along so well initially and why we still spend so much time together outside the group.

But we don't usually do it at my place, alone, where I have no roommate or neighbors on the other side of the wall. We have on occasion, sure, but not after I stroked her hair in the bar and spent the night on her couch. Not after she's sketched me *and my dick*.

I'm a bubbling mix of unsure and electrified when I hit send on my end, Sure.

———

I'M ON THE patio basting the ribs on the barbecue when I hear Lola's voice carry down the hall.

"I'm here!"

The front door closes. There's the sound of her shoes hitting the floor as she kicks them off just inside, bare feet making their way across the room, and the ring of keys as she hangs them on the kitchen hook next to mine.

It's such a domestic habit, and I'm unprepared for the strange sensation that rolls through my stomach. With a nervous glance toward the house, I close the barbie through a cloud of charcoal-scented smoke and try to remind myself that I'm Lola's *friend*. Nothing has changed, not really.

When I step inside, she looks up at the sound of the screen door and smiles. "Brought some stuff," she says, and nods to a pile of grocery sacks covering the counter.

"You didn't have to do that," I tell her, closing the door

with a wave behind me. "Ribs are almost done, was just about to take them off."

She holds up two pints of ice cream. "Well now we have dessert, too." Rocky Road and strawberry. Our favorites.

My chest feels tight and uncomfortable, as I cross to the cupboard and pull out a platter. The calm distance is unraveling, and I can sense the impending explosion. I just have no idea what shape it will take.

Lola putters around behind me, and when she walks over to the freezer to put everything away, I absolutely don't look at her arse.

———

THE EXPERIENCE THROUGHOUT dinner puts me as close to torture as I've ever been. It never occurred to me that serving Lola barbecued ribs might have been a bad idea, and that for what watching her eat them does to me I might as well have handed her a banana, or reached across the table and had her suck my finger.

And so I spend a good part of the meal half-hard—again—and shifting in my seat as Lola sits across from me, working through some thoughts on her new book, and completely oblivious to my struggle. She's clearly avoiding thinking about Austin's ideas for *Razor Fish,* and I want to give her useful feedback, but it takes superhuman strength to drag my eyes from her mouth while she licks sauce from her fingertips.

Finally I give up, claiming a need to use the bathroom so

I can get some air. I splash water on my face and give myself a long, hard look in the mirror.

This is exactly why I didn't let things go too far between us in Vegas. Why—as much as I wanted to punch myself in the face at the time—I turned down her invitation to join her in a hotel room. Lola is smart and beautiful, and, knowing we were going to be living in the same city and I would really, *really* want to be her friend, I didn't want to ruin things or make them weird by fucking her.

But things are definitely weird now.

We clean up dinner together, working side by side in companionable silence as we load the dishwasher and wipe the counters. She isn't talking, but there's a determination in the set of her jaw that says she's thinking, plotting. It's an expression I'm familiar with, though it seems different tonight. I'm not sure why but my stomach twists with nerves as the number of things keeping us in the kitchen and away from the comfortable sofa in my dark living room dwindles down to nothing.

What is she planning?

I tell her to go ahead and pick out a movie, and I watch from my spot near the stove as she scrolls through the choices on my iPad, her mouth turned down into a frown until she finds exactly what she wants.

"Point Break?" she says.

"Go for it."

Bank robbery and explosions, guns and testosterone? Exactly what I need to keep my eyes and hands to themselves.

I start the dishwasher while Lola heads into the other

room. Grabbing the popcorn and a couple of beers from the fridge, I flip off the light with my elbow.

The previews are playing as I get to the living room. Both lamps have been dimmed, and the couch is huge, big enough for at least four grown adults. Lola is sitting squarely in the middle.

Okay . . .

"Comfortable?"

She pats the spot next to her. "Almost."

My heart slowly melts into my gut.

I take a seat and after a moment of hesitation, she crowds a bit closer, tucking herself neatly into my side.

I go still, holding my breath before exhaling and molding into the shape of her against me.

Lola and I have always had what Finn and Ansel call a *touchy* relationship—lots of playful shoves, pinky swears, and high-fives—but cuddling on the couch? Definitely new.

"Do you want me to grab the ice cream?" Lola says, lifting her chin to look up at me.

I imagine her this close, eating ice cream from the carton and licking melted strawberry from the spoon.

That would be fucking catastrophic.

"In a while," I say, and she nods, taking the popcorn and stretching her legs out in front of her. I think I hear her exhale in one long, calming breath.

She's wearing a soft gray T-shirt that slopes off one perfect shoulder, a pair of black skinny jeans, and her bare feet rest next to mine on the coffee table. Lola is small-boned but tall, with curves that make my mouth water. I'd never describe her as delicate—and that may be primarily because she exudes a certain steely aura—but I'm so much bigger than she is, so much longer, and I've never been more aware of it than I am right this very moment.

Picking up her hand, I place it over mine, palm to palm. "You're so small."

Lola laughs, looking down at our hands. "I am not, you're just a giant. Is that how all men are made in Australia?" She tilts her face up to mine. "I might have to plan a visit and go hunting."

"You're cheeky tonight," I say, reaching with my free hand for the bowl of popcorn in her lap, and shift my eyes to the television.

But I can feel the way *her* eyes linger on me, and can't resist looking back at her face. We're so close, shoulder to shoulder. Out of the corner of my eye I catch the jerking rise and fall of her chest as she breathes.

"Still picturing me in my boxers?" I whisper.

"Is it that obvious?" she says. There's a hint of a smirk on her lips, but her cheeks grow warm and pink. She clears her throat.

"Pipe down and watch the movie," I tease dryly, feeling my cock tighten in my jeans. "You've already made me miss the first ten minutes—you know, where we really get into the nuances of Keanu's excellent characterization."

"I can tell how upset you are," she says with a small laugh

and sits up. Each point of contact we just shared cools and I use every ounce of my mental Jedi skills to wordlessly coerce her to sit back close again and touch me.

My skills are apparently far more powerful than I imagined because, after she takes a long pull from her bottle, she sets it on the table in front of us and swings her legs onto the couch so she's lying down.

With her head in my lap.

I take a deep breath and keep my eyes on the screen, waiting with fire in my veins while she shifts around and makes herself comfortable.

After a moment she's settled in and looks up at me with smiling eyes. "You're so comfy. Is this"—she swallows—"is this okay?"

"Pretty comfy yourself," I say, and try to set the bowl on her face, anything to keep my focus off the fact that her head is practically on top of my dick. Her ear is almost pressed against it.

She *has* to realize what she's doing to me.

"Hey," she says, stealing the bowl away from me. "Be nice or I'll tell Harlow."

Lola reaches for a handful of popcorn and goes back to watching the movie. Swayze runs by, along with the rest of his Ex-Presidents bank robber crew, and she laughs. "Why does that seem like something Not-Joe would get himself involved in?"

My hand wanders to her hair, innocently at first—just to

brush it away from her forehead—and then with more intent as I smooth the strands back. If we're doing this, I am fucking doing this. "Because if we asked him to sit in a running van at the curb while the rest of us ran into a bank, the only question he'd ask is if he could change the radio station."

Lola tilts her head and looks up at me, and it would probably be best for both of us if she'd keep her head still. "Or to bring him a lollipop."

"Exactly," I agree.

We're silent for a few more minutes and I twist a lock of hair around my finger, watching the way the light from the TV flickers across the strands.

"So things are good at the shop?" she asks, moving her hand to rest near her head on my thigh.

"Wouldn't you know?" I ask. "You're practically employee of the month."

"That's because I have a thing for Not-Joe," she says, glancing back at me again. I shift minutely—trying to move her away or get her closer, I'm not really sure.

"Don't ever say that to him or he'll think you're going to get married."

"No, actually," she says, laughing. "Not-Joe says he could never marry a divorcée, though I think he forgets we were married."

"I've ruined you for him. This gives me a small touch of pleasure." Things are getting a bit too honest, so before she can say anything else, I go back to her original question. "And things at the store are great, really. Heaps more business than

I anticipated, might even bring in an extra hand to help on weekends."

"Wow, really? That's great!"

Something warms in my chest as I gaze down at her. "You looking for a job?"

"Ha ha," she says, moving around again so she's on her back. I can see her now, which is nice, but if she turns her head, my dick will be mere inches from her face. It's never wanted anything more in its life. I'm not really sure if this is an improvement. "I'd be better company than Not-Joe, I'll tell you that right now."

"He's not so bad. But you look a hell of a lot better in a pair of jeans."

"Not-Joe wears something other than board shorts?" she asks, closing her eyes as I massage her scalp.

She moans a little and I have to work to not stumble over my words. "If this international stardom thing doesn't work out for you," I say, "you could always sell comics at Downtown Graffick."

She goes quiet, and I take it as a cue to ask, "Do you want to talk a little more about Austin's idea? Or do you think you're just going to pull the veto card?"

The more I think about Austin's suggestion that Razor be turned into a Martian, the more irritated I get. For someone who claims to be obsessed with the books, Austin doesn't seem to understand the heart of them at all. And it's a suggestion Lola would have laughed at a week ago. Is she honestly considering it?

She shrugs and gunfire rings out on the television. Lola rolls to look at the screen, taking my free hand with her. "I love this part," she says.

Stress avoidance. Lola's superpower. "Of course you do," I say. "Patrick Swayze is about to be shirtless. Hell, *I* love this part."

"Keanu Reeves would have made a great superhero," she says.

I look down at her in shock. "Have you forgotten Neo?"

She shakes her head. "No, I guess I mean he has this special blankness that could be great for a villain. Like, Sabertooth. Maybe Ra's Al Ghul or General Zod."

"Ugh, Zod?" I say. *"No."*

Lola giggles. "I love the way you say that."

"Say what? 'No'?"

"Yeah. It's like . . . I can't even do that sound you make at the end. It's like four vowels at once."

"You're a dag," I tell her with affection.

"It's the *o*, I think. Whenever I try and mimic the way you say something, I can never get that part right. Say, '*Go blow the garden hose.*'"

"I'm not saying that, Lola Love."

"See? Right there! *Luuuooarrrla,*" she says, dragging out the word and changing the shape of her mouth dramatically. "I don't even know what letters you're using, to be honest."

"Just the normal ones," I tell her.

After a moment, she rubs at the back of her neck.

"You okay there?" I ask, taking my hand from her hair to rub the tops of her shoulders.

"My neck is just at a weird angle like this."

"Do you want me to move or—?" I start to say, but Lola sits up, surveying the couch before standing.

"Maybe . . . um. You move right here," she says, lifting my feet from the coffee table and swinging them to the cushion. "Yeah, like that."

I set the popcorn down and do what she says, stretching on my side along the length of the couch. Does she seem nervous? Am I imagining it?

She carefully lies down on the sliver of space in front of me, the back of her body pressed along the entire front of mine. And well . . . this is also new.

"You've made me your big spoon," I say, hoping to ease some of the strange tension that has settled between us.

She reaches back to pinch my hip, and I grab for her hand, intending to stop her but somehow ending up with my arm around her ribs. We lay there in silence for a moment, the sound of the movie ringing around the room, and when I shift slightly, she slots her legs with mine.

Oh, fuck me.

No longer interested in the movie, I close my eyes, feeling myself sink farther into the couch as she traces shapes along the back of my wrist, her nails scratching, slowly at first and then slower, slower, until they feel more like caresses than casual touch.

I've been so careful around her, careful to keep the depth of feelings from ever being too visible. I don't want to push her. I don't want to ruin what we have, but right now it feels like we're balancing on the tip of a mountain; if we lean too far one way we could slide into something wonderful that I've wanted for what feels like years. But if this is only a friendship for her, and I step the wrong way, I could fall off the cliff into a void: without her friendship *or* her love.

I'm not sure I'm willing to risk that. I need to let her decide.

"Lola?" I say, and I hear every one of my fears and doubts in those two, brief syllables.

The entire length of her body tenses, starting at her shoulders and moving down like a wave, until she's pushing herself to sit.

"Holy crap, I didn't realize it was so late," she says, and stands from the couch. "I have panels I want to finish. I should get back to Austin tonight, too."

It takes me a moment to catch up with how quickly the moment has shifted. "You can call him from here," I tell her, watching her absently tie her hair into a knot atop her head. I don't want her to go. "I'll stay out of your way."

She moves to the kitchen and I can see her shadow against the wall. Lola pauses as she gathers her things. "It's cool," she says lightly. "I need to think about what I want to say, anyway."

I stand and wait while she retrieves her keys and slips her shoes on at the door.

"You'll text me when you get home?"

She nods, smiling up at me. "Of course. And thanks for dinner."

"It was no problem."

She swings her keys around her index finger and looks back toward the living room. "Thanks for more than just dinner," she says, staring at where we were just cuddled together. There's a carcass composed entirely of sexual tension lying abandoned on the couch. I wonder if she can see it, too. "Thanks for being so badass. I know my life is a whole lot of crazy right now and you've got your own stuff going on. I appreciate that you put up with me making you be my big spoon tonight."

I smile but don't reply, because honestly, what can I say? That I'd put up with crazy around the clock, if it meant it was *her* crazy?

Finally she turns, reaching for the door. "You're like my blanket fort."

"I've been called worse things," I tell her.

With a small smile, Lola pushes herself up on her toes and leans in, pressing her lips quickly to my cheek. "Night, Olls."

"Night, Lola Love."

And then she's gone.

Chapter FIVE

Lola

WHAT DOES ONE do after a night of intimate cuddling with a *friend* on a couch and then going home to a very cold, very empty apartment?

Well, first one pulls one's vibrator from the bedside table. But the *next* day, one goes directly to said friend's store and pretends not to watch him all day.

I honestly don't know what is wrong with me. I vacillate so starkly between *keep it in the friend zone* and *jump him immediately* that I feel a little locked up every time I think about it. And the fact that, last night, Oliver didn't seem all that opposed to the cuddling and the flirting? Encouraging, even? I just . . . I honestly don't know what to do, and the person I most want to talk it out with—Oliver himself—is also the last person I want to talk it out with. I want to push, just a tiny bit, to see if things have changed and he'll make a move. It's just that I can never quite tell what's going on in his head.

"Do you live here now, Lola?" Not-Joe asks from behind the counter as I walk past him to the back of the store. "Because if so, I could show you how to run the register so I can go smoke a blunt."

"I heard that," Oliver mumbles from across the store. He looks up as I pass and gives me a little smile.

There are a thousand words in that tiny expression, and I don't speak the language.

"Stalking you two is one of the many perks of being a comic writer," I answer, stretching out with my sketchpad on the new couch in the back corner. Lately, the front reading nook is almost always full of Oliver's fangirls and high school kids sneak-reading *Sex Criminals.* "I get to hang out here all day and call it research."

"She's hiding from the paparazzi." Oliver lifts his chin to the front window to indicate the lone man standing with a note-pad near some parking meters. "It's only eleven in the morning and he's been there for two hours now," he tells me. "I think he's hoping to get an interview with you for his tiny free paper with a circulation of about five thousand in Chula Vista."

I'm grateful for the steaming Starbucks cup in his hand because I suspect the time he took to go get that is the only reason I missed him on my way in.

Although the press release got widespread coverage, trending hashtags, and the Tumblr memes are already out in full force, so far the buzz is all about casting, and there doesn't seem to be much more interest in me. Writers are boring. Introverted writers who don't seek attention are even more so. I've been able to forward all of the big interview requests to Benny so far, or answer questions via email. Thankfully, for now, Angela Marshall was wrong about how my day-to-day life would change.

"What'd you do last night?" Not-Joe calls to me, handing a customer a bag and closing the register.

"Went to Oliver's for dinner."

The man in question doesn't look up when I say this, and again I wonder what's going through his head. Is he thinking about how it felt to lie front to back on his couch? Is he thinking about how he maybe ate all the ice cream by himself after I left? Is he wondering what the hell got into me? I know I am.

I can't say I regret it, though.

"Din-ner," Not-Joe repeats.

"Joe." Oliver's voice is a gentle warning.

"This guy here made barbecue ribs," I tell Not-Joe. "They were fantastic."

Oliver's eyes meet mine for a brief second and then he looks away, fighting a smile.

"So, eating meat off some bones, then?" Not-Joe asks, grinning at me. "Sucking off the hot juices?"

I love Oliver's easy laugh that follows, the subtle slide of his eyes over to me again. I love that the pace of his work doesn't change even when we look at each other, breathing in, breathing out. He pulls a stack of books from a box and puts it down on a counter. Lifts another stack and puts it down.

"You're a menace," I say. I blink over to Not-Joe when I say it, but can pretend I'm saying it to Oliver.

Because he is a menace. A calm, steady, sexy-as-fuck menace.

Not-Joe shrugs, moving on, and bends down to inspect a

book. "Say, this new issue of *Red Sonja* features a lot of breast curve. I mightily approve."

Oliver turns around to look at him across the room. "Show me both of your hands, Joe."

Not-Joe holds up his hands, laughing. "You're the guy who wanks to comics, not me."

"You're the guy who gets asked 'is it in yet?'" Oliver drawls.

"You're the guy who keeps asking, 'Is it good, baby, does it feel good?'"

"Don't need to, mate," Oliver tells him, looking back down at an inventory sheet. "I *know* it's good."

Not-Joe laughs but I feel my eyes go wide at the growl in Oliver's voice, the casual way this fell from his lips. I'm choked by the weight of jealousy and longing when I think about him having sex. Or maybe it's the leftover *needneedneed* from last night.

Last night was weird.

I blink, turning to look at a rack of new releases and urging my brain to reboot.

"Just because it's good for you doesn't mean it's good for them," Not-Joe says.

"Well," I answer absently, "there were the lesbian roommates who made him practice, practice, practice. . . ."

I trail off, having felt the store go completely still.

Reboot fail. I can't believe I just said this.

The story of Oliver and his lesbian roommates was one I heard when we were all hammered—from Ansel, no less, and he had on his adorable troublemaker face when he told me—but Oliver and I have literally never talked about it. Shocking as that may be.

I can feel him staring at the side of my face, and one of his fangirl customers basically eye-fucks him from across the store.

"How did—?" he begins.

"Wait." Not-Joe stops him. "*Lesbian roommates?* Why am I just now hearing this story? I feel betrayed."

Oliver continues to watch me, and lifts his eyebrows as if to say, *Well? You were saying?*

"According to Ansel," I tell Not-Joe, trying to sound casual, like this information doesn't make me itch under my skin whenever I think about it, "Oliver had two female roommates at universiy in Canberra. Both were into other women, but being that it was college and we're all sort of loose about things in college, they took it upon themselves to show Oliver the ropes, as it were. Ansel says that *loads* of women have just raved about Oliver's—"

"No one has ever raved to *Ansel*," Oliver cuts me off, looking flustered. "I mean, it's not like that at all."

"Well, it sounded exactly like that," I say, giving him a playful smile.

But he doesn't return it.

In fact, he looks really tense, like he doesn't like that I'm talking about this. And of course he doesn't; we're in the middle of his place of business. But . . . wasn't he just the one talking about knowing sex with him is good?

Confused, I blink down to the book in my hands and read the same dialogue bubble over and over.

"That . . ." Not-Joe claps a hand on Oliver's shoulder. "That is *legendary*. Remind me of this the next time I give you shit."

Oliver doesn't say anything; he just scowls down at his clipboard.

And now it's weird. I *made* it weird, but when I think about it, it's been weird all morning. I took a leap and crossed an invisible line last night at his place. I exposed the farce of this Just Friends business, at least my end of it. *Just friends* works as long as everyone is on the level. As soon as it's clear one person wants more, the entire house of cards crumples. Saying I wanted to draw him a few days ago . . . last night, with the spooning and the hand-petting, and now here with the knowledge about his former sex life when he and I *never* talk about those things . . . I've probably knocked down the entire carefully constructed fortress and doused it with gasoline.

I walk over to him, lightly punching his shoulder. "Sorry," I mumble. "I just opened my mouth and dropped a whole lot of awkward on this moment."

He doesn't look at me. "S'okay. I just don't want you to think . . ."

"Yeah, I know," I say when he trails off. I get it. He doesn't want me to think about him like that.

The panel shows the girl, staring down at the beating organ in her hands.

We fall silent as another customer approaches, and I turn

away, headed back toward my things on the couch. I slip my sketchbook back into my messenger bag and sling it over my shoulder, ducking past Oliver and around an aisle of comics so I can discreetly escape.

"Where you headed, Lola?" Not-Joe calls.

"Just going out," I mumble, pushing open the front door.

Outside on the sidewalk, I carefully dodge the reporter and pull my phone from my bag, quickly dialing my dad just to look busy.

He answers on the second ring. "What's shaking, baby girl?"

I duck, speaking quietly into the phone. "Hey."

"Hey." He pauses, waiting for me to say why I've called. I did it as a cover, but now that I've got him on the phone, I realize how it feels like water is building behind a dam in my chest. Art and writing and the film and Oliver. My fits and starts of flirtation, the way I'm terrible at reading Oliver and even worse at trusting my own instincts with guys. It's too much all at once on my plate.

I could have called one of the girls, but I almost regret talking to Harlow about it the other day and don't want her poking me about Oliver right now. London is at work, and Mia can't help but pass along everything she hears to Ansel.

"What's up?" he asks again, prompting.

I grimace, closing my eyes. "I'm just short-circuiting."

"Tell me about everything that's got you."

"Who gave me a grown-up card? Like who thought that was a good idea?"

Dad laughs. "They give out grown-up cards? Huh. Must have passed me right up." He inhales again, voice tight with a held breath when he says, "Spill."

God, where do I even start? Dad would have opinions about Austin—*he sounds too slick, do you really think he's the right guy for this project?*—and the idea of Razor as an alien from Mars—*is he fucking kidding? Did he read the damn story?* Talking to him about my work always triggers his protective don't-let-them-screw-you instinct and, while I do love how proud he is of me, he has no experience with Hollywood. His opinions would be loud and unhelpful.

But the weirdest bit is that I don't need to talk that out yet; work is always the one realm where I've felt confident, and besides, my reaction to Razor-as-Martian is still percolating. *Oliver* is what has me the most tangled and I may as well talk about *that* with someone who's the least likely to dig too deep.

I chew on my nail before saying, finally, "I guess I'm in a weird place with Oliver."

"Ah." I hear him inhale sharply on the other end, can imagine the way he squints as he holds the cigarette between his lips. He blows out his breath. "We're talking about this now?"

"I guess."

When Mom left, Dad had to take over all the aspects of raising a girl that would normally have gone to her—helping me sort through minor dramas, crushes, and heartbreaks, getting my period. He did it all with the kind of straightforward stoicism I've come to absolutely adore about him. He's a teaser, a jokester, and uses sarcasm as a defense, but inside I know he's soft. Inside, his heart is too big sometimes.

He laughs, a short exhale. "So talk."

"So . . ." I start, squinting up at the sky. "I think I might want more."

Dad clucks his tongue. "I don't know, Boss. I can't read that kid. I think he adores you, but is it more for *him*?"

This is the exact kind of honesty I need. Dad likes Oliver a lot, but he isn't invested in the idea of us being romantic the way Harlow is. Frowning, I admit, "I don't know. In Vegas it was pretty clear he wasn't interested."

"And Oliver's a good friend," Dad says. "You always gotta be careful when you try to make it more."

I shrug, kicking at some dried leaves on the sidewalk. Dad is a mirror to my own thoughts on the matter. "Yeah."

I hear him inhale and blow out smoke again before saying, "But I know we all got itches that need to be scratched."

"*Dad.*"

He laughs. "You *do*. Come on now. Keep things light and fun. Your life is nuts right now. First *Razor Fish*, now you're writing more? And they're making your goddamn movie?"

I look up at the skyline. I've worked so hard for all of this, but I find myself suddenly wanting to change the subject. "What are you doing tonight?"

I hear the scratch of his shoe on the concrete back porch as he puts out the cigarette and the bang of the screen door as he goes back inside. "I think Ellen is coming over here for dinner."

Ellen. Dad's new girlfriend, whom I trust about as far as the distance between my bent elbow and my middle finger. Dad is one of the smartest and best people I know, and deserves someone special. Ellen is a gum-addicted, fake-breasted cocktail waitress at T.G.I. Friday's.

"Awesome."

"I can tell you don't like her."

I chuckle. "I *told* you I don't like her."

"She's fun, Boss," he says. "And she's got a great rack."

"Gross. I'm hanging up now. This was one hundred percent unhelpful."

He laughs. "Love you."

"Love you, too." I shove my phone back into my bag and climb the metal stairs to the loft.

I know what I said is a lie: it wasn't totally unhelpful. Sometimes Dad's straight shot of honesty is exactly what I need. It may not be more than a friendship for Oliver, but even if it is, is that the best thing for us?

But almost as soon as I've slid the loft door closed, someone bangs on the other side. It's two short hits with the side of a curled fist: Oliver.

I'm right there, pulling it open while his hand is still returning to his side.

"Hey," I say.

He's out of breath and swipes a hand through his hair. "Hey," he says. "Can I come in for a minute?"

I step aside. "Of course."

He walks past me into the living room and stares out the wall of windows for a few seconds until he catches his breath. He doesn't seem to have come here for a sandwich, or to use the bathroom because the one at the store is broken, and the longer he takes to start speaking, the more anxious I become.

Finally, he turns to me. "Are you okay?"

I stare up at him as a blur of images from the past hour flips through my head. Why would he think *I* wasn't okay? "Yeah. Why?"

"You just left really abruptly. Like something was wrong."

I groan inwardly, turning to look out the window. "I just felt like kind of an asshole for saying that thing to Not-Joe about you in college, and—"

"Fuck, Lola, I don't give a shit if Joe knows about that."

Shrugging, I tell him, "You seemed annoyed."

Clasping his hand around the back of his neck, he says, "I don't want you to think of me as this guy that would hook up with his roommate just to learn how to be with girls." His big bespectacled eyes look at me softly. "It sounds sketchy."

I smile. "I didn't really think of it like that. It's college. People do things in college."

"That whole thing happened over a single, *very* drunken weekend over a decade ago. It wasn't like"—he winces as he looks for the right words—"like, a nightly thing."

"It's okay," I say quietly, wanting him to know he doesn't need to explain this to make me feel better. "I don't need you to—"

"And knowing you're hearing those things about me from someone else . . ." he cuts in, scratching his neck, "that doesn't sit right with me."

"Well, to be fair, it's not like you and I really talk about those kinds of things."

He doesn't reply to this, and I quickly add, "I mean, it's fine. We don't need to. I just—that's why I left. Because it felt like I was being sort of intrusive. I don't want to get into your personal business, Oliver. I totally respect that space."

When he looks down at me, he seems confused. "I feel . . ." he says, and then shakes his head. "Fuck. I feel like maybe we need to talk."

Something sharp wiggles in my stomach. That is never the way a good conversation starts. "Aren't we talking right now?"

"I mean," he says, pacing, "last night was sort of . . . different for us. Was it just me?"

I look down at my shoe and poke at the carpet with my toe, awkwardness pushing its way into my posture. "No, I think I know what you mean. I'm sorry about that."

Stepping closer, he says, "No." And then more quietly, "Don't be. That isn't what I mean."

His hand comes up, slowly cupping the side of my jaw. I feel the sweep of his middle finger against my pulse point and he stares at his own hand, lips parted as if he can't quite believe what he's just done.

Like trying to see through thick fog, I'm trying to remember why I thought kissing Oliver might not be a good idea. Because right now I know without a doubt he's thinking about it, too.

My phone blares in my back pocket, so loud it startles us both. I step back and reach for it. "Sorry, I forgot I've been turning the ringer on lately. . . ." When I pull it out, we look down in unison and see the name *Austin Adams* on the screen.

"Jesus, how often does he call?" Oliver asks in a thick whisper.

"Sorry, just . . . one sec." I hold up a finger as I answer. "Hi, Austin."

"Loles!" he yells. Oliver turns to face the window, but I'm sure he can hear everything Austin says because I have to hold it away from my ear it's so loud. I can hear wind in the background and imagine him zipping through the Hollywood Hills in a convertible. "Wanted to see if you were going to be up in L.A. this week? Langdon is chomping at the bit to start. I'd love for you two to meet ASAP."

"I can come up anytime," I say. Oliver turns back to me, and I smile up at him, but he seems too distracted to return it.

"Great," Austin says. "There's a small studio party tomorrow night at the Soho House in West Hollywood. He'll be there, and I'd love if you could come. We could do the introductions, maybe start to hash out some of the bigger questions: What is Razor's origin story? How old is Quinn? If she's eighteen in the opening—"

"Wait. Quinn is fifteen," I cut in. "What do you mean?"

I can practically imagine him waving a hand. "Don't worry about it now. There are just a lot of angles to consider in the film adaptation. Questions of strength, sexuality, balancing normal life and the desire to continue her work as a vigilante."

Sexuality?

I look up at Oliver, whose brows are now drawn.

"So," Austin continues and the background noise decreases, as if he's just pulled into a garage. "I'll make sure you're on the list. Eight. Tomorrow. You can make it?"

"Yes," I say, quickly adding, "I think so."

"*Great,*" he says. A door slams and a car alarm chirps in the background. "I'll try not to hog you all to myself."

"Sounds good," I say.

"Until then!"

The line goes dead.

I slide my phone onto the coffee table and look up at Oliver, giving him a wide-eyed *what the fuck just happened* face. A tiny smile flicks up the corners of his mouth, but it quickly melts away, and then he just studies me in the ringing silence.

"You all right?" he asks quietly.

I feel the cold prick of panic spread across my neck, nausea bubbles in my belly. The two conversations—with Oliver, with Austin—are oil and vinegar, splashing around in my thoughts.

I blink, trying to figure out which one to tackle first. My brain trips on the idea of Quinn as an eighteen-year-old at the start of the story, and I feel my breaths grow shallow and tight. It doesn't work; she's young for her age even at fifteen; she's immature and innocent. Making her older would completely change her journey.

I blink harder, sliding my thoughts toward Oliver, but instead of being able to relish the idea of touching him, feeling him, being *his*, my brain snags on the instinctive fear of losing what we have now, the inevitable changes to *us*, the possibility of a life without him.

"Lola." Oliver says it so quietly, so free of emotion that I'm not sure if he's checking in on me after what Austin just dropped, or trying to return to what we were discussing when he first got here.

The panel shows a girl, hunched over, scribbling on a page so furiously the pencil snaps.

"Can we take one thing at a time?" I ask, finally looking up at him. "I'm sort of frazzled all of a sudden, and this is a big conversation."

"I wouldn't expect you to be able to talk about last night after . . . *that*." He nods to my phone, smiling a little.

"I'm not saying we shouldn't have the conversation. I just . . ." I sigh. "I'm inarticulate at the moment."

Oliver nods. His face is calm, eyes warm and engaged. He really does seem to understand. Even so—and maybe it resides only in me—but there's a residue, some film left between us, like I took this perfect glossy moment of potential and smeared a greasy hand over it.

"I get it." He digs his hands into his pocket and his jeans

dip, exposing the top of his boxers. I look over his shoulder, out the window, and he adds, "One thing at a time."

I walk over to the couch, collapse on the seat, and throw an arm over my face. Sometimes the fantasy of getting everything you ever wanted is so much easier than the reality pressing up against the glass.

"Do you want to talk through it?" he asks. "Quinn as an eighteen-year-old, that is," he adds quickly. "The idea really fucks with me. I feel like they might be setting up Razor and Quinn as love interests."

The cool stab of panic returns. "I know. I know. *Fuck.*" I rub my hands over my face, feeling too overwhelmed to think about it right now. Tilting my head I ask, "And maybe we can talk about it on the drive to L.A. tomorrow?"

His brow furrows. "You want *me* to come?"

I hesitate for just a moment. The rational part of my brain is holding up warning signs while the emotional part insists I need him by my side. "Of course I want you there," I tell him. "Who else will help me remember all the names and elbow me when I start doodling on a napkin? Unless you don't want to co—"

"I do. Just wondered if you'd rather go with one of the girls."

I feel my gaze narrow slightly. "No . . . I want to go with you."

He swallows, nodding as he looks to the side. "Well, then . . . sure."

"I'll meet you at the store at six?"

"Sounds good," he says. He's blushing. I've never seen Oliver blush before. "Anything specific I need to wear?"

My heart is beating way too fast and I'm reminded of the time Harlow convinced me to go bungee jumping, and those terrifying, thrilling seconds before we took the leap. I push my palm against my chest and struggle to sound casual when I say, "Just look pretty for me."

Chapter SIX

Oliver

I RARELY TAKE A day off—in fact, I haven't taken an entire day away since the store opened four months ago—but I need it today.

I sleep in, have coffee on the back porch, and watch a mourning dove build a nest in my eaves.

I run a few miles along the water, to Cove Beach and back.

I get the car serviced and washed.

I clean the house, shower. Eat and dress.

And I give myself the entire day to think about what's happening with me and Lola.

I want it to be conscious—*intentional*—between us. I don't want to slide into something with her without thought, not only because our friendship is one of the best and most important of my life, but because even though we don't talk about it much, I know her relationship history isn't particularly positive.

Harlow has hinted that Lola's few relationships have ended after only the briefest life spans, that Lola tends to keep men at an emotional arm's length, and that she spooks easily.

Even if I hadn't seen the spooking with my own eyes two days in a row—at my house, at the store yesterday—I could have figured it out after a single conversation with her father where I learned the most telling detail of Lola's life: her mother left when she was twelve, without even saying goodbye. It's like a bruise that sits just under her skin, one that darkens whenever she lets herself get too close.

The store is pretty dead when I stop by just before I'm supposed to meet Lola. Joe is a great employee, but instinct tells me to not let a full workday go with him alone here.

"You missed a dude with a huge box of Tortured Souls figures about an hour ago." Joe watches me drop my keys onto the counter, adding, "I feel unclean. I've seen some crazy shit in my day, but that stuff scares *me*."

"Says the man who pierced his own cock."

He laughs, stepping aside as I log in to the computer system. "I know," he says. "But have you seen those figures? They're babies in bottles of liquid and tortured people gestating their own murderer."

"So what did you tell him?" A good deal of our business is the buying and selling of collector's items: action figures, comics, graphic art. Joe has a good eye for stuff but doesn't really have the same background in the scene that I do. The official rule is that if Joe isn't sure whether he should buy something, he tells the person to come back when I'm here. In the first few weeks, he rarely knew what to buy and what to leave, but he's a quick learner and I no longer panic that he'll let something unbelievable slip through our hands.

"I told him we get a lot of kids in here and it's not our thing." He shudders visibly and then does a slight double take. "Why are you so dressed up?"

"I have a thing," I say.

I can practically hear his eyebrows go up. "'A *thing*'?"

Sliding my eyes over to him to give him a mild glare, I squat down, and cut open a box of office supplies. To be fair, I don't ever have *things*.

Joe steps into my peripheral vision and then bends down until his face is about five inches from mine. "A thing?" he repeats.

"For fuck's sake," I grumble, handing him a few boxes of pens. "A thing up in L.A. tonight with Lola."

The three seconds of silence that follow communicate a good deal of incredulity. "Is it a date?"

I shake my head.

"Are you *sure* it's not a date?"

I reach up, sliding a new box of business cards onto the counter. "Pretty sure."

"Because lately she's been looking at you like she might want—"

I cut him off. "It's not a date, Joe."

The bell rings and I hear someone walk in, heels clicking on the linoleum floor.

"This is the last time I'm going to ask you," Joe whispers. "Are you sure it's not a date?"

I open my mouth to say something sharp, but stop when I hear Lola ask, "Where's Oliver?"

"On his knees under the counter," Joe says breathily, and I look up to see him smiling widely down at me.

Her unsure speechlessness fills the room.

I shoot Joe an annoyed look. "Down here," I tell her, and wave a roll of receipt tape over my head. "Just putting some stuff away."

"Uh-huh," she says, leaning over the counter so I can only see her face. I realize how utterly fucked I am if I think I can play it cool tonight. She looks bloody gorgeous. "Hi."

I put the last roll of tape away and almost swallow my tongue when I stand and finally see the rest of her. Lola wearing leather pants should be illegal. Couple that with shoes I would happily die impaled on and a top that hints at everything underneath but shows nothing? I have zero chance of not making a fool of myself in one way or another tonight.

"You look amazing," I tell her, and without thinking, walk around the counter, lean in, and press a kiss to her cheek.

She doesn't react as if what I've done is out of the ordinary, just smiles and says a quiet, "Thank you."

Her eyes slide to where my wallet and keys rest on the counter, but I'm not done taking her in yet. Her hair is up in a high ponytail, sleek and black. Her bangs cut straight across her forehead, and her makeup isn't heavy, but I can tell she's wearing it. Soft black lines her eyes, pink flushes her cheeks, and her lips are an unholy, nearly sinful red.

"Oliver?"

My words come out sort of shaky: "You look really pretty."

This time she laughs. "Thanks," she says, adding, "*again.* London helped. I swear giving the two of us makeup is like giving a monkey a hammer."

When I step away to grab my things, she makes a show of slowly looking me up and down. I follow her eyes as they linger on what I'm wearing: slim trousers, simple, dark button-down shirt. I even polished my boots for this woman.

"Damn," she says. There's *appreciation* in her voice and I realize that we've always done this—flirted, dropped subtle innuendo—but it's never felt this loaded before.

"I'm glad you approve," I say. "I'm parked around the corner."

She follows me out, saying goodbye to Joe. And then she takes my arm and smiles up at me. "I definitely approve."

Yep. I am fucked.

I'VE ALWAYS KNOWN Lola to grow quiet when she's thinking about something that's troubling her. I assumed that the reason she doesn't tend to talk out her problems the way Harlow and even Ansel do is that she wants to take the time to sort through it on her own first. But when she brings up the conversation with Austin in the car, and wants me to list some of the pros of his ideas, I lock up, wondering whether the reason she likes to take so long before talking about things is that she doesn't always trust her own judgment.

"I'm not sure I could argue the merits of either suggestion," I hedge, merging onto the 5 North freeway.

"Just for the exercise," she says. "Why might it be better for Razor to be from another planet?"

I sit quietly, thinking on the question. But my mind reflexively fights it; they're both shit ideas. Quinn shouldn't be made into a sexual creature. Razor isn't an alien. There's no reason to change it.

The tires trip easily over the road and Lola stares out her window while she also thinks about it. It's these easy moments where I seem to plummet deeper in love with her.

"I guess it could allow them to do something cooler visually?" she muses after a few minutes of silence. "Some more creative way to flash back to his life before without just a panel shift."

Shrugging, I say, "I guess, but Razor's alternate time in the book is just as visually different in flashbacks as another planet would be. I mean, the way you do it is unique, but time shifts are done elsewhere, too. The Multiversity collapses all parallel timelines into the Hypertime."

"I know, but maybe that argues Austin's case. Multiversity collapses all of the DC timelines to explain how they all could exist. Maybe the idea of parallel time is easier to grasp there because people want a way to reconcile all the various takes on the same characters."

"I think *yours* is simpler," I say, adding, "more elegant, I mean. It *starts* with the idea of a parallel time loop. It doesn't use it to explain things in hindsight."

She hums, nodding at this. "I guess I'll just need to hear what they say. It's so easy to do something when it's just me and a book and my ideas. It's different when I expose it all to this larger collective consciousness."

This thought lands heavily between us. She's going to let Austin and the screenwriter try to convince her? And maybe she should. But I can't help but feel like I wouldn't. Like a man in her position maybe wouldn't.

"It's not because you feel cowed by him?" I ask her.

Lola tilts her head. "It's not my expertise," she says, adding, "Film, I mean."

"But the *story* is. Razor is. _Quinn_ is." *Quinn is you,* I want to say. *Don't let him change you. Don't let him sexualize your journey from ruin to triumph.*

Nodding, she looks back out the window. "I know. I'm just thinking about how I want to handle it."

"What if he insists Quinn be eighteen?" I ask her. "What if he says without a romance angle in the story, it won't float in Hollywood?"

Lola turns and looks at me, and I catch a flash of fury in her eyes before I have to look back at the road. "He might be right," she says. "That's what sucks. It might need romance to work as a commercial film. We didn't sell this to an art-house indie. We sold it to a major studio. Profit is the key. And I knew that going in."

I see what she's saying but it twists me, tightly. "You wouldn't push back?"

"Of course I would," she says. "And I know what you're saying, but I guess I want to make sure I do it right. You should have seen the meeting. Angela and Roya got maybe three words in, and they're the executive producers here. And contractually, I only have so much input."

"Really?" I'm aware of the comic community's ongoing discussion about feminine representation on the page and in creative staffing, but I still find myself surprised that Lola's *film* might not be hers after all.

She nods. "I'm twenty-three. I'm the first female comic creator to have a major motion picture, and I'm one of the few people out there writing *and* illustrating it all. If I was Stan Lee or Geoff Johns walking in there—or even just some nobody guy with my age and experience—I could tell them what the fuck to do and they would listen. A man having strong opinions and pushing back right away is someone with *sound business sense*. If I walk in there as Lola Castle and push back, I'm pushy and hard to work with. Maybe someone will even use the word *bitch*."

I feel my jaw go tight. I know she's right, but still. "That's fucking bullshit."

"It's the way the world works," she says. "The first question I always get asked is what it's like being a woman in the comic industry. Every single interview. The second question is whether any of my *girl*friends read comics."

Fuck. I never thought about the interview aspect before. They seemed like reasonable questions, but with a step away from it, I can see it's utter shit.

"Do you think anyone would ever ask Brian Michael Bendis whether he has any male friends who read his comics?" she asks.

I laugh, but it isn't really from humor. "Probably not."

"We fight these perceptions one meeting at a time, but it's why I want to be strategic about the battles I pick," she says. "I need to convince myself first that these changes are absolutely unacceptable because I'm sure there are other things down the road that will floor me, and I don't want to be excused from the conversation before it even starts."

And there, right there, I want to propose.

I want to pull over and climb from the car, and get down on one knee on the dusty, narrow shoulder of the freeway. Because Lola knows it's bullshit, she knows she needs to tread carefully. And she's figuring out the best way to fight for what she's built.

MILLION-DOLLAR HOMES PEEK out from behind lush trees and iron gates before we turn onto Sunset, parking in a sleek underground lot.

The lifts are spotless, marble floors polished to a shine. We're on a list in the lobby; another list is checked upstairs. Lola takes my hand as we walk in but it isn't romantic; I'm sure that much is clear to both of us. It's what we would do before stepping off the side of our world and into another. It's about having an anchor.

This is the kind of party where everyone is wearing black, and the waiters—most likely models or actors—wind their way through the room with silver trays covered in beautiful hors d'oeuvres and flutes of champagne. Music is loud so peo-

ple are forced to speak over it. The room isn't bursting with
partygoers, but it sounds that way.

Some guy spots us from over near the bar and throws his
hand in the air, calling out to Lola.

He's shorter than I am by several inches, and is dressed so
casually—in a T-shirt and jeans—in a roomful of meticulous
people, it strikes me as a bit douchey.

"Loles!" he calls and comes up to hug her tightly . . . and
for a while. *Jesus.* If my math is on, this is only the second time
they've met. "I'm so glad you could make it!"

She thanks him for the invite and turns to gesture to me.
"Austin, this is my friend, Oliver."

"Oliver," he says in surprise. It gives me no small pleasure
that he has to tilt his head to look up at me. I can tell immediately from his little smirk that he'd planned to fuck Lola tonight, and I certainly hope he is recalculating his odds. I may
not know if I claim Lola's heart, but I sure as fuck know that
this man could never claim a single inch of her.

Sorry, friend.

He extends his hand, shakes it firmly. "Nice to meet you."

"You as well."

There's no more for us to say, really, and after a few
more seconds endured of silent eye contact, he turns back
to Lola.

"I want to introduce you to some people." He scans the
room, pointing out a few names we might recognize from
where we stand.

The guy in the black pants and shirt is a screenwriter. The other guy in black pants and shirt is a director. The woman in the black cocktail dress is VP at some studio.

And Lola just fits in. The girls always joke that Lola looks like some kind of badass superhero, and it's true. There's a strength about her, a quiet confidence that comes from setting out to do something and getting it done.

"Now come on," Austin says to her, and she grabs my hand. Her palm is clammy, fingers trembling. "Let's go find Langdon."

I hold back and because we're now attached at the hand, Lola is gently jerked back, and looks at me.

"Go do your thing," I tell her quietly. "I'm going to get a drink and something to eat. I'm fine."

"You sure?" she asks.

"Totally." It occurs to me only now that it's going to be late when we're done, and neither of us may be up for the long drive home. "But should I book a couple of rooms at a nearby—"

"Already handled," she assures me with a smile.

My heart starts to thunder in my chest, and Lola doesn't immediately turn. "Thanks for taking care of that." It feels right to bend down and kiss her jaw, just shy of her neck, so I do.

I may have just crossed a line, but I can tell when she smiles at me and squeezes my hand that she doesn't mind.

———

AT THE BAR, I drink, I eat, I people-watch.

It's a fascinating study, and in such stark contrast to my everyday. I have the most casual of clientele; have always run in circles that were more comfortable with grub than polish. Literally no one I know other than Harlow and Ansel—and now Lola—would blend in here. But this is Lola's new reality and so, in some ways, it's also mine.

She finds me after about a half hour and slides onto the seat beside me. "Hey you."

"Hey." I put my drink down and take her hand, squeezing. I'm relieved to have her back. Despite my confidence that Lola would never go off with someone like Austin, I didn't particularly relish being separated from her. "How did it go?"

She smiles and nods at someone across the room. "It was good," she says through her grin, holding it. "I think. They have a lot of ideas. I sort of tried to listen." She looks back at me, adding, "Without judgment."

"That bad, huh?"

Shaking her head, she says, "Not all of it. It's just weird when something so personal isn't just mine anymore. Langdon already has a lot written, I guess. I'm trying not to knee-jerk all over the place."

"Want to talk about it later?" I guess.

She nods, and when the bartender checks in with her, she leans in to order a drink over the din of the crowd. He mixes it in front of her while she watches in silence, looking like she very clearly needs it. She takes the glass from him with a smile that's returned a little too enthusiastically for my liking, and turns back to me.

"So what *do* you want to talk about?" I ask.

"We're at a pretty fancy party, and you just sat at the bar alone for a half hour while about fifteen executives checked you out and mentally took you home to their creepy L.A. sex dungeons."

I laugh. "Lies."

"*Not* lies," she says, leaning in and making a funny face. "What's your best pickup line?"

"I don't really have a line. I just sort of sit there, like this." I shift my knees apart and give her the blue steel.

"Wide stance," she says, with a grin. "I like what that communicates to the room."

I make a show of straightening my glasses and motion to myself. "I mean, you put out the honey, you're going to get some bees."

Lola smacks my shoulder, laughing.

Nodding at her with a sexy little wink, I say, "Baby, I know we're gonna fuck, it's just a matter of how we get back to your place." I lean in, for dramatic effect, whispering, "I don't have a car."

When Lola laughs, her head tilts back, exposing her perfect skin, long, slim throat, and the sound is higher than one would guess from hearing her sultry voice, more girlish. Her laugh, when she's at ease, is adorable in a way Lola would never admit.

"That's my new favorite," she says when her laughter dies down.

I love when she says *favorite*. The way her mouth forms the *f*. She kisses the air. It makes me think about moving over her, capturing those lips in a kiss when she gasps out a pleading *"Fuck."*

Her eyes meet mine and they're smiling, unaware of how far my thoughts have taken me. "How could anyone ever say no to that?"

"Honestly," I tease, "I haven't a clue."

"What's this like for you?" she asks me and then looks around the room.

I shrug, following the path her eyes have taken. "Weird, I guess. But not. It's not altogether different from what I expected. Sort of a departure from the shop, I reckon."

She smiles at me. "You're the biggest geek I've ever known." When she says it, I hear pride in her voice. To Lola, this is the ultimate praise.

The bartender sets another whiskey in front of me and I thank him with a nod. "This is true," I tell her with a bit more mocking in my voice. "And yet, here you are, enjoying this evening with me anyway."

"It must be the alcohol," she says, sipping from her little straw.

I nod to her drink. "That's your first one."

She smiles. "You're observant, I like that."

"One of my many attributes. Along with hardworking, good at maths, and punctual."

She shakes her head, swallowing a sip quickly so she can

contradict me: "Hey, at the top of that list should be the accent."

"You're saying my accent is more important than my ability to do multiplication tables in my head?"

Lola laughs, and if I'm correct, leans just a bit closer. "Why don't you date more?"

I hesitate with my glass perched on my lips, and then take a drink before setting it down again. Lola absolutely sounds like she's teasing me, but there's an edge there, like she's inching closer to something she finds a little scary.

"Shouldn't I be asking you that?" I tilt my head, thinking. "Austin seems interested."

Lola grimaces, folding her arms on the bar and looking at me. "You're not answering my question."

"Neither are you."

"And why is that?" she asks, watching.

"Probably for the same reason you don't."

Lola stirs the straw in her drink, using the tip of it to pierce the lime slices one by one, and just beside me, someone opens a door to a patio, letting in a blast of cold air.

"Do you want to leave?" she asks, looking up at me. "Go someplace more our speed?"

I open my mouth and the cool air hits my tongue like a spark of electricity. "Sure." I wonder how it's possible that the hammering of my pulse feels louder than the music around us.

Holding out her hand, Lola gives me her secret little smile. "Well, then . . . let's get out of here."

Chapter SEVEN

*W*E DRIVE OLIVER'S car back to the hotel and leave it there, walking a couple of blocks to what the concierge has assured us is a perfectly humble venue. And he's right: it's dark and nondescript, with an oval bar in the middle of the room, some high tables on one side, and space for a band and handful of fans. Except tonight there is no band, no fans. Hardly anyone else here.

I only had one drink at the party, but I feel silly, clumsy, distracted by the *thump-thump-thump* behind my breastbone, and know it's the way it feels like being here with Oliver is a mini-vacation. There's something about getting away from home and routine, and suddenly *anything* is possible.

We could stay here for a week.

We could pretend we don't have responsibilities here or back home.

We could change everything between us.

The panel shows the girl, falling backward: arms out, eyes closed.

He picks two seats at the bar and helps me with my coat and purse before sitting down. The way he touches me trips my pulse into overdrive; his hands are firm and sure, fingers not shy about reaching for the collar of my coat, gently dragging it down my back. He cups my bare shoulder, asking, "Is here good?"

I want to ask him *good for what* but when he nods to the seat I realize he means geography. Not whether here is good for this flimsy barrier of still-platonic to melt away.

"Perfect."

He catches the bartender's eye, waves him over, and we sit in silence while the man wipes a glass dry, puts it away, and makes his way over to us.

It feels like a date.

"You want a Manhattan?" Oliver asks.

"Yes, please."

He orders for both of us, gives his thanks, turns back to me. My heart wants to escape, to flap out of my body and into his. And, *God.* Is this what it means to become infatuated with someone? A heart becomes a hybrid, half yours, half theirs. Mine beats like this because it wants out. My chest aches to let his heart in.

"How do you feel about all of this?" Oliver asks.

The pounding in my chest intensifies and the swoon of it, the reflexive joy brings another, less pleasant sensation with it: fear.

When I smell fresh bread, my mouth waters.

When I see a pen, I reach for it.

When I want someone, I worry.

What happens if the brains decide to walk away from it

all? Does the hybrid heart wither, leaving us with only half of what we need?

He must sense the shift in my posture because he touches my jaw with one finger so I'll turn my face up to his, adding, "I meant the movie, Lola Love. The book. Tonight."

"Oh." I am an idiot. The panic dissolves and I smile, letting it grow from a grin to something that makes Oliver laugh. "I think it's all pretty awesome."

"I only got the tiniest glimpse of you before it all started," he says. "*Razor* was released not long after Vegas, and it was a whirlwind from the get-go. You didn't seem to really believe it was going to happen at first. I'd love to get a peek at Lola from before even that. Before it sold."

"She was a college kid," I remind him. "Stressing about finals and rent money."

He nods, and moves his attention to my mouth. Without embarrassment; he does it intentionally. "I sometimes forget you're so young."

I'm not sure why, but I love that he's said this. It feels kinky, in a quiet way, like he's corrupting me a little. "I don't feel very young."

He exhales slowly through his nose. "You had to grow up early."

"You did, too, didn't you?" I know so little about his life before college. He never speaks of siblings, of parents. He's mentioned grandparents once or twice, but it's not in our nature to push. At least that's how it's been until now. I want to crush that pattern with a brick.

Oliver looks back up to my eyes but we both turn to the bartender when he slides our drinks in front of us.

"Want me to open a tab?" he asks us.

"Yeah, sure," Oliver says, pulling out his wallet and handing him a card.

The bartender turns and realization smacks me. "What? Wait." I reach behind me for my purse. "Wait. I should be paying for this! You're doing me a favor coming up here."

"Lola," he says, stilling me and shaking his head to the bartender to indicate he is still paying. "Stop. It doesn't matter who pays."

"It does, but thank you."

Oliver grins. "You're very welcome."

I hang my purse back on my chair, smiling guiltily. "Is it weird to forget that I can afford to pay for drinks now?"

"I don't think so." He runs his finger over the rim of the glass. "God, I remember how long it took me to get out of the starving-student mentality. My father died five years ago, left me this sum of money." Long fingers curl around his tumbler, and he lifts it to his mouth, sips his drink. I want to taste the scotch from his lips. "It was this huge shock. I hadn't seen him since I was seven. I lived with my grandparents. I figured Dad was off doing heroin most of my childhood."

I blink, jerked out of my Oliver Lust Haze. "What?"

He nods. "So when his lawyer contacted me, telling me my father was dead—but good news! He'd left me money—I was furious. He'd got his life together enough to earn money, to *save* money, but he hadn't bothered to come back for me."

I feel the pressure of tears in my head, the heating, tightening of it in my throat when I look up at his pained expression. "I didn't know that."

"Well, anyway." He hands me my drink, gently clinks my glass with his. "To finding your people," he says.

I nod, drinking when he does, but even the sharp burn of whiskey doesn't really register. His dad left him, too. Even his mom. I feel like we're two wires, wound around and around and around together, propagating current.

"Lola?" he says.

I look up at him, try to smile. "Yeah?"

"Dance with me?"

I nearly choke on my pulse. "What?"

Oliver laughs. "Dance with me. Come on, live a little."

He holds out his hand and after what he's just told me, what else can I say, but "Okay"?

We put our drinks down and slide from our stools, walking over to the empty floor. There are three other people here, not including the bartender, and they don't give a single shit what we're doing or why we're standing in the middle of the empty floor staring at each other.

"There's not really any music," I tell him.

He shrugs. "S'alright."

But then music comes on, too loudly at first and we both flinch. The bartender has put on the sound system, and after he adjusts the volume, Aerosmith drifts down over the dance floor.

"Oh boy," I say, laughing.

Oliver grins in playful apology. "This will have to do."

"It's almost so bad it's good again," I tell him and hold my breath when I feel the slide of his hand around my waist, feel every single one of his fingers against my spine. His other hand comes just beneath it, to the spot low on my back that suddenly becomes the convergence point for all of my nerve endings. Oliver pulls me in, flush against him. I can feel the waistband of his pants against my stomach, can feel how my breasts press against his solar plexus.

My hands are curled around his biceps and I'm staring up at his face. The dark of his brows, the light of his eyes, the shadow of a beard at his jaw . . . somehow it comes together to make my favorite face in the world. Oliver's lips come apart just the smallest bit when he looks down at me and I see his jaw flex, feel his fingers press more firmly into my back. *This* is tension. This, right now, is lust, and I've never wanted anything more than I want his kiss. It's nearly painful, the wanting. Something inside me is rebelling, stabbing itself with need, telling me it won't let up until it gets what it wants. I'm being held hostage by my own heart.

We move, shifting feet, very, very slowly turning.

"This is nice," he says. "I haven't danced in ages."

I keep waiting for the oddness to descend, the realization that what we're doing is a little weird, but it doesn't happen. It feels like I'm holding my breath, waiting for a sneeze to come.

"Breathe, Lola Love," he whispers, and something inside me trips.

I *haven't* been breathing. I've been standing here, hold-ing my breath, waiting for him to kiss me and for my body to relax and for time to stop and for me to suddenly know what it is to be in love with someone.

"I'm terrified," I tell him. We've shifted so close now I can't really make out all of his features, but I can feel his breath, can nearly taste the scotch he's had.

His eyes move back and forth between mine; his voice is a gentle reassurance: "I know, pet."

"I've never been good at romantic relationships. I *want* to be," I add quickly, "but it scares me."

"I know," he says again, bending to press a kiss to my temple. One of his hands slides up my back and into the hair at the back of my head. "But I just want you. I don't need easy or perfect. I don't need to rush anything."

And there, laid out so bare and easily between us, it is. His honesty breaks a dam in me and I feel my own truths tumble forward, messy and raw.

"My first time was with a total stoner," I tell him in a burst, closing my eyes and nearly crying out when he turns his face, pressing his stubbly cheek to mine. His ear is right next to my mouth; I can whisper right into the confessional. "He worked at the 7-Eleven on the corner, and just wanted to get high and have sex. We didn't even really talk."

Swallowing, I tell him, "I was only fourteen. He was twenty." I can feel Oliver tensing against me. "No one knows about him, not even Harlow or Mia. They think I lost my virginity senior year. But Dad worked until dinnertime, and I'd go over there a lot of days after school, just looking for some kind of"—I shake my head—"distraction or, I don't know. After Mom left, I wasn't great with decisions."

"How could you be?" he asks, kissing my jaw. His lips leave a streak of fire on my skin.

"But how horrible is it to admit that that relationship was the easiest one I've ever had? Everyone I've dated since then has ended up mad at me." Pulling back to meet his eyes, I tell him, "It's always when things get serious that I start to . . . I don't know. Short-circuit. I don't want it to be like that with us."

He's watching my mouth when he asks, "You don't want it to be serious, or you don't want to short-circuit?"

"I don't want to mess this up," I say. "Our friendship is too important to me. What if we . . . do *this,* and it changes that?"

Oliver nods, bending and pressing his cheek to mine again. "I don't have a choice but to want to do this, Lola. I'm in love with you."

The words incinerate my lungs and I stop breathing again. There isn't a word for what I'm feeling. It is the direct, razor edge of ecstasy and terror.

"Shh," he whispers. "Don't panic, okay? I'm just being honest here. I love you. I want you." He exhales, and it's a massive, trembling gust against my neck. "Fuck, I want you. But I understand it isn't simple, and I don't expect simple. I just want you to try. I mean, if—"

I nod quickly—my heart is lodged in my throat, pounding, pounding, pounding with need for him—and he jerks me tighter into him, relief evident in his posture. I didn't think it was possible to be any closer, but it was. It just required our bodies to collapse, air to evacuate lungs.

We go quiet and I realize I've been dancing without thought. I'm not a natural dancer, but I haven't considered what my feet are doing, how my arms or hands or hips are moving. But now that I am, I can imagine how it would be to be with Oliver: how he would fit against me, over me. He's taller, broader, but his hips would still feel sharp on my thighs. His hands don't do tentative; I can imagine the pressure of them sliding up and over my curves. I want the hand in my hair to form a fist, pull my head back. Even though he wouldn't do that here, the promise is there, in the flexing of his fingers, in the way they haven't shifted away. He found a spot, buried deep.

"I saw Aerosmith when I was fourteen," he says, and I wonder if he's thinking about how young that is, thinking about *me* at fourteen, alone in an apartment with a burnout guy. Or, if he's just talking to get me to remember that this is us. This is what we do, with or without *I love yous.* "It was after they had that ballad out from Armageddon—"

" 'I Don't Want to Miss a Thing'?"

"Yeah, that's it," he says, laughing. "We went by ourselves and felt so fucking mature. We took a bus to Sydney— it's nearly two hundred kilometers away and my grandparents were like, 'Yeah, sure, go for it.' I'm not kidding when I say every crazy personality in the world is represented on buses."

"Wow."

"I know," he agrees. "Such kids, right, but I reckon it was the best night of my life up to then. My mate got tickets from his cousin. I didn't even know any Aerosmith songs—well, I did," he says, "I just didn't realize they were Aerosmith. But it was brilliant. Maybe that's when I decided I wanted to travel. Maybe it was before that, I don't know. I think I learned to be a little fearless on that bus. Figured if I could head up to Sydney for a weekend, I could go anywhere."

"My first concert was Britney Spears."

He laughs outright, pulling back and smiling down at me. "That's awful."

"It was *awesome*," I tell him. "I swear. Me, Harlow, Mia, and Luke—Mia's ex." I shake my head, remembering us dancing our asses off and Luke smiling through his teeth, being a good sport. "Poor Luke."

"Taking three chicks to a concert? He could do worse."

"Only one of us was putting out. Well, back then," I say, reconsidering. "I think Luke gets more action now than 1979 Steven Tyler."

Oliver laughs at this, but the song ends and he stops, easing his arms from around me.

"You did it," he says, looking down at me with a half smile. "You danced with an Aussie in an empty bar and the world didn't end. Check it off your list."

"And we . . ." I start.

We talked. We *admitted*. We took that terrifying single step forward.

He waits to see how I'm going to finish this, expression

warm, but neutral. "Yeah, we did," he says finally, tilting his head toward the bar. "Let's finish our drinks."

And like this, it's easy again.

――――――――

I WAKE UP alone in an enormous white bed, in a bright pool of sunshine.

In the past few months I have traveled so often that the dusty blue walls and wide, white chair in the corner don't immediately trigger a context for where I am. I roll over, see my leather pants folded on the chair, my shirt and bra lying neatly on top.

Obviously, Oliver is down the hall, in his own room.

My stomach feels low and small in my body, missing him. Wanting him closer.

Over our second drink we easily shed the tension of the We Are Totally Into Each Other admission. We were interrupted by a perfectly timed call from Not-Joe telling us how his date passed out drunk on her couch, and only after he left did he realize his phone was dead and he left his wallet in the store so he had to give a taxi driver his watch in order to get a ride home.

At around one in the morning, we left the bar, hand in hand, and walked the two blocks back to our hotel. I had five missed calls from Austin, none with voicemails, so I let them be. I wanted nothing but Oliver on my brain. He pointed out his room when we passed it on the way to mine, but before I could stutter my way through an invitation inside, he bent and kissed my cheek.

"Let's take it slow," he said. "See you in the morning."

The words immediately formed in my head, but I couldn't exactly say them out loud: can't we have sex but *otherwise* take this slow?

I roll over, unplug my phone from the cord on the bedside table, and check my email. Shoving up onto an elbow, I squeeze my eyes together, struggling to read the words in front of me.

"Holy fuck." I sit all the way up, crossing my legs in bed and zooming in on my screen so I can be sure I'm not imagining what I'm seeing. It seems that while Oliver and I were flirting and clinking glasses and avoiding the discussion of dating, Columbia-Touchstone cast the leads in the *Razor Fish* film. I have over three hundred emails, and at least ten voicemails from media outlets wanting a statement.

I tried to get a hold of you last night after you left. There's a script, Austin wrote in an email. Thank God I've flagged his name; otherwise who knows whether I would have even seen it? Just something Langdon drew up in the past week. But don't stress, we did it so we could cast quickly, and you're going to do all the polish.

He didn't think to clarify this *last night*? He told me Langdon had *started* writing, not finished.

The check also deposited in my bank account, and seeing that much money there makes me want to vomit. It triggers some instinctual panic, like I should have it all made into gold bars and hide them in my mattress.

There's a knock at my door and I stumble up, pulling on a robe. Outside in the hall, Oliver looks rumpled, a little nervous.

I immediately see it on his face—a soft, vulnerable happiness that flashes in the tilt of his mouth, in the narrowing of his eyes—for only a breath before he can carefully tuck it away.

Even though I was just with him last night, it feels like it's been a week, and he looks different somehow. Less like this wonderful face of a friend, and more like this man in front of me who has a body under his clothes that I'm growing desperate to see again and even more desperate to touch.

Neither of us has spoken, and I'm afraid last night changed everything. I don't want things to be awkward between us.

"How's my favorite comic book store owner named Oliver Lore?"

He smiles, wide enough that it shifts his glasses and I can see his eyes crinkling fully at the corners. "I wish I could answer in emoji. I'd just say the fried egg icon out loud."

Okay, so that was sort of perfect.

"Do you want to grab breakfast?" I ask. "Or . . . order room service?"

This option feels decidedly more intimate, and Oliver seems to agree.

"Nah," he says. "Let's hit the restaurant downstairs. They have a buffet. I think I'll eat it all."

"Come on in," I tell him, running over to my overnight

bag and grabbing my clothes. "Give me five. I've got to call Benny real quick."

Oliver walks into my room, and I notice when he gives a lingering glance to my clothes from last night, so neatly placed on the chair. I wonder if he's thinking what I'm thinking, that if he'd been in here with me, those leather pants might have been sacrificed to the sex gods.

"Lola!" Benny answer-yells through the speakerphone, and I cringe, staring at the screen as if it burned me. It's not even nine in the morning; how is he so chipper?

"Hey, Benny."

"I bet I know why you're calling," he sings. "*People* magazine's Sexiest Man Alive is playing Razor and you want to come up to Hollywood to celebrate tonight."

Oliver turns to look at me, eyes wide. I hold up a finger, indicating I'll update him in a second.

"I'm already up in Hollywood," I say. "But I'm headed home. Austin didn't mention the script last night when I saw him."

"Probably because he knew you'd ask to read it on the spot, and then would request edits before it went out, but it was already out."

I chew my lip, suppressing a grin. "What happens now?"

"I release a statement on your behalf," he says. "How's this? 'Management has confirmed Lorelei Castle is absolutely delighted with the casting news.'"

I wait for the rest of it and realize that's all there is. Across the room, Oliver seems to go through the same process before tilting his head like, *Eh, not so bad*. It accurately shows my level of engagement on the media side.

"That's perfect, actually," I say. "I *am* delighted with the news. I also don't really think I need to be interviewed. But Benny, can you really push for them to send me the script today? If they want my polish on it—and I hope that's code for letting me at it with a scalpel—then I should see it sooner rather than later. I have other things due and will need to get my time organized."

"I'm already on it. Go do your thing. You'll be mobbed at your signings from here on out, and all I ask is that you kick ass when you're expected to."

I thank him, blow a kiss through the phone, and set it down on the bed. My hand is shaking. "I wasn't sure I loved Benny," I tell him. "But I do. I don't know what I would do without him right now."

"They *cast* it?" Oliver asks. "And Austin didn't mention anything last night?"

When Oliver and I left the party, we mostly left the subject of the movie behind. "Austin mentioned they were talking to people. Langdon said he's tinkering with a draft. I guess when these conversations happen, things move quickly. Or," I add, thinking on it some more, "they never really gave me the full story to begin with." I lift my hands in front of my face and watch them, still shaking like leaves. It feels like my brain needs a moment to catch up.

"Come on," he says with a calming smile. "Get dressed and let's talk about this downstairs. I'm starving."

I grab my clothes from my overnight bag and slip into the bathroom, pulling my hair up in a bun, dressing simply in jeans and a white T-shirt.

When I come out, Oliver is standing at the window, looking out. He's wearing a dark blue shirt that's worn over time, making it thin and soft on his back. I can see the muscles defining his shoulders, can see the sturdy lines of his torso. My heart does this dipping-squeezing thing that nearly makes me cough.

He turns at the choking sound and smiles, walking toward me.

"Ready?"

I look up at him but I can't hold my eyes there for very long. He shaved this morning, but even so, I can already see the stubble shadowing his jaw. He's at least six inches taller than me and so I get a good view of his neck, his throat, the curve of his bottom lip.

"Ready."

We walk down the carpeted hallway in silence, and Oliver reaches forward to press the elevator call button before stepping back, putting his hand on my lower back. His instincts are so tender.

"Do you have a finance person?" I ask him. "I need help."

"Yeah, but he's sort of more business? I guess that would work for you," he says, gesturing that I lead us in when the elevator opens for us.

"The studio money came in."

He nods, watching the floors tick down. "I remember that feeling when my dad died. It's a good thing but terrifying. I felt like I had to go from being a slacker living with his grandparents and eating tinned baked beans to being a bona fide adult. I didn't really have the mental tools to know how to budget or plan or save."

"Yeah," I agree, slumping into him a little. Oliver makes me feel so . . . safe.

"So, I put it aside until I was ready. Until I knew what I wanted to do with it."

"The store?"

He nods. "You'll figure it out. Just leave it alone until you do."

The elevator stops at the third floor and we get out, following a sign to the restaurant. "I should probably get a new car," I tell him.

He laughs.

"And I do know I want to get my own place."

Oliver goes quiet for a few steps and then asks, "A house?"

"I think so." And then my brain trips on the thought, because Oliver has his own house, and if anything happened with us, and it became more, would we live together? Would we want to own two houses?

"I can help you look," he says, popping the rapidly expanding balloon of my thoughts.

We walk into the restaurant, and are seated at a table facing Santa Monica Boulevard. Oliver and I have had meals together dozens of times but it's different right now, and I'm terrible at this kind of situation so I have no idea if it's all in my head. Maybe because I'm letting in this floodgate of *feelings*, everything feels loaded and special.

What would Harlow do? I wonder. She would ask. She would say, "Is everything okay?"

Is it really that simple?

"Is everything okay?" I ask, giving it a try. Oliver looks up at me, brows pulled together in question. "I mean, after last night . . ."

He smiles and puts his menu down. "Everything is brilliant."

Harlow would elaborate. Harlow would explain why she asked. Hell, Harlow would probably be in his lap right now.

"Okay, good," I say, turning my eyes down to study the long list of waffle choices.

I can feel his eyes on me a little longer, and then he picks up his menu again.

I put my menu down. "It's already different," I say.

"It's *not*," he says immediately, and when I look up at him, I see he's smiling. He *expected* this version of my panic.

I laugh. "It *is*."

Shaking his head, he looks back at the menu and mumbles, "You're a head case."

"You're a jerk," I shoot back.

The waitress comes by and fills our coffee cups. Oliver watches me with a smile while I forego the buffet and order pancakes. He orders pancakes and eggs.

She leaves and he plants his forearms on the table, leaning in. "What do you want, Lola?"

Way to start small, Aussie.

"What do I *want*?" I mumble, pulling my coffee closer.

I want to feel a better sense of what shape my life is taking.

I want to draw every single story my brain is churning up right now.

I want to have Oliver, and not lose him.

"I don't know." I pour three creams into my mug.

He exhales, a tiny skeptical sound, and nods. "You don't know."

I look up at the sound of him scratching his jaw, the stubble *scritch-scritching* against his short fingernails.

And fine.

I want to make out until my lips are raw from the scrape of that stubble.

I want him to fuck me into next week.

I want the press of his cock to wake me up in the middle of the night.

"Well, Lola Love, you let me know when you figure it out," he says. The tip of his tongue peeks out to wet his lips, and he sees me watching.

He knows.

It's that easy? "That's it?"

"That's it."

I realize he's walked over to my side of the court and carefully placed the ball directly in the center.

"You're a jerk," I repeat quietly, fighting my grin. I adore him, so much. It's this massive, blooming emotion making my cheeks heat and my stomach curl with pleasure. I don't know how I'll manage once I let go of the rope and float.

The panel shows the girl holding a glowing meteorite in her hands.

Oliver lifts his coffee to his mouth, smiling.

———

I FALL ASLEEP in the car somewhere near Long Beach and Oliver gently jostles me awake when he's parked just outside the store.

"Thanks for the ride," I say as he pulls my duffel bag from the trunk. He sets it down on the curb and digs one hand into his jeans, tugging them down at the waist.

His boxers are red today. Stomach flat. Hips defined.

"Thanks for coming with me," I say, blinking to the side in a completely unsubtle attempt to stop trying to get an eyeful of happy trail. "I wouldn't have had nearly as much fun by myself."

"Anytime," he says, adding in a nerdy voice: "I think you're wonderful, Lorelei."

I smile up at him. "I think you're wonderful, too, *Oliver*."

He surprises me, cupping my face and bending to press his lips to my cheek. It's far too close to my mouth to be innocent, but not actually touching my lips. It doesn't quite count as a kiss. Does it? My pulse explodes in my neck and

I have to hold my breath to keep from making a sound. He holds there for the length of a slow, quiet inhale before moving away.

"So," I say, "maybe we can hang out later?"

"Did you guys just *kiss*?"

On instinct, we both practically explode apart and turn to see Not-Joe squinting at us. His hair is a total wreck, more spiky cactus than mohawk, and his shirt is on backward.

"No," I tell him. "We were just . . ."

Okay, maybe we were about to kiss. Fucking Not-Joe.

"Goddamnit," he half-yells, half-groans. "If you're not making out then move out of the way so I can get in. I need to lie down."

It's Monday—the only day of the week the store is closed—so Oliver unlocks the door and we watch Not-Joe stumble over to the reading nook.

"I need to start using a hurricane naming system for my hangovers," he mumbles, stretching out on the couch. "I'm calling this one Abby. She's a total whore."

Oliver watches Not-Joe with a justifiable degree of wariness: I'd give eight-to-one odds Not-Joe is going to barf on the furniture.

"What are you even doing here?" I ask him. "Why aren't you at home?"

"I think someone needed his wallet." Oliver picks it up from behind the counter and tosses it onto Not-Joe's chest. "There you go, Ace."

"Too loud," Not-Joe groans. "Too bright. I think this is what autism feels like."

Oliver barks out a horrified laugh before saying, "Motherfuck, Joe, you can't say shit like that!"

"You can't tell me I'm wrong."

With a small, exasperated shake of his head, Oliver moves behind the counter to put on some music. Journey blasts through the store and Oliver pulls out his air guitar.

"Yes!" I air-drum on the counter.

"What the fuck, man?" Not-Joe rolls over, face-first into the cushion.

Oliver walks around to the reading nook and yells, "Time to rock out!" right next to his head. Not-Joe convulses into a tiny ball and I burst out laughing.

"Is this 'Revelation'?" I ask Oliver.

He nods, tongue poking out as he tears through a guitar solo.

"Have you ever thought about that, though?" I ask, and Oliver walks back around the counter to turn it down a little.

"Thought about what?"

When I look at him—wide grin, fingers flying in a ridiculous air guitar, lip curled like a rocker—I realize his glasses break up his looks, cool them down, add ice to the glass. Without them, he's all bone structure and color: brilliant blue eyes, warm lips, coffee-brown stubble.

"Steve Perry versus Arnel Pineda." At his confused expression, I explain, "The guy on YouTube who gained a following for covering Journey songs . . . then eventually became the new lead singer for the band?"

Oliver's head bobs in an enthusiastic nod along with the music. "Right. I think I heard about that."

"I mean, would you rather see the real thing or the best tribute band?"

"Wait, I thought you meant Arnel Pineda *is* the real Journey."

I make a play-exasperated face. "You know what I mean."

He shrugs. "I guess it depends on who we're talking about."

"Dylan?"

From the couch, Not-Joe moans a little *mmmh?* and opens one eye. He looks at us momentarily, blinking slowly, resulting in the most awkward three-person silent stare in modern history. Eventually he rolls his head to hide his face and returns to his hangover.

"Aw, come on," Oliver says, shaking his head and returning to our debate. "Bob Dylan is a legend. Besides, *everyone* is a Dylan tribute band."

"Okay, then," I say. "What about Heart? You could get these young chicks belting out 'Barracuda' or you could get the Wilson sisters in their sixties—"

Oliver looks horrified. "You are a terrible feminist."

Laughing, I tell him, "This isn't about *feminism*. I'm just saying. Imagine a reality show where they make the band compete with the tribute band. How much would you hate to have this amazing forty-year career and then compete with your tribute band?"

He walks over to me, musses my hair. "This is why I could never leave you."

I freeze, my breath catching in my throat as the cautious part of my brain snaps to attention again.

My reaction must be written all over my face because Oliver knows immediately what he's done.

"Fuck, Lola." He wraps his arms around my shoulders, pulling my face to his neck. "I just meant you were being rather sweet. Of *course* I would never leave you." And it's true, I tell myself. He means it.

"Will you two just bone and get it over with?" Not-Joe groans from the couch. "Jesus Christ, *someone* needs to christen the storage room."

We pull apart, but it's different. Our hands slide apart more slowly: palms then fingers then fingertips.

"I need to go make some calls," I tell him. "What are you doing later?"

He shrugs, looks at my mouth. "Dunno yet."

I walk backward toward the door, watching his slow-growing smile. Something clicks over in me. I bend and pick up the proverbial ball from the middle of the court. "Okay, I'll check in with you in a bit."

Chapter EIGHT

Oliver

I'VE LEARNED THAT Lola rarely does anything on impulse. Our Vegas wedding aside, she takes her time—be it seconds or days—to weigh every angle of a situation. I've never known anyone so deliberate.

The first time I noticed this, we were at the beach on a perfect August night. Her book had just been released that day, and already it was topping the charts in her genre. Drunk, I'd sprinted to the water and kicked off my shoes before diving fully clothed into the surf.

Lola had been drunker than I, but she'd staggered toward the foamy edge of the water and hesitated, teetering on her toes, before plunking down onto her bum on the sand.

"I don't have clothes to change into," she'd slurred. She'd fallen back, arms outstretched against the sand. "I'll be wet, and sandy."

"You're sandy *now*," I pointed out, pushing the dripping bulk of hair off my forehead.

"But I'm not wet. And I don't have clothes at your house."

I'd wanted to celebrate with beer and declarations and

some rowdy fucking. I'd wanted to say, *Fuck it, Lola, you can wear my clothes. Or you can wear nothing at all.*

But I hadn't, and I hadn't because I knew already not to push. She didn't want to swim, didn't want to trip home in soggy clothes that seemed to weigh eighty pounds.

It's this trait that makes it easier for me to let her walk out of the store after she's asked me what I'm doing tonight with such intent, I have to step behind the counter to let my body calm. And it helps me understand why every interaction with her the past week feels like two steps forward, one step back. But when she texts me only fifteen minutes later asking if she can come over later . . . I feel in the pounding of my heart that Lola has reached a decision. I just have to hope it's the one that I want.

I text back a simple Sure.

ONLY THREE HOURS later, the doorbell rings as Ansel reaches for his keys.

"Expecting company?" he says, and looks in the direction of the door before turning back to me. He's stopped by to borrow my Wet-Vac for the new house, and stayed for about an hour, waxing on about the place, wanting to get Mia knocked up, all sorts of utopian Ansel dreams. Lola's silhouette is clearly visible through the window, and this is exactly the reason I've been trying to get him out of here before she showed up.

"Just dinner with Lola," I tell him.

" 'Just dinner with Lola,' " he repeats with a smug tilt of his mouth.

"Go home, Ansel."

"I'm going," he says, and laughs to himself the entire way down the hall.

I open the door and my heart jumps at the sight of her standing there, dressed like she's just come from some sort of media interview or event.

"Oliver's grouchy tonight," Ansel tells her.

"Is he?" she says. "I was going to suggest we play some poker but now I'm not sure this competitive maniac could handle it."

"Get him drunk and take all his money. It's the least he deserves."

She turns her smile on me, obviously pleased with this idea. "I was planning on it."

I give her a small grin. "Best of luck."

"As much as I would love to stay and watch what I'm certain will be a bloodbath, I'm taking Mia to dinner. Good-bye friends," Ansel says, and bends to kiss her quickly on the cheek. I'm almost certain I hear the words, "Finish him," before Ansel is bounding down the front porch, and it's just the two of us. Again.

Lola walks into the house past me, and there's something new in the way she moves. Something more feminine, more *aware*.

"All good?" I ask.

Near the kitchen she turns and looks at me.

"All good." She slides her thick hair behind her ears. It immediately falls forward again and she grins up at me, looking even younger than she is. "Did you have a nice visit with Ansel?"

I give her a confused smile. "Yes? It was a *nice visit.*"

Her smile stays put, eyes glued to me. "I'm glad you guys got to see each other today."

"What's going on with you? You're as terrible at small talk as my aunt Rita from Brisbane."

With a laugh, she turns into the kitchen, and I hear the refrigerator open, bottles clinking, and the door closing again. "Maybe I'm nervous," she calls.

My pulse is rolling thunder in my neck. "Nervous about what?"

There's more rustling in the kitchen, more glass, and the sound of liquid being poured before she returns.

In a few of those long, hip-swinging strides, Lola hands me a beer and a shot of tequila, and looks up at my face.

"We have a lot to talk about tonight," she says.

I swallow, wanting to melt into her. Smiling reflexively with her this close, I say, "We do?"

She nods, using her free pinky to free a strand of hair from where it's caught on her lip. "You said a lot of interesting things up in L.A."

"Surely nothing you didn't already suspect?" I say quietly.

"I may not have suspected it," she says, mimicking the low volume of my words and looking at my mouth for a lingering moment before blinking back up to my eyes. "But I'd wanted to hear it for a long time."

I open my mouth to respond, but she cuts in, brighter now. "But rule number one tonight: no making out." She takes the shot and winces, chasing it with a swig of her beer.

I choke on my own shot, coughing. "Pardon?"

"You heard me," she says.

I take a long pull of my beer, and swallow through a grimace. "No making out *when*?"

"Once we're drunk," she explains. "I want to *talk*."

My chest feels too full for everything inside it; lungs, heart, the expanding emotions inside don't leave enough room to breathe. Is this it? Is it happening now?

I reach for a strand of her hair and ask, "Is there a rule number two in case rule number one gets broken?"

Her smile is a slow-growing work of magic. "Don't be cute."

Smiling back, I whisper, "I'll try." Every single drop of blood in me is rioting. *Fucking finally.* "What's happening here, Lola Love?"

She gives me an innocent shrug. "We're playing poker."

"I'll clean the floor with you," I warn, before tilting my bottle to my lips and sipping my beer again.

She watches me swallow. "You can clean the floor with all of your clothes while I watch." I raise an eyebrow at her and she adds, "We're playing *strip* poker."

With a surprised laugh, I say, "We really do have a lot to discuss tonight if we're playing strip poker but we can't make out."

Lola turns and retrieves a deck of cards from the drawer in the kitchen, and then gestures for me to join her at the dining room table.

This all feels so *sudden* . . . but at the same time it seems I've waited an eternity for this. I want the friendship barrier to dissolve. I want the next step, and the one after that. Lola has entered my house like a bulldozer, and although I've never seen her like this, not in a million years would I try to slow her down.

A determined Lola is a sight to behold.

She pats the tabletop to rouse me from my thoughts and I blink, carrying my beer to the table. Sitting across from her, our eyes lock, and neither of us breaks the tension by looking away. We've danced around each other for so long and I swear my skin is on fire, my brain thrumming as I wonder how this night will unfold.

"Ante up," she whispers, reaching beneath her hair to remove her earrings. She drops them in the center of the table and looks up at me expectantly.

I glance down at what I've got on. A watch. Jeans, a shirt, belt, glasses. I'm not even wearing shoes or socks. "This seems a little uneven."

"Lucky me."

She has no idea that I consider myself the lucky one. To have earned her trust. To have earned her affection. To witness her take-charge attitude. I smile at her, wanting to just say it again right here: *I love you.*

Instead, I unfasten my watch and drop it on the table as she begins to deal out five cards each.

We look at our cards, shifting them into our preferred order, and *holy fuck,* I have two fucking pair: two jacks, two threes, and a seven.

"Your *actual* poker face is so bad," she says, giggling. "This is the shock of a lifetime."

"I may get you naked with this one hand," I say, waving my cards at her, and feeling everything inside me pull to the middle in a warm tightness when I see she catches my double meaning. "I'm going to open." I reach for my belt, slowly pulling it free and coiling it before dropping it in the center of the table. "See or fold, Castle."

"Do you know if we'd stayed married I would be Lorelei Lore?"

I nod. "Thought about it once or twice, though I always assumed you'd keep your name."

"I'm traditional in weird ways," she says, putting her cards facedown. Just when I think she's folded, she reaches for the hem of her sweater and pulls it up and over her head.

She's wearing nothing but a bra beneath.

"Raise or call," she tells me and I realize I'm staring.

Looking down at my cards, I know I really *could* get most of her clothes off right now, but I need to savor this as much as I can. "Call."

I lay the seven facedown and she hands me a fresh card. I peek at it: the three of hearts. And now I've got a full house.

She gives herself three new cards—the maximum—and grimaces. "Oof."

"You've also got a terrible poker face."

Lola looks up at me, saying, "You can raise, if you want."

My shirt is off, dropped in the middle of the table. "You can fold, if *you* want."

Her bra comes off, landing on top of my shirt, and I stutter out a few sounds before reaching for my beer with a shaking hand. I can barely process the sight of her bare breasts. They're so full, so firm. My mouth waters, and I rest my lips against my beer but don't manage to tilt it fully to get a sip.

"You're staring," she whispers.

"I can't help it; you just took off your bra."

"Let's see your cards."

What cards?

I blink hard, squeezing my eyes closed, and then look down at my hand again before laying it on the table. She groans, showing me a pair of fours and then a trio of missuited jack, ace, and six. Dropping her head onto her arms, she shakes with laughter, looking back up only when she hears me sweeping the pile of clothes over closer to me. I put my shirt, belt, and watch back on. I put her bra on my head, her sweater around my shoulders, and her earrings stay on the table near my beer.

When she sits up, her long dark hair slides over her shoulders, covering her breasts. It's the contrast of the black against her milky skin, the way the ends of her hair just cover her nipples. Now I know why this view of a woman has been drawn a million-million times.

Her voice cuts into my trance. "Staring again."

"Still braless."

"I lied," she says, rubbing her finger absently across her lower lip.

The way she says it tells me it's a game, at least a little. "When?"

"When I pretended I didn't want to kiss you."

I feel my brows pull together. "The no-makeout rule?"

"That." She drops her eyes to where her finger traces circles on the tabletop. "And every time I saw you."

My arteries can't dilate fast enough for how much blood rushes into my system, and I feel lightheaded. "Come here."

She shakes her head, pushing the stack of cards to me before standing to get us each another beer. "Your deal."

After another round loaded with innuendo and tension, Lola loses, but this time is smart enough to only ante up her shoes before she folds. The next hand, she wins back her earrings and my watch, but after that, she loses both of these things as well as her socks.

"You've only got two more items, if my calculations are correct," I tell her while I watch her shuffle the deck. "Pants and whatever you've got beneath."

She laughs. "I don't mind the jeans but I can't lose my underwear."

"Then you've got nowhere to go. It's my turn to open after the deal."

She ponders this, eyes warm with the effects of two beers consumed relatively quickly. "Text Harlow. Have her tell us what the consequence is for losing. Don't let her know who's losing, though."

I nod, reaching for my phone and sending the question to Harlow. We need a consequence for losing at poker. One of us is out of clothing.

Barely thirty seconds pass before she answers, Dance on her goddamn lap, kid.

Laughing, I tell Lola, "She thinks this is my punishment, not yours."

"What did she say?"

"I'll tell you when you lose."

LOLA SLIDES HER losing hand into the middle of the table, looking up at me with fear in her eyes. "Wait. I need another beer before I hear this. Oh, God."

"You're going to need music, too."

Her eyes go wide before she grabs another beer from the middle of the table, chugging it down, then picking up my phone. She knows my passcode, entering it without thinking.

Her mouth drops open when she reads Harlow's text. "I'm not going to do that."

"Then give me your underwear."

"Fuck no."

I laugh, standing and walking over to the stereo. "Do you want rock and roll or something more club appropriate?"

She groans. "Oliver, I've never in my life given a lap dance."

"Club it is!" I crow, pressing play. Walking back, I nearly

trip at the full view of Lola standing near the dining table. I couldn't see her from the waist down when we were sitting, but *Lord*.

Lola is in nothing but her underwear. Black silk. *Minuscule*. Her body is so smooth; I want to sink my teeth into the soft flesh of her upper thigh.

My skin is on fire.

I can feel my pulse in my throat as I lower myself into a chair.

She smacks my arm as I tuck my shaking hands beneath my legs. "You even know protocol."

"So do you, it would seem."

Lola steps closer, staring down at me. "Why couldn't you have been the one who lost?" Her knees touch mine and I feel the pressure reverberate along every inch of my legs.

"Wouldn't be nearly as good now, would it?"

"Is it weird to see me topless?" she asks, sliding one leg to the side of mine, and then moving closer, straddling me.

It's hard to breathe, hard to think.

I look up and down the length of her body. Her waist is narrow, hips perfectly curved. She has a tattoo along her side that I can't read in the dim light, but I'll read it later. Right now, I'm one breath away from putting my face in her tits. "It's fucking bliss is what it is."

The music rolls through the room, slowly taking over my pulse until it seems to do the same with Lola, and her hips tentatively rock forward, and back. Her hands come around my shoulders, anchoring there.

"Lola . . ." I whisper. "Just do whatever you're comfortable doing."

She leans in, looking at my eyes so closely as if searching for a stray eyelash, to steal a wish. Her gaze swims a little, but I like tipsy Lola. She cracks out of her shell and looks at the world around her. Right now I want to be that entire world. I want to be all she sees.

"What's your tattoo?" I ask.

She licks her lips and studies my mouth as she answers. *" 'It is better to light a candle than curse the darkness.' "*

I scan my thoughts to place the quote, but with her nearly naked body over mine, the smell of her shampoo, her skin, and even the hint of her lust . . . I'm obliterated. "What is it from?"

"The goddess of wit, the woman who made generations of women put on their big girl pants: Eleanor Roosevelt." Lola anchors her hands on the back of the chair and tilts her head as she moves.

The heat of her body against me makes my words come out thick: "How old were you when you got it?"

"Seventeen."

Her hair slides over her shoulder, tickling along my bare arm. When her eyes lock on mine, my chest clutches at how her makeup has smudged slightly, making her appear sweetly rumpled, as if I've already had my way with her. Just the thought tips me into a desperate, trembling sort of hunger.

"Is this awkward?" she whispers.

My words are propelled by an incredulous burst of air: "Fuck no."

Her brow twitches. "You mean because you're used to having half-naked friends dancing on your lap?"

"I think you are at least one article of clothing past 'half-naked,'" I tease. "And perhaps more than a little past *friend*."

She stares down at me, worrying her lip with her teeth.

"It's not awkward because it's *you*, Lola Love. And you look amazing half-naked."

A long stretch of silence passes where she's still just looking at me. Staring, eyes fixed on mine. But it isn't static. It's an enormous transition in her expression from playful to sincere, and watching each step seems to pluck at a vibrating, urgent thread between my ribs.

"Are you hard?" She lowers her hips and slides over me, just once.

Oh, fuck.

I lose my breath when my heart climbs into my throat. She *knows* I am; my cock is rigid and pressed right against her.

"Are you wet?" I volley back.

I know she is. When she rocks forward again, I can feel it in the easy slide of her over me.

She laughs and her attention shifts from my eyes back to my lips. She's so close, it isn't just a flicker of her gaze; it's an intentional drop, a mile-long stretch that seems to take forever as she looks at my nose, my cheeks, my lips, then snags there. If she looked any lower she would no doubt see my pulse frozen in my throat.

"Are you thinking of kissing me?" she asks.

I stare right back at her mouth. Lick my lips. "Are you thinking of being kissed?"

"Will you answer *any* question I ask?"

"Yes, but only that one."

She gives me my favorite laugh: the quiet thrust of breath from her mouth. The sound she probably doesn't even know she makes. And then she bends, time stops, and after a tiny beat of hesitation where she holds her breath, Lola presses her full lips to mine.

Warm, soft, and just the tiniest bit wet: it's the sweetest first kiss I've ever had. Lola gives me a blissful few introductory kisses before the eventual parting of her lips, and the careful capture of my bottom lip between hers.

When she sucks, gently bites, and makes a tiny rough growl, I am wrecked.

When the tip of her tongue grazes mine, my heart seems intent on punching its way out of my chest.

I am totally fucking ruined.

I can barely keep my hands beneath my thighs on the chair when she pulls away, licking her lips.

"I kissed you," she whispers.

My voice shakes: "I thought we weren't allowed to do that."

With a tiny one-shouldered shrug, she whispers, "I think I'm going to do it again."

My pulse is hammering so hard, I can barely manage an "Okay."

When she comes back, I groan, pulling my hands free and

so desperate for the taste of her that I stretch forward, meeting her halfway with my palms cupping her face. It's explosive: the feel of our skin touching just here. I perceive the kiss in every tiny hollow part of me, filling me up with her sweetness, and lust, and abandon. I want to devour Lola, but this first series of kisses is remarkably gentle. Aimless. Everything wild and tense is held in our muscles: in the tight clench of my quads under her ass, and my hands barely holding her face. In *her* hands in fists in the shirt at my shoulders, her legs trembling over me. It feels like sex, the way she's kissing me, the way her tongue slides across mine, but slower, and infinitely more innocent.

"I can't believe you're doing this," I murmur into her mouth. "I've wanted this for so long."

The words cause her to tense and she sits back, blinking slowly. "Will this mess everything up?"

I move my hands from her face and rest them, carefully, on the outside of her thighs. "It can make everything better. We can do whatever you want." I stretch to kiss her again, repeating, "Whatever you want. We can put on a movie and relax. We can stay here and kiss. We can play some more cards."

The clock in the hall must tick at least a hundred times before Lola speaks.

"I don't want to stay out here and play cards."

My lungs have evaporated. "Okay," I agree.

"Or watch a movie."

I nod, choking on my own breath. "Whatever you want, pet."

"And I don't want to just kiss." She stands, pulling me up with her. We're so close my exhales puff against her hair as she stares, wide-eyed, up at me.

Her hand comes down the inside of my arm, fingers curling with mine, and she turns, tugging me down the hall.

Chapter NINE

Lola

I'VE ONLY BEEN in Oliver's room one other time—when he was fixing something in the garage and needed me to grab his phone from his dresser—but I didn't take the time to look around and take in how he'd put his secret space together. That time, it felt too personal to be in his sanctuary; I located the phone and dashed out. Back then, too, I hadn't really let the enormity of my feelings sink in. We were still Just Friends. Being in his room wasn't intense because he would be naked here, or sleep here. It just felt like a level of personal that Lola + Oliver didn't do.

But right now—after that perfect kiss, after the feel of him rock hard beneath me, and knowing what we're about to do *in this room*—my heart is a banging drum in my ear.

This is really happening.

I'm not dreaming.

Oliver's hand is wrapped around mine, the memory of his mouth still makes my lips tingle, and his bed is mere feet from where we stand. It's on the far side of the room, near the window that overlooks the ocean, which is a couple of blocks away. His window is open and it smells like salt water and ocean air and the clean pine scent of his laundry detergent.

I lead him over, and with a shaking hand pull back the covers and carefully slide in. His sheets are clean, the cotton cool beneath my back, and it makes my skin feel charged. Oliver watches me turn and lie down, and waits only a moment before he moves, slowly prowling over me and settling between my legs. His expression is so full of wonder when he looks down at me; it gives me a dizzying rush of power. He wants this as much as I do. I knew it, because he'd told me, but until just tonight, I didn't truly believe.

The cold of the sheets is gone in only seconds and I'm too warm in an excited, frantic sort of way; the prick of sweat rises on my neck, down my chest. My nipples feel swollen and sensitive, and the heat of his skin when I rub against him pulls a soft gasp from my mouth.

"Lola." My name is an urgent whisper on his lips, and I reach up, pulling his glasses from his face. He takes them from me and slides them onto the nightstand with so much caution that I wonder if he also feels so deliberate in every movement, it's like moving through water.

"There," I say when he turns back to me.

While my eyes adjust to the darkness of his room, I let my fingertips trace the outline of his face, the sharp line of his jaw. He's angles and slopes; his skin is smooth along his cheeks, rough along his jaw. I stretch into him, pressing my bare chest to his, and Oliver lets out a shaking groan, sliding his hand down my side, along my thigh to my knee, where he pulls my leg over his hip. Beneath the denim of his jeans, his cock is rigid against me, and I feel the shape of it as we press together and apart, together and apart, rocking.

"You sure?" he whispers.

"I'm sure."

The panel shows them prone, entwined, afire.

My breaths are violent jerks sucked in by necessity and pushed out by a wild beast in my chest. I'm completely naked except for the cotton of my underwear, and I relish the scratch of the denim on the soft skin of my thighs, but I want to feel *him*. The warmth, the skin, the tickle of hair. While his mouth plays along my neck, to my collarbone, and over the top swell of my breast, I slip my fingers between our bodies, unfasten his jeans, and work them as far as I can down his hips. I feel the rumbling groan in his chest before I hear it. He rocks his hips forward, making me gasp sharply when he presses himself—now only in his boxers—directly against my clit.

Oliver bends to move his mouth up my neck in a hot trail of teeth and lips. "Holy fuck, Lola—"

He cuts himself off when his mouth finds mine already open and searching for his, and I know the second I taste him that we're skipping the slow exploration. His lips are soft and strong, sliding with mine so urgently we quickly grow messy—teeth grazing and chins captured in the hunger of it.

Want hits me like the lash of a whip, propelled by adrenaline. I grip the back of his neck, urging him to kiss me harder, to touch me. The sound I make when his thumb slides across my nipple is nearly one of pain; it pulls every nerve ending into a tight bunch, stroking me into fire, and he does it again, and again, in small, pressing circles. My heart pounds beneath his hand as he holds me there for his mouth and bends, sucking wetly . . . biting sharply . . . and his hips press forward and back, pushing himself right up against my clit until I'm scratching at his shoulders trying to get his weight to push me into the mattress, push my legs farther apart, push into me.

I tickle my fingers down his stomach, feeling both frantic and terrified.

"Yeah. Touch me," he begs into my open mouth.

I slip my hand inside and gasp at the warmth. He's urgent in my grip and exactly how I imagined he would feel: silken skin wrapped tight around iron and fire. Oliver's face falls in relief as I stroke him, gently slipping his foreskin down and up, over the crown, and he begins to move, forward and back, lips distracted and hungry over mine.

The last eight months have been the slowest, most torturous foreplay, and there's a fever beneath my skin that makes me impatient, lets me release him only long enough to push his boxers down far enough for him to kick them and his jeans the rest of the way off.

He's unable to remain still over me, stubbly jaw razing across my sensitive nipples as he kisses down my ribs, under my arm, teeth scraping over my bicep as he rocks into my hand.

He fumbles between us, pulling my underwear down so I can free one leg and then his fingers are there, sliding over and into me and it's like being plugged into the solar system, everything inside me is light and fire, and I'm squirming under him to get there because, already, I'm close. I want to know what he feels, how he feels when he's touching me and I'm there, too, one finger twisted around his and he laughs into a kiss, telling me how amazing it is. How can he find words when I'm completely speechless? His thumb grazes my clit again and again and I'm so swollen and desperate and pushing up off the bed so he can reach deeper with his forever-long fingers. His cock brushes against our hands and then he shifts his hips and moves our fingers out of the way and then it's there, closer, and with a tiny synchronized catch in our breath he's pushing forward and he slides into me.

"Oh, fuck," he says

and

"Lola. Oh fuck me. Oh *fuck me.*"

And it turns to frenzy.

He's moving

not just moving but

absolutely *fucking* me

and

it's *Oliver* and he's inside me already

and he's moving so deep in and out, groaning into my neck.

Oliver plants his knees into the mattress and moves— there is nothing but sound in the darkness around us: the headboard slams against the wall, the hinges of the bed groan in protest. He's grunting in my ear because it's *work*, fucking me like this: fast and messy. His fingers slip over my chin and my mouth and he's following with his tongue, licking my taste from my skin.

We're laughing into kisses because it's good—*it's so good*—and my hands are everywhere between us: his chest and hips and stomach and the base of his cock. Somewhere deep down I knew it would be like this, I did. In the corners where I let myself imagine being close to anyone in this way, it was him. Always the fantasy had a flash of dark hair tucked into my neck, long fingers wrapped around my hip, *his* mouth curved into a knowing smile when I start to come—

"Oh, God—"

My words are cut off by pleasure. Smoke runs through my veins, hot and weightless until I feel like I'm floating, grappling for him with hands and nails, begging with unintelligible sounds to keep doing whatever he's doing that's already so good, so good, please, I'm screaming under him, so loud I hear the echo bounce sharply back to me.

Pleasure fills every limb until I'm mindless and I'm melting, burning, dissolving into relief.

His rhythm is frantic through my orgasm but as soon as I quiet, choking for air, he's jerking back and pulling out so abruptly I feel immediately hollow.

"Fuck," he gasps, sitting back on his heels with his chest heaving as he wipes a hand down his face. He bends, tucking his chin to his chest as he takes several gasping breaths.

Panic and bliss react oddly in my blood and I can barely find the words to ask: "What's wrong?"

He curls a shaking palm around my thigh. "I'm not wearing a rubber. I nearly came."

My heart is pounding, skin damp with sweat, and I'm reeling from the reality of what just happened.

We just had *sex.*

We fell into his bed, and within only a few minutes *we were completely fucking.*

Instinctively, I reach to touch his forearms when he smooths his hands up and down my spread thighs.

"Did *you* come?" he whispers.

I still can't really find words, so I nod and manage, *"Yes. God."*

In fact, I think I nearly passed out.

His hand moves up my hip, over my stomach, to my breast where he covers me with a warm palm. "I can't believe." He swallows, closing his eyes. "That we're . . ."

Now that my eyes have fully adjusted in the darkness I can see more of his body. It was one thing to see him in his underwear in the bright light of daytime in my living room, but it's nothing compared to the shape of him over me in the shadows, kneeling between my spread legs. I take in the expanse of his torso, the ridges of his abdomen, the sharp curve of his hips leading down to the heavy, wet weight of his cock.

His thumb strokes over my nipple in tight, pressing circles. "I thought I would savor it more the first time we . . . if we ever did this."

Coherent thoughts are tiny, buzzing flies in the background. "I feel too crazy right now to savor."

"Me, too," he admits, laughing. "Clearly."

I want him back where he was twenty seconds ago, covering me in his weight and his sweat and pivoting his hips between my legs. Sitting up, I cup the back of his neck, kissing his swollen, wet mouth before asking, "Do you have condoms?"

"Yeah." His fingers slide between my legs, mouth moving with mine in deep, searching kisses. When I reach for him, he's covered in me, and I relish the wet slide of my hand up and down and the way he moans into my mouth, nearly whimpering. His free hand comes around mine, not guiding, just feeling the way my fingers wrap around him the same way mine did earlier, for a few long strokes before he begins to move with me, kisses growing more urgent as he leans in, nearly sliding back inside.

"Hurry," I whisper, and he shushes me with his lips.

"Hang on, hang on," he says, gently pulling my hand away. "Hang on. This . . . I want to slow down and feel all of this." His kisses narrow into small, sweet tastes of my mouth. "I don't want to come as fast as I will if we fuck like that again."

I don't know how sex with Oliver can ever be slow now that I know how it feels when he's unhinged. Forever now, when he tries to be gentle I won't have it. *No,* I'll think. *I know how you feel when you absolutely* fuck *me.*

He reaches for the bedside table, fumbling with a box that I notice, with a small rush of satisfaction, was sealed shut. Returning with a foil packet, he drops it on the bed beside me. When I reach for it, he covers my hand with his before covering my lips with his smile.

"Wait." He laughs into a kiss. "Wait."

Lowering his body over mine, he bends and kisses me, slowing me down, heating me up, showing me what it feels like to savor.

The full mouth, his shoulders, and the strong, ropey lines down his arms.

The lean muscles of his back, his ass bunching in my palms as he slides wetly across me, fucking me on the outside.

The soft, dark trail of hair pressing against my navel.

We aren't having sex yet, but we are; penetration is a technicality at this point, and I feel in his gaze that he's telling me something with every kiss, every slide of skin over skin.

He watches me in a way that feels like he's seeing more than my face looking up at his or my breasts shifting with his movements. He's seeing *me*. The heat of it makes me wild, like skin singed, blood simmering.

"I feel like we have forever to 'savor,'" I whine quietly. "I don't—"

He reaches for the condom, putting it in my palm and kneeling between my legs. "I know."

I tear it open, feeling it briefly to orient myself. I'm suddenly nervous and know my hands are a little fumbly, my fingers unpracticed at this. "It's been a while since I did this."

He smiles but says nothing, holding his breath as he watches me cover the head, anchor the condom with one hand, and roll it all the way down with the other. There's a good couple of inches of him left uncovered and I feel the skin there, marveling until he leans forward, hands planted beside my head.

I can tell he wants to say something, but I also get the sense that it's nearly too much to articulate without sounding trite or overly sentimental. It's probably why I'm not saying much, either.

When he leans in, kissing me softly, he asks, "You want me like this?"

I assume he means on top of me again. "Yeah."

His cock feels warmer than any other part of him, like fire barely contained. The feel of it in my hand makes everything inside turn liquid, makes my brain turn fuzzy. I close my eyes, bite my lip as I guide him in, shutting off some of my senses so I can process how he feels, the stretch of it when he shifts forward and into me. He's shockingly hard where I am so soft and tender and it crosses wires in my body, makes me feel crazy, makes me wonder whether I could take him everywhere, where else he could possibly fit.

He exhales a low curse, pressing his mouth to the skin just below my ear. *"Fuck,"* he says again.

When I roll my hips under him, pulling him even deeper, he stops me with a rough hand on my hip. "Wait. I'm too—"

I still beneath him, except for the slow roaming of my palms up his back when he pushes himself up onto his hands. It's the most surreal feeling, to feel *joined* to someone else like this. Not just rutting or moving together but actually connected.

With a slow exhale, he pulls back slightly and pushes in, groaning and giving in to the act as he starts to really move.

And I find I was wrong: slow and deep is just as perfect as Oliver's frenzied fucking.

I'm amazed how he looks, moving over me. I've seen him from every angle a friend could see: standing side by side, seated across a table, in my car or his, on my floor while I've sketched him. I've even had my head in his lap looking up at him, and seen him roll out from beneath my car after he's checked a suspicious leak. But I've never seen him like this. Naked, damp with sweat, with his hands propped beside my neck as he stares down the length of our bodies, watching himself. Arms flexed, lip snared between his teeth . . . enjoying just looking, feeling as he slides lazily forward and back.

I close my eyes, let out a tight choked breath, and his body snaps forward, so deep.

"Lola. Fuck. I . . ."

My hands find his hips, guiding him when he falters and I want him closer, want all of that skin on mine, sliding up and over and all around in me. One hand trails up his side, to his shoulder and around to his neck, pulling, urging him lower.

Oliver bends, his hair brushing my forehead. "I can't. I can't believe it. I can't stop looking at you."

He's so hard inside, stilling as he catches his breath, and I know it's more from emotion that he's lost it in the first place. This time certainly isn't rigorous sex. It's so slow it's almost embarrassingly intimate.

Still, I would have expected to feel self-conscious to look

him in the eye while he's inside me. He seems even more naked without his glasses. But it's not weird, not even a little, and in an explosive burst of emotion I adore him so acutely it's nearly painful. This is the man I've spent nearly every day with, joking, talking, unloading my triumphs and fears. Without warning, my body clutches him, needing, and he groans, finally bending his elbows and carefully lowering his chest to mine.

"Did you know how long I wanted this?" he asks.

I smile into his neck, before sucking it gently. "No. Harlow says I'm so oblivious it's painful."

He laughs, and when I laugh, too, he gasps and pulls his hips back, nearly leaving my body before he slides back in. So deep.

"I didn't think you were interested," I admit. "I asked you to sleep with me that night, you know."

He stills, kissing my shoulder. "When I met you, I didn't think you were the kind of girl I'd fall for, because of the Vegas situation. Then you *were* the kind of girl I'd fall for." His mouth makes its way up my neck, to my ear. "And then you were the girl I *was* falling for. I didn't want our story to start in some cheesy-ass Vegas bullshit. I didn't want to fuck you that night in some crusty hotel room. That's the quickest way to ruin something, by rushing in like that."

"Not for our gang."

He growls out a little laugh. "True."

I kiss his neck, sucking. He tastes so good, he's firm and warm and I imagine biting down onto the smooth, strong skin.

"I've loved you for a while now," he says. So simply. God, it's so bare and straightforward and it makes me want to be brave.

I'm terrified of loving him.

I don't know how to keep it from happening, though.

"You don't have to say it back," he adds in a whisper before kissing the corner of my mouth, and I can tell he's sincere.

"I've had feelings for a while, too," I say, and it sounds like a lame admission but it *feels* big. I love him for so many reasons, I'm not sure my heart is ready for that kind of love yet. The biggest kind of love.

"Have you ever been in love before?" he asks.

I swallow thickly before admitting, "No."

He hums into my neck, sucking. I want him to move, but I also don't. I've never had a conversation like this at a café or in a car, let alone while someone was over me, inside me, moving in a way that makes me want to beg.

"Can I make you come again?" he murmurs, sliding closer to kiss me, and I hear his smile in the words. His mouth moves from mine and down, sucking at my jaw. "And then we can talk some more?"

I nod and he shifts over me, back and in, kissing my chin, my cheek, and then my mouth, his hand sliding into my hair and the other at my hip to hold me in place as he begins to move harder, in earnest. I'm seeing this side of him that feels dirty and secretive: his firm hands, the deep shove of his body in mine, his unapologetically wild mouth. Someday we'll sit with all of our friends and talk about mundane everyday things while the entire time I'll remember the way he tilts my hips, greedily thrusting into me, fingers slipping between us to rub me, his rasping voice, accent thicker with pleasure when he tells me to keep fucking up into him, that it feels so good he might keep me spread under him all night.

He talks about how soft my thighs are, how warm and slippery I feel.

He rolls to his side, fucking me hard with my leg over his hip, and he grunts hoarsely with every deep, hard shove. Biting my neck, he wonders absently how it's even possible my cunt feels better than it tastes.

My skin ignites, shock and lust curling tight inside me at his words.

He grates across my clit again and again, each time with more intent, and I can tell he knows exactly how close I am when he pulls back to watch, his eyes so close to mine, teeth pressed to my jaw as he growls out tiny sounds of encouragement.

I close my eyes under the weight of the looming explosion, but he bites down into my jaw, hissing an *Open*, and cupping my ass, rocking me up into him.

I gasp, my wide, thrilled eyes meeting his calm, knowing ones and an electric storm builds in me, curling my spine and pulling my legs apart. He groans when he feels me go off like a bomb all around him. A million tiny eternities pass with his teeth pressed roughly against my jaw, my body liquefying beneath him.

The panel shows the girl dissolving into a sky full of stars.

"Lola," he gasps, hips faltering and then gaining speed, and if he ever managed to iron out that accent I would crumble.

He grunts into my neck, hand moving up my body, gripping my breast somehow too hard and just right and then he's moaning, "I'm coming . . . fuck, here I come," and I feel him shake over me, pushing deep. The sound he makes when he does—a choking, rasping approximation of my name—carves itself deep into my heart.

I can hear the ocean in the silence that follows. The distant hum of cars, a palm frond scratching against the side of the house in the wind. Oliver's breath is warm and rapid against my neck, his hand sliding up over my breast and down my waist, along the curve of my hip, my thigh, to my knee, and then back again, over and over, as if measuring me with long, sure sweeps of his hand.

"I don't need you to love me yet, Lola, but I can't do casual with you," he whispers when my eyes open and I return to orbit. "I'm completely in love with you and if this is only—"

My heart catches high in my throat and squeezes so tight I cough. "It's not. It's not casual."

Oliver's eyes stall on my lips, and he grins with relief, kissing me once, softly, before pulling out of me, pushing the covers back, and sliding the condom off. He reaches for a tissue and I watch him the entire time; there's so much *man* to his movements: the easy comfort he has touching his own cock, knowing exactly what to do with the condom, the shadow of dark hair on his chest, the muscular line of his shoulders as he turns and climbs back between the sheets with me. His hand slides down over my stomach and between my legs, where I'm still warm from the friction of him pounding into me. I love the possessive flat plane of his palm, the confident command of his fingers when he touches me.

"You okay?" he murmurs into my neck.

"Yeah." But my hips instinctively shift away as he slides his fingers inside me.

He moves his hand back up my body and he runs his knuckles between my breasts. "When was the last time you were with someone?"

It might feel intrusive or weird to be asked this so soon after sex with any other new lover, but with him, I don't mind the question; I want to unload it all. Every event, everything else that happened before him. We've shared all of the every-day details of ourselves but not these: the most sacred, the barest.

Turning his hand, he brushes the back of his fingers over my breast, before sliding the index and middle apart and cap-turing my nipple between them. He bends to lick the very tip. I close my eyes, struggling with the mental calculation while he's doing that.

"Um . . . March?"

"March of last year?" His fingers tease their way down my ribs and there's no jealousy in his voice when he asks, "Who was he?"

"This guy I saw a few times, from my digital cinema class."

"Was it good?"

I trace the shape of his jaw from his ear to his chin. "One of the times it was pretty good, I guess," I say. "The others . . . it wasn't particularly memorable." I close my eyes, finding bravery. "What about you?"

"A woman on the bike trip."

"This last one? In June?"

He nods as he kisses my collarbone. "It was at the end of May, actually, but yeah. That trip."

"Before you met me?"

I know the answer to this. Of *course* it was before he met me. He met me in Vegas, at the end of their journey. But I guess I want to somehow acknowledge that after me, he wasn't with anyone.

"Mm-hmm. Albuquerque. She worked at the hotel restaurant."

"Was it good?" I echo.

"Nothing particularly memorable," he echoes back. "For her, either, I don't think. We were all pretty lit." He laughs, admitting, "I was too drunk to finish."

We haven't given these other people names. I can barely remember the last guy's face or how his body felt under my hands. With every possessive touch, Oliver erases the trace of any other men from my skin.

"No one since?" I ask.

He smiles as he kisses me. "No one since."

"Is it weird for you to go that long?"

He answers this with a shrug. "I wanted this gorgeous woman named Lorelei Castle too fucking much to play around."

I pull back enough to meet his eyes. "You've had options." I hear the tiny sting in my voice, jealousy over the could-have-beens.

His smile dissolves my tension like sugar in hot water. "So have you, pet."

"Fewer."

He laughs. "Hardly."

"I have five hundred things going on right now; who wants to put up with that?"

"I do." Oliver's expression straightens and he bends to kiss me again, lips pulling at mine. With a groan, he's over me again, pressing his nose beneath my arm, grating his teeth up over my bicep, sucking each of my fingers and biting the tips. His cock is already an urgent presence between us again, heavy and pressing.

He groans when I grab him, shaking as I squeeze and pump.

Already, again, it feels feral, grabbing and biting. Oliver flips me to my stomach, sliding his cock between the cleft of my ass as he bends and sucks at the back of my neck, hands coming between my body and the mattress to play with my breasts. His touch is frantic but somehow assured. There's no *Can I*. No *Do You Want*. A million tiny fantasies play out with his teeth on my skin and with his hands full of me.

I hear the tear of foil again, the wet slide of a condom over him, and then he's lifting my hips, thighs still bracketing mine, and he's pushing back into me, groaning at the warmth, the softness, the view he has over and behind me.

With my thighs pressed together and the stretch of my body around his I'm pressing up and grinding and making these wild, desperate sounds, feeling like I might shatter. I am light shot into a prism, scattering in a thousand directions. Oliver is riding me, hands curled around my hips as he pistons forward and back, hitting deep.

I'm screaming into a pillow, arching at the sensation of his sweat hitting my spine, wanting to spread my legs to take him completely into me, but forced together to hold the pleasure in a tiny radius of contact.

It's too much.

I need more.

Oliver smacks my ass hard, grunting at the surprised clench of my body around his.

"It's good," he grates out. "It's fucking *bliss.*"

I nod, pressing into him and feeling like I'm fraying at the edges when he takes my ass in his grip, short nails digging, hips moving wild and fast behind me. His hands spread me, thumb slides closer, circling and I don't know . . . I like it but—

"Shh, it's okay." He reaches for my face with his other hand, cupping my cheek and turning me toward him so he can kiss the side of my mouth. "You've never . . . ?"

I shake my head.

"It's okay." His kiss turns wilder, an urgent match struck somewhere inside him.

I press into his palm, desperate for more: for his kiss, his weight, the sound of him coming.

"Whatever you want," he says, his breath warm on my lips. "I'll give you whatever you want."

"I want to see you."

Oliver withdraws, rolling me onto my back again. His hands slide from my ankles to my knees and he cups them from behind, bending them to press them to my chest. His elbows come underneath, hooking, holding me open as he stares and then slowly eases back into me with a groan. The sound is pain and joy, his relief dragged along the edge of a knife.

He fucks me tender then brutal, hips circling to make me scream before my hands are pinned at the side of my head and he hits deep in tiny, sharp stabs that shove the breath from my lungs in these blissful forced gusts.

I am mesmerized watching him like this: my calm, gentle friend unleashed. My lover now, so tender with me, so brutal in his drive to make it good. He waits until I'm shaking, until my cries are cut apart by relief, and then he lets himself come again with his mouth open and groaning against mine.

Sweaty, chest heaving, Oliver lands heavily on me.

As soon as he rolls me to my side and tucks in behind me, exhaustion hits me like a physical blow. His lips press to my neck, voice thick with the approach of sleep. "I'm fucking exhausted, but I don't know how long I can sleep knowing you're in my bed."

I hum, smiling into the arm he's tucked under my neck and wrapped around my front.

"I'll wake up wanting more," he whispers with a tiny catch in his voice, part preemptive apology, part warning. His cock is still half-hard, pressing warm against my thigh.

"Me, too."

I fall asleep feeling my breaths synchronize to the easy rise and fall of his chest behind me.

―――――――

THE WORLD INVADES first with the sound of a car horn, then the wind, then the distant sound of waves. I open my eyes and relish the slow appearance of the sun in the eastern sky.

I stretch in Oliver's arms, too warm. Somehow I'm curled up facing him now. He was an octopus in his sleep, endless arms that gripped me deliciously when I tried to move even an inch away.

I feel when he wakes—that tiny startled twitch in his arms around me—and quietly wait for it to become awkward: we left nothing hidden last night. His room smells heavily of sex and still we're entwined, completely naked. There's a condom wrapper somewhere near my left foot, another visible behind Oliver at the edge of the mattress.

Last night comes back to me in scattered flashes of sound

and sweat and sensation: the low hiss he made when he pushed inside. The rise and fall of his shoulders as he moved above me. The way his mouth covered mine, tongue skilled and urgent.

I ache between my legs. My skin still feels the friction of his hands and mouth all over me. I knew sex could be like that, I just never knew it could be like that for me.

He's so solid beside me, so vital. The idea of moving out of the circle of his arms is almost as appealing as cutting off an arm or leg.

What happens when emotion is too big, when it fills the chest and the veins and the limbs? I imagine sunshine filling me until I shatter—leaving starburst-coated girl shrapnel strewn across this bed.

I close my eyes, mentally drawing the way the sun slants across our bare legs instead. I count to ten, and then twenty, focusing on pulling air into my lungs. It will never be what it was before. Oliver and I are forever changed. Something clicks inside me, something permanent and concrete, and it's both thrilling and terrifying. . . .

I'm wildly, deeply in love.

He lifts his head from where it was buried between my neck and shoulder, kisses me, and whispers, "Good morning, Lola Love."

I pull the sheet up over my mouth. "Morning."

He kisses me again through the sheet. "I love you still." He pulls the sheet away, kissing my chin, and watches me as his smile straightens a little but doesn't leave his eyes. "Whatever else you're thinking . . . that's not changed with the sunup. I loved you before last night. I'll love you tomorrow. I've just said the words now."

I saw my teeth across my lip, feeling the sunshine fill my chest and bleed up into my eyes.

"I've wanted to fuck you long before last night," he says, playful smile back in place as he climbs over me, spreading my thighs with his knee. "And now that I've had you, I want it even more."

This is a sentiment I can easily reciprocate: "Let's fuck for the rest of the day."

His laugh is a happy, warm sound. "Week."

"Month."

"Year."

He's said it. It's longer than I've ever been with anyone else, so easily assumed. We stare at each other, neither of us saying it. It's too soon, even with all of the declarations rising like smoke in the air. But the longer Oliver looks at me, the more I know he's thinking it.

Life.

"All right then," he murmurs.

I answer against his mouth: "All right then."

Chapter TEN

Oliver

$\mathcal{A}$N ALARM ON Lola's phone goes off halfway through her first cup of coffee. I tried to keep her in bed for the agreed-upon duration, which I considered an ironclad contract, but eventually we both needed a bathroom, caffeine, and food.

"Oh, shit," she says, reaching for it and opening the calendar app.

We're sitting side by side at my dining room table. I'm in jeans; she's in nothing but the shirt I wore yesterday. It's long, but not so long that I can't see all of her, especially with one of her legs on the ground, our ankles pressed together, and her other leg in my lap. Caffeine is slowly bringing my brain to life and I still feel warm and slow, like well-worked clay. I really don't want her to have to leave quite yet.

"What's wrong?" I ask.

"I have this thing I'm supposed to do at eleven." She frowns, and I look up at the clock. It's nearly ten.

"'Thing'?"

"It's a chat with the UCSD Arts publication." Steam rises up from her mug and twists in the space between us, dissolving in a beam of sun overhead. "Shit. I completely spaced it," she says, and then more to herself, "I never forget this stuff."

I set down my cup and lean forward, taking her free hand in mine. "Can you do it from here? The Wi-Fi can be a bit spotty, but my laptop's in my room. You're welcome to it."

She's already shaking her head. "It's a video chat," she explains, pointing to her hair. Lola's hair is naturally smooth and straight. Right now it looks like it might house a family of small birds.

Laughing, I lean forward, kissing her nose. "I have to get to the shop this morning to check on Joe, anyway. Maybe we can meet up for a late lunch?"

Reading my expression, Lola pushes closer, tilting her head to my mouth, speaking between each kiss: "I'm not sure how long I'll be." She pulls back, rubbing her thumb over my stubble. "I have to shower and then I have a call with Benny after—but I'll text you when I'm done?"

"Yeah. Text me." My words are tight, and I lean back in, kisses growing more desperate. "Stay here again tonight. I need . . ."

I need to drink, and drink, and drink of her. I'll never get my fill.

A rush of breath escapes her lungs and she pushes off her chair and onto my lap, whispering against my mouth. "I don't want to leave," she says, and her hand slides over my bare chest. "Let's go back to bed."

My jeans have slipped so they're barely hanging on, and all I can think of is how easy it would be to push them the rest of the way down, lift my shirt up, and make her come, right here on my kitchen table.

She grinds into me, sliding wet across my button fly.

"Get up on the table," I say into her open mouth. "Let me kiss that little cunt."

She pulls back, blushing. Her lip is trapped between her teeth. "I like the way you say that word."

"I can tell. It makes you get all squirmy and bashful. . . ." I lick her mouth, saying, "Not entirely sure yet—need to do a few more studies—but I believe there's a direct correlation between me saying it and how fast I can make you come."

I notice she hasn't, in fact, climbed up on the table. Slipping my fingers under the shirt, I rub my hands over the warm, soft skin of her waist.

"I know you're sore," I tell her. "I'll be sweet, I promise."

Her phone goes off again and we both grow still.

"Alas: real life invades," I murmur.

Lola pouts. "I really hate interviews."

"And here you are, getting better at them every day." I help her up, standing after her and holding her face, kissing her once. "Just let me know when you're done."

I go for a long ride after Lola leaves, taking the road that leads down to the beach and biking the trail as long as I possibly can. Although we slept in tiny bursts broken by two more rounds of frenzied, wordless fucking, I'm full of an energy that feels nearly limitless. I go from Pacific Beach to Carlsbad, legs pumping, heart propelling blood in enormous, victorious spasms.

I hurt when my mum left. I was angry and sullen, and upset with the world for a long time. I hated my dad for leaving me. I couldn't imagine that I would ever experience true contentment or joy, but now I have both. The store is situated. My home is mostly paid for. The love of my life slept in my arms last night—in my bed, where I hope she will stay forever. I want for nothing.

THE BELL RINGS over the door to the shop as I step inside, and a strange calm settles over me. It's barely half-past eleven and the aisles are pretty packed for a nonrelease day, people spilling off the couch in the front reading nook and crowded around the pinball machine near the back. Joe is at the register, a line of customers behind him.

He nods in my direction but everything from last night is too fresh, and I'm not sure I'm ready to put my game face on, especially with Joe. For all his flaky mannerisms, I'm often surprised by how acutely he pays attention.

I return Joe's nod and round the counter, stepping into the back office and hanging my jacket on the hook. Only now that I'm here does it occur to me that I'm not clear what the rules are. If I'm reading things correctly, Lola and I are *together*—I'm just not sure who else is supposed to know that. Lola isn't guarded in a stereotypical way; she shares things, but she does so in inches rather than miles, and not always immediately. It's entirely possible she'll wait to tell Harlow about this until whenever she happens to see her next. Lola isn't exactly a close-the-door-behind-him-and-call-the-girlfriend-to-dish kind of woman.

Which puts me in a weird spot: If I tell Finn, and he tells Harlow, and Harlow hears it from Finn before she hears it from Lola, Lola will be in trouble and I may be, too. If I tell Ansel, and he mentions it to Mia, which he definitely will, there is no way Mia won't call Harlow immediately.

So there is absolutely no way I can let on to Joe what is going on: *Joe* hearing about this before anyone else would make Harlow's head explode. Not to mention the *Not-Joe is Always Right* Tumblr he'd probably start and fill with illustrations of every time he told us to "just bang and get it over with already."

Luckily I have experience hiding this . . . though who am I kidding? There's not a single person—except perhaps Lola—who didn't realize I'm wildly in love with her.

I head out to the front of the store and begin helping customers. One of my regulars is searching for the newest issue of *Hawkeye*, but when I check I see we've sold out. There's a man in his forties looking to sell a box of miscellaneous junk he got at a garage sale, and after poking through it, I know there's nothing I'm interested in buying. I help a couple looking to buy their first big comic together, and I sell them *Captain America* 61. Released in 1947, it depicts Cap and Bucky discovering that the Red Skull, believed to be gone, is indeed still alive. Classic.

And through it all, I can feel Joe watching me.

The crowd thins a bit and I walk to the counter, reaching under for a rag to wipe down the pinball machine.

"Place has been crazy lately," Joe says, pulling a stack of twenties out of the register to face them.

"Yeah, was thinking of bringing someone else in."

He pauses for a moment and looks up. "Someone else to work here?"

"Sure."

Joe perks up. "Would I train them?"

He follows me toward the back, and I look at him over my shoulder. "Sure."

"So, I'd be in charge. Second in command, even. Wong to Doctor Strange."

I laugh. "Absolutely. Robin to my Batman."

"Batman? Let's not get too far ahead of yourself. Foggy Nelson to your Daredevil. The *movie*."

I stop near the back and start straightening a shelf of Choose Your Own Adventure books. "Sure," I say again with a shrug.

Joe knocks on the counter, *loudly*. "Okay what is *up*?"

"Up?" I repeat. "Nothing's *up*."

"*Ben Affleck's Daredevil?* You're just going to let me throw that out at you?"

I move back to the front of the store. "What? It was an okay movie."

"An oka—"

The bell over the door rings, cutting him off, and I hear one of our regulars up front call out to Lola.

My body goes tight, heart taking off in a sprint.

It's one thing to decide I'm not telling Joe, or Finn, or Ansel, or even letting on to *anything*, but am I expected to act like nothing happened? Is that even possible? I feel like one look at her and all of last night will be written all over my face.

Glancing over my shoulder, I see Lola's hair is pulled into a dark ponytail that swings behind her as she walks. When she isn't in a hurry, her stride is even and serene and her hair rests gently down the middle of her back. But when she's moving like this—with purpose—it swings behind her, propelled by the sway of her energy.

She's headed straight toward me, and she's definitely moving with intent.

I turn fully to face her. "Hey, how did the video chat go?"

Casual, calm. Nothing out of the ordinary here.

Joe watches as she breezes by him, ignores my question, and stops just at my feet before reaching for the back of my neck and pulling me down to her. With a tiny sigh, her lips meet mine and all other sound in the room is sucked out in one giant rush of air. My blood heats, and lust flashes through me, hot and dizzying.

Lola smells exactly like she always does—the sweet honey scent of her soap—and her lips are just as soft as they were when I kissed her goodbye through the open window of her car only hours ago. My brain spends so much time wondering at these things that it takes a moment for me to realize that Lola is *kissing* me. *Now*. Right here, in the middle of my shop.

Fuck it.

My hands push into her hair to tilt her head, my tongue slides against hers, and it feels like the perfect way for us to announce what's happening. I only wish *everyone* was here to see it, to get it over with in one fell swoop.

A throat clears somewhere nearby, and when Lola takes a step back the rest of the world slowly comes into focus. Joe is leaning against the register, ankles crossed, with his eyebrows raised to the ceiling.

Lola smiles and looks up at me with the adoration I feel for her mirrored in her eyes. "Can we talk for a minute in your office?" she asks, breathless.

She follows me to the back, and her presence behind me feels radioactive, buzzing. I want to turn and kiss her as we walk. It's a heady infatuation, that need I have to touch touch touch until our skin is sore and the need for food and water takes priority. I crave it, I crave *her*.

Inside the office, she closes the door behind her back and leans against it, grinning at me. "Hey."

"Hey." I'm not sure I've ever smiled so wide; it feels too big for my face. "Nice show out there."

She gives a little one-shouldered shrug. "Thanks."

"I wonder if Joe will ever move from that spot now that you've shocked the life out of him."

Laughing, she says, "We'll have to tell the others soon, I guess."

She looks around the room, and I try to see it from her eyes. She's been back here only a couple of times, and in the past few months the space has become my little, calming cave. Before we moved into the shop, it was a pretty fancy boutique, and some of those original fixtures remain in the back office. The walls are painted a soft cream and there are outlets where glass chandeliers used to hang from the ceiling. A row of mirrors lines the back wall but is partially covered in boxes I've yet to unpack. Even so, it makes the space feel larger than it is. My desk is situated along the long wall behind me, facing the door, and a small row of windows cuts a dusty sunbeam across the room.

When our eyes meet again, I know we've silently agreed not to talk about the hardest part of all this, that there's new pressure there now. Ansel and Mia are married. Finn and Harlow are married. We don't have the luxury of crashing and burning in a fiery mess.

There's an unspoken sense among our friends that Lola and I are somehow more together—the store, her comic career—as if we've had it all figured out more thoroughly and for longer than they have. But looking at Lola now, I can easily tell she doesn't trust herself at all in this. As much as I sense she *does* feel for me, I also know she would rather illustrate a comic for Frank Miller with him looking over her shoulder than navigate emotional territory when a group of friends is involved.

I move to her, giving her a soft kiss. "What brings you to my office today, young lady?"

Wincing, she tells me, "I'm headed to L.A."

My heart trips over her words. "Today?"

"Yeah. The car is coming for me at five."

"They sent a *car*?"

"I think that's mostly because Austin isn't sure mine will survive the drive there."

"You're still hot shit," I tease, and then look over my shoulder at the wall clock. It's three seventeen. "When are you home?"

"I'm staying tonight, tomorrow, and Thursday, back sometime Friday night."

Well, that blows. "Can we plan for dinner Friday?"

"I'm supposed to go over to Greg's. Come with me?"

I bend, kissing her again. "Sure."

There's tension in her eyes, and I lean back, studying it. "You okay?"

She swallows, shaking her head quickly as if to clear it. "I'm fine. I have a book due next week and I've barely started. We're supposed to finalize the script this week, but I haven't seen it yet. I don't know how I'm going to get everything done."

"You take it one step at a time."

She leans into me, resting her chin on my chest as she looks up at my face. "I'm a little distracted."

"The feeling is mutual."

She pushes her lips out in a sweet pout. "And I don't feel like going to L.A. for a few days."

"I don't feel like having a girlfriend in L.A. for a few days."

Biting the side of her lip, she repeats, " 'Girlfriend'?"

"Fuck buddy of whom I am rather fond?" I offer instead.

Lola smacks my chest, laughing.

I put my hand over hers to keep it in place, right over my breastbone. "*Girlfriend* is certainly my preference."

She stares up at me, quiet, unreadable.

"Want to go to your place for the next hour?" I ask, and I know my meaning is obvious when Lola flushes.

"London is there."

"London is going to have to get used to me staying over," I remind her.

Leaning back, Lola levels me with an amused look. "We're not quiet."

"She'll have to get used to the noise then, too."

"*Especially* you."

I shrug, lifting her hand to kiss the center of her palm and still trying to wrap my head around the fact this is a thing I'm allowed to do now. Lola watches with wide, blue eyes as I kiss up her wrist, to the inside of her elbow, sucking lightly at the delicate skin there. "So, we won't go to your apartment. . . ."

"London doesn't date much," she blurts, and I recognize it for what it is: nervous babble now that it's becoming clear we're going to fool around back here. It's so un-Lola to ramble, it makes me smile in surprise. "Like, she gets asked out all the time and always turns them down."

"Why's that?" I ask before biting her gently, though to be

honest, I'm not really all that concerned with London's dating life right now. I'm pretty sure we both know this.

Lola blows out a breath. "I don't know, really. She had a boyfriend for most of college. Not sure what happened." She pauses. "Anyway, I don't really want to talk about her right now," she says, a hint of a smile pulling at the corner of her mouth.

"Oh?"

She watches me kiss her arm again. "No."

"What would you prefer to do?"

She pulls away gently before walking to my desk, and I follow. Reaching for my belt loop, Lola pulls me closer. "I don't know. . . ."

My fingers graze her sides and toy with the hem of her shirt. I wait for her to stop me, to give me some sort of sign that she wants to take things slower today. But before I can ask, the fabric is pulled from my hands and her shirt is gone, a blur of blue that lands somewhere in a pile behind my desk.

Her bra is black and covered in white polka dots, her tits pushed up so the swells are full and round. She pulls my shirt up over my head and then stretches, brushing her chest against mine, and even though I know what's about to happen, I could never anticipate the way it feels when her hands move down to the front of my pants, gripping me over the denim. Her thumb moves back and forth along the tip and my head falls forward, forehead resting on hers as I force myself to hold still, not to rock into her palm or rush this.

Lola pulls my head back down to hers, her warm lips

opening against mine. I want to figure out how to go faster and slow down all at once, how to spend an eternity feeling everything. We kiss, lips and the slippery slide of tongues, vibrations of noise, and tiny explosions of realization that seem to pop like flashbulbs in my mind over and over again. I'm an amnesiac: I still can't believe this is happening. Twenty-four hours ago we didn't kiss or touch—we definitely didn't see each other naked—but here we are.

My heart is racing, and when I pull back for breath, I see that Lola's mouth is red and swollen from the drag of my day-old beard. She looks up at me as her fingers move to the fly of my jeans and unbuttons them one by one. I can feel each teasing pop. I bite down on my lip and try to stay quiet, knowing that if I let myself make even a sound it will be the tiny crack that shatters my control. I'll throw her down and fuck her, unprotected, messy, half-dressed.

She stretches to suck on my neck and then steps back, bunching her skirt in her hands and pulling it up her thighs. I watch the slow reveal: milky skin, soft curved hips . . . She's not wearing underwear. Still, she's fresh-faced, eyes carrying a clear innocence I'm sure she has no sense of whatsoever. Never in my life have I felt more like I'm doing something very naughty with someone very, very sweet. Sliding onto my desk, she spreads her legs and leans back, giving me a rather perfect view of her pussy.

Heat slides through my veins and I step between her thighs, desperation licking at my skin. I slide my hand up the inside of her legs, wondering idly about how many men she's been with. It could be one or one hundred and I wouldn't begrudge her any of them, but something tells me this type of relationship is new for her. I know from overhearing her with her friends the past few months that she has no compunction about sex, no sense that it should be held off for some larger declaration, no issue with one-night stands. But I also get the sense that for Lola, it takes more than a momentary desire to let someone into this secret, honest place.

She shivers as my fingers trace the shape of one breast, the pad of my thumb brushing over the taught peak of her nipple until she arches, wordlessly begging for the pinch I know she wants. I lean down and run my tongue over the sheer fabric before I take her between my teeth. Her back bows, pushing her chest to my mouth, and I use the opportunity to reach around, slipping the hook free. I pull the fabric away and watch as she's unwrapped like a fucking present.

With my gaze locked to hers I drag the tip of my tongue over her skin. She sucks in a breath, reaching to part the denim of my jeans and pulling my boxers down just enough to take me in her palm. I almost bite through my lip when she swipes her thumb across the head, and then reaches up, sliding her fingertip into her mouth.

Her hand returns, thumb even wetter now, and I blink down to where she holds me between our bodies. There's the flat plane of my stomach and the soft curve of hers, and my cock, hard and swollen at the tip, jutting straight up between us.

I'm almost too warm, and feel the prickle of sweat at the

back of my neck as Lola leans in, lips brushing over the shell of my ear. "Do you have a condom in here?"

"Yeah. Middle top desk drawer. Brought some in today."

She gives me a triumphant *you're-a-genius* grin and then lies back, stretching an arm over her head to reach to the other side of the desk and open the drawer. It would be easier for me to do this, but there's no fucking way I'm missing the chance to look at her stretched out and almost naked on my desk.

When she sits up, I step forward, taking her face in my hands to press my mouth to hers.

"I want you to put it on," she says against my lips.

"Yeah?"

"Watching you roll that thing on in the middle of the night might have been one of the sexiest things I've ever seen."

With my cock in one hand and the condom in the other, I pause with the latex poised just over the tip, and look up to make sure she's watching.

She is. In fact, I'm not sure she blinks or even breathes the entire time, her eyes glued to me while I slowly roll it down. I love the way she looks at my cock: eyes a little wide, lips parted.

I reach up, cupping her breast. "You look surprised."

"I think I'll be surprised every time you take your pants off," she says absently. "Your cock is unreal."

Hearing Lola say my cock is unreal will never get old. Never.

She slides her fingers between her legs, slipping them back and forth along either side of her clit. I both see and hear what this does to her, in the way the muscles of her stomach flex and her thighs squeeze my hips, in the soft sounds she makes.

"Wet enough for me?"

Lola nods, bringing her hands from between her legs to my mouth, where she slips them between my lips. I can feel for myself how wet she is, can *taste* it. My eyes nearly roll out of my head with how good this is, how dirty I want to be with her and all the things I want us to do. I moan and Lola pulls her fingers away with a quiet pop, staring up at me with a hunger I've never seen in her before.

I wish I could pinpoint why her expression tugs at a tender part of me, what feels off.

It isn't the way our hands trip over each other in their quest to touch every inch of skin, or the way she digs her fingers into my hair, exhaling in relief when she feels me slip barely inside her. It isn't the way her head falls back, the way she pushes her breast into my hand, or how her legs spread wide to take more.

But maybe it is in the way she won't let her eyes hold mine for too long, the way it feels like she's holding her breath. It's the same thing I do before I tilt my bike over a steep hill and barrel down.

I ease into her—in, out, in deeper, out a bit more—and she's with me, fuck I know she is, I can feel it in the rocking of her hips, the curl of her fists in my hair—but the hot film of protectiveness won't leave me. Every move she makes screams that she's new to this, that this type of intimacy is different, blissful, and terrifying.

I've had sex with many women, and have had loving, intimate sex with some of them, but I've never felt for them what I feel for Lola. Still, the depth of the emotion is a relief, not at all disorienting. Last night was the perfect combination of making love and fucking, but here I wouldn't dare be so rough with her as I'd been. She feels like blown glass in my hands, looking up at me almost as if she needs to know what to do.

So I give her a task. My lips press to her cheek, teeth bared. "Don't make a sound."

I feel her exhale in relief against me, and she nods, turning, seeking my mouth, but I pull away.

"Stay quiet, be good, and I'll kiss you."

She nods again, quickly, urgently, and it can't be that simple, but it is. The drifting tension in her eyes is replaced by focus. But now that I've said it, there isn't a thing on this planet or any other I want as much as I want her mouth, open and wet against mine while we fuck.

I fill my hands with her tits, suck at her neck, and grind my body into hers until I feel her sweat under my lips, and she's tight everywhere.

Growing tighter, still quiet, breaths shallow and sharp.

"That's it," I tell her. "I can't hear you. I can only hear the fucking."

I love her sounds, but right now her silence means so

much more. Her silence and the begging in her eyes is the admission that she needs me to ground her, to help her focus down on this and *only* this. Not L.A. Not the book she needs to write. I always suspected she looked to me to center her, but to *know* it so surely right now, when we're making love, pulls at a tight band in my chest.

Lola's skin is creamy and pale, even paler against the dark of her hair. Her ponytail has come undone and now strands fall forward over her shoulders, brushing along her nipples, the ends curling over her breasts. A sheen of sweat breaks out on her chest, her upper lip, and around me her cunt squeezes tight . . . she's close. Her breaths come quicker when I thrust up with just a little more force and I bare my teeth on her jaw, feeling my own control fraying, growling, "Not a sound. Not one *fucking* sound."

I find her wrists, draw them behind her back, and plunge so deep, grinding where she likes it. Her mouth goes wide, expression nearly pained, and then it's like tapping the first domino down and watching in wonder: She squeezes her eyes closed, head back and teeth clenched with the effort it takes to hold in her cries. Around me, her body comes with a series of wild, tight spasms. Lola flushes red and her pulse is a wild animal in her throat—but my girl doesn't even let free a tiny gasp of air.

Pride swells so fast in my chest I'm covering her mouth with mine, fucking her fast and shallow, and she's wrestling free, finally crying out at the feel of my tongue on hers. Her hands dig into my hair, eyes open so she can watch me.

"It's so fucking good." I hear myself grunt on every shove, the sounds of sex making me harder—the wet slide, skin slapping, the creaking of my desk.

"Fuck!" I can't help but yell. *"Fuck!"*

I'm grateful to the traffic on Fifth, the constant bustle of the shop for muting the noise we must be making.

Harder, faster, she's gasping and clutching me at my neck, nails digging into my skin. Her legs are wrapped around me, sweat making us slippery, and I grip her ass to pull her onto me at the same time I shove as deep as I can, going off with a hoarse yell, in a flurry of wild thrusts. Light bursts behind my closed lids, bliss racing down my spine, tiny explosions of pleasure spreading across the map of my entire body.

I slump against her, pressing my teeth to her neck as my hips slow and eventually stop. It's a miracle my desk is still in one piece.

Lola catches her breath against me, holding me tight. Her legs don't let up; she doesn't want to let me go, and, fuck, I don't ever want to leave the warmth of her body.

The room is suddenly so quiet, and I can't seem to pull in enough oxygen. My breaths feel too fast, too loud. Lola slumps forward on my chest and I wrap my arms around her. She feels tiny in my arms: willowy and delicate. I feel like I'm made of nothing but basic instincts—fuck, breathe, sleep—but I manage to remain upright. The pleasure slips away gradually, and I run kisses up her neck, pausing for a breath so I can tell her how fucking good it was.

Before I can get the words started, I stop, listening.

An odd stillness seems to have surrounded us, and I'm hit with a restless awareness: the magnitude of the quiet is nearly dystopian, almost as if the world outside ended while we were in here wildly fucking.

Lola's eyes meet mine and I know the thought hits us both at the same time.

I close my eyes, waiting for the explosion. "Oh sh—"

Suddenly Def Leppard's "Pour Some Sugar on Me" blares from the front of the store. It's so loud it may as well be playing in the room with us.

I look at Lola, who is still flushed from her orgasm. She claps a hand over her mouth to keep from laughing. "Oh, my God," she mumbles.

Motherfucking Joe starts yell-singing along with it: *"Demolition woman, can I be your man?"*

Finally, I pull out, quickly tying off the rubber and dropping it in the trash bin. Together, we start putting our clothes back on: I pull my pants up my legs, tug my shirt over my head. Lola slides from the desk, straightening her skirt, locating her bra and shirt.

"Television lover, baby, go all night!" Joe sings.

At least four other voices join in for the rest of the chorus.

Lola hooks her bra behind her back, adjusts the straps, and then presses her hands to her face. "Oh, my God. Oh, my God."

The music dies down and Joe proclaims, "Show thyself, mighty stallion!"

Laughing, I call out, "Shut the fuck up!" I help Lola get her shirt back on as laughter trails through the door.

Pulling her hair into a bun, she says, "I guess that answers that question."

"The soundproofing in here?" I ask.

She nods, rubbing her face again, but behind it I can see her smile. "Is there a secret way out or are we doomed for a walk of shame?"

This makes me laugh. "*Shame?* I'll be strutting. We nearly broke that fucking desk fucking."

"Seriously."

I cup her face, kissing her once. "Sorry, pet, we can only escape through that door, right there."

Lola nods against my hands, eyes holding mine.

"Was it good?" I ask quietly. "Did you like trying to be quiet?"

"*So* good," she whispers, stretching to kiss me again. "I don't want to go to L.A."

My arms come around her, and I feel the warmth of her breath on my neck. "I'm not wild about this plan, either."

She's shaking, and I want to look at her face, but she has it determinedly pressed to my shoulder.

"Look at me," I say. "Let me taste that pretty mouth."

She tilts her face up to me, lazily sliding her lips with mine: warm, heavy, wet.

"I love you," I tell her. Her eyes flutter closed, her kisses deepen. And I don't need to hear the words from her in return because this—her body language, her response when I say it, even the fact that she's confirmed to anyone in the store that she's mine—tells me she feels it, too.

After another ten seconds where I'm debating having her again, but this time on the couch near the window, I pull back, kissing the top of her head and coaxing her arms from around my waist. It's time to face the inevitable.

I cross the room and look over my shoulder at her; she swipes away the smudged eyeliner from beneath her eyes, and then gives me a tentative thumbs-up. The squeak of the door-knob seems to reverberate in the quiet and I pull the door open, letting in a gust of cool air.

My heart drops when I see Harlow first, Finn just behind her. I expected Joe. Not this.

"Well, well," Harlow says as a smile spreads across her face. "If it isn't my two favorite nerds."

I step out, working to keep my expression neutral. "You know two *other* nerds?"

Harlow's mouth tries to form a few words. Finally, she manages, "How long have you been—"

Finn gets his hand around her and over her mouth just milliseconds after she releases a loud *"Fucking?"* into the entire store.

"Roughly for the last eighteen hours," Lola answers, coming up behind me, and I look down at her, surprised by the poise in her voice. She slips her arm around my waist. "Though we took a break between ten and three today to get some work done."

Joe whistles from behind the counter, and then looks

down at a book he's reading, as if he weren't behind these shenanigans.

"Think you could have started the music a few minutes sooner?" I ask him with a grin.

He laughs down at the book. "Probably. But where's the fun in that? This is your punishment for taking so long to do that."

"And leaving him in charge," someone calls from the front reading nook.

"Wong to Doctor Strange . . ." I remind him. "*Wong* would have been a team player."

Joe looks up at me, feigning insult. "That hurts, boss."

Harlow is staring at Lola, brows raised in expectation. "Do you have a minute, *friend?*" she asks, fighting an enormous grin.

Lola looks warily up at the clock behind the counter. It's nearly four, and I'm sure she's thinking the same thing I am—that a conversation with Harlow about this is unlikely to be quick. "I have a few. But I need to pack for L.A., so just come to the loft with me for my interrogation."

She turns, gives me a pained look, stretches to kiss me in front of her best friend—who gasps—and then whispers, "I'll see you Friday."

"Friday," I repeat, holding her hand until the last possible moment. With a last wide-eyed glance over her shoulder at me, Lola allows Harlow to march her out of the store.

Finn watches the two women leave with a mixture of amusement and concern. Harlow is already shouting excitedly on the sidewalk. "So," he says, turning to me.

I smile. "So."

He lifts his cap, scratching his head. "Lola's headed to L.A. again?"

My smile widens. I can always count on Finn to keep things easy. "For a few days."

"I hate L.A."

"You do?" I ask through mild sarcasm.

He ignores this. "You either spend the entire day driving from meetings on one side of town to another or you get up there and do everything over the phone and could have stayed home anyway."

"Well, I think they're working on the script."

He nods. "Probably better to be up there, then." Finn walks around the counter and looks in the mini-fridge we have stashed in the corner. "Lola will figure it out, I bet." I hear him slide a couple of cans out and he tosses me a beer. "So things are good?"

I grin at him for several beats of silence before asking, "Finn, did you just ask me a personal question?"

Laughing, he says, "Forget it," and cracks open his beer.

"Yeah things are good," I tell him, opening my own. "Bloody *great*."

"So last night . . . ?"

He lets the question hang between us. This is the deepest Finn is willing to pry.

"Yeah." The reality of it—of Lola as mine—makes me feel like sprinting from the store and running a marathon.

"Fucking *finally*," Finn says with a small lift of his brow.

I laugh, taking a deep drink. "Do you ever stop and think how crazy this is?"

Tilting his chin up, he asks, "The wives, you mean?"

"Well, yeah. I mean, from Vegas to now."

"Part of me suspects Harlow masterminded the entire thing," he says. "I wouldn't be surprised if she was the one to slip us each the Bike and Build info years ago."

"The long con." I acknowledge this by lifting my can to him. "How *is* the esteemed Mrs. Roberts?"

He grins. "Crazy as fuck. She's probably up there giving Lola the third degree."

I think *third degree* is probably an understatement, but if Lola can handle anyone, it's Harlow.

"It's a good time to be a man," I say. The clink of our cans echoes dully through the store.

Chapter ELEVEN

Lola

I EXPECT AN INTERROGATION from Harlow, but I definitely don't expect to find London and Mia also waiting for us at the loft. My brain is still fuzzy from the sex, from the impending trip, from the deadlines looming on my calendar; I don't seem to have any extra space in my thoughts for what's happening right now.

I stare at the three women just inside my door, blinking in confusion.

"I texted them," Harlow explains with a wave of her hand. "During the fuckfest. After you came—I think—but before Oliver did."

"You called an emergency meeting because I was having sex with Oliver?" Pressing my palms against my face, I mumble through a laugh, "Oh, my God."

Harlow pulls my hands away, shaking her head. "I'm just relieved you're getting pounded."

"Harlow," Mia says, pulling me away from her. "You're ridiculous."

"Says the girl who can barely walk today."

Mia ignores this and pulls me inside. It's true: she's limping. But it's not her bad leg. Harlow would never tease her about that. Mia's walking like an old woman, or a very, very pregnant one. Delicately, like her back might snap in half.

"What's with you, Blanche?" I ask, grinning.

"Shh." Mia waves me off.

The girls crowd around me in the living room—London and Mia next to me on the couch, and Harlow sitting on the coffee table, facing me.

"The thing we need to discuss," Mia says with dramatic sincerity, "is how we failed you."

Harlow turns to look at her in thrilled amusement.

I lean away from Mia, skeptically observing the three of them. "You what?"

"All this time," Mia says, lifting a delicate hand to her throat, "things were developing with Oliver, and we have to assume if you weren't telling us everything it's because we weren't *available* to you. As friends."

I level her with a flat look. "Are you being a passive-aggressive troll?"

London and Harlow nod.

Mia shakes her head solemnly. "We've just been so *busy.*"

"You were buying a house, asshole," I remind her.

She agrees with a smile. "So busy signing all those papers for days on end, I couldn't answer my phone, *asshole.*"

I lean back against the couch, laughing. "It just *happened.*"

"No thought at all," Harlow deadpans.

Nodding, Mia says, "That sounds like our Lola. Impulsive."

"No, I mean, last night—" I begin.

"Last night was the first time you guys ever flirted and then boom! Sex?" Harlow asks, nodding as if she's got the answer right.

"The three of you are enormous dicks," I say, grinning. "And I need to pack."

I push up from the couch and start walking down the hall to my room.

"But we still need details," Mia calls out as she follows.

Details.

My head swims with them. I still feel full of Oliver. I want to tattoo every *detail* on my skin: The curve of his mouth when he's coming. The soft brush of his fingers on my shoulders when he's moving to touch my hair. His shoulders over me, shifting up and down, up and down as he moves.

"It was nice."

Harlow snorts from my doorway, watching as London and Mia settle on my bed. "He broke your vagina and—from the sounds of it—almost broke furniture, and it was 'nice'?"

I look up from where I'm pulling clothes from my dresser. "Can you not say 'vagina'?"

"It's an awesome word," she argues. "You should be proud—"

"God, I'm sure my lady parts are unbelievable," I cut in, turning back to my packing, "but it's *not* an awesome word. It's an awesome thing, but it's a horrible word."

"We need a better one," London agrees. "I do like *pussy*, though."

"But we wouldn't just casually refer to our pussies the way guys refer to their dicks," Harlow says.

"Is that a bad thing?" Mia asks. "Do we *need* to casually refer to them?"

Harlow looks insulted.

"Like, how about . . . *sock*." London angles both hands to point between her legs and looks at us for agreement. "This is my 'sock.'"

"Maybe something that isn't already a *thing*, and doesn't rhyme with *cock*?" I suggest.

"Oh." London deflates. "That's so weird. I didn't even think about that. Clearly it has been far too long since I thought about cock."

"How's the new house?" I ask Mia, changing the subject. I zip up my duffel bag and drop it near the desk.

She shrugs, grinning with bliss. "Gorgeous. We got the keys yesterday."

"Did you spend the night there?" I ask.

She nods. "No furniture, no electricity, it's about two degrees inside, and Ansel ran around the entire place naked before attacking me on the wood floor of the living room." She grips her lower back, wincing. "Is twenty-three too old to comfortably have sex on the floor? I thought we'd have more longevity than this."

"Well, that explains the geriatric curve to your spine," I say.

London sighs. "I would have sex on a pointy rock right now."

I high-five her, but she immediately grabs my hand and swipes her palm across mine. "Wait. I'm taking back my high-five. You got *superbanged* last night. And today."

"It was nearly a year ago that I was last banged!" I protest. "And I'm headed to L.A. for three days with no banging. Give me that high-five back."

London limply wipes her hand back over mine and the four of us fall into silence at the mention of L.A. The quiet tells me they're done giving me shit. But their continued presence tells me they're not leaving until they get some more details.

So I give them what I can.

I tell them about drawing him, about the tension that seemed to be let loose after that, about how my feelings seemed to grow exponentially as soon as I gave them air. I tell them about the night at his house, cuddling, about the party in L.A., the bar afterward, and Oliver's bare admission that he's in love with me.

My heart seems to balloon until it's hard to take a deep breath.

Harlow's hand is pressed firmly to her chest. "He *said* that?"

I nod, chewing a nail and speaking around it: "He said it."

"And you didn't have sex with him *immediately* that night?" Mia asks.

"In a *hotel* room," Harlow adds, horrified at my missed opportunity.

It's too much, and I feel months of longing crash into everything else going on in my life right now. "It's a big deal to me," I say. And, inexplicably, tears fill my eyes.

Pushing past a surprised Harlow, I rush into the bathroom, closing the door behind me.

"What—?" I hear London say.

Harlow's voice is a calm murmur: "I got this."

I hear her knock quietly on the door as I fill my cupped palms with cold water, splashing it on my cheeks before pressing my face into a soft towel.

Breathe.

It's just a lot all at once, I tell myself. *Breathe.*

"Lola?"

"Just give me a second."

I don't know why, but I have this dark sense of dread. My blood rushes cold in fear and hot in thrill, wildly alternating between these two poles. This is *good.* Everything is good. So why do I feel like I'm trying to contain a hurricane in the palm of my hand?

I take a few minutes to brush my hair and put it back up in a neat ponytail. I put on a little makeup. I stare at myself in the mirror, and try not to worry that the woman staring back at me is going to fuck all of this up, every last bit of it.

"Lola," Harlow whispers through the door. "Lola. It's okay for it to be intense. Oliver isn't going anywhere."

THE CAR PULLS up in front of the Four Seasons Beverly Hills and the driver lifts my sad little duffel bag from the trunk, smiling blandly when I give him a pathetic tip because I only have ten dollars in cash.

I'm startled when the bellhop reaches for my bag before I can pick it up and we apologize in unison. He gives me a sympathetic smile and nods to the opulent hotel entrance. I must look like I've just emerged from a cave: I'm going on a night with little sleep, and napped like a milk-drunk newborn the entire drive from San Diego. But even with the darkening sky all around me and the promise of a comfortable bed, unfortunately I know I will be up for hours now.

The room is already paid for, and with my key in hand I head upstairs. It's a lavish suite, decorated in soft neutrals with bright flowers in a vase on the desk. A giant king-size bed takes up much of the bedroom floor, and just beyond is a set of French doors to a balcony overlooking the Los Angeles skyline.

It's beautiful, and this week promises to be exciting, but my stomach feels a little low in my body. As desperate as it sounds, I don't like the idea of being away from Oliver for the next few days. Things are so new between us still; it isn't time yet for interruption.

I pick up my phone to call him, and see that in the past three hours, I've missed two calls from my editor, three from Benny, and one from Oliver.

I listen to Oliver's message first as I walk into the bathroom and undress, needing a shower, some room service, a full night's sleep.

"Hey, pet. Just missing you. Hope the drive went smoothly. Havin' dinner with the group tonight. Will miss you there, and

later." His voice drops. *"I don't want to sleep alone in my bed tonight. I want you in it, on top of me. Lola, I'm obsessed. Call me when you've arrived so I can play with you. I love you."*

I listen to it again, and again, and again, until I turn on the water, lips curled in a smile as I remember every single one of his touches, and forget that I have other messages waiting, red and urgent on my phone.

A CAR PICKS me up outside the hotel at nine the next morning, and I look out the window as we weave our way through downtown L.A. traffic. I called Oliver last night after my shower, talking to him for three hours until both of our words were coming out thick with exhaustion. I suddenly want to see a picture of him, of us—something to stare at other than the monotony of cars merging into our lane, the endless view of sidewalk and taillights.

But when I pull out my phone to scroll through whatever pictures I have stored there, my screen is already lit up with another missed call from Benny.

"Fuck," I breathe, feeling with my thumb that my phone has been on silent since I left San Diego yesterday. "Fuck, fuck, *fuck*." I'd forgotten that he called. I never listened to his messages.

Lola, it's Benny, give me a call.

Lola, sweets, I just talked to Erik. He's needing an update on the delivery of the manuscript.

My editor? What?

Hi, Lola, it's Erik. Give me a quick call. I wanted to check in about the progress on Junebug *and see if you needed some extra time.*

"Extra time?" I say out loud. The driver glances at me in the rearview mirror. My hands are shaking when I open my calendar app.

There is no way I got this wrong.

No way I got this wrong.

I look, blinking. I *know* my book is due next week—I've been stressed about being behind on it while on the road—but it's not on the calendar. I scroll forward one week, two weeks, three . . . nothing. I scroll back through this week, and last week . . . it's not there, either.

The driver pulls up in front of the studio offices and I trip out of the backseat with a distractedly mumbled thanks. My fingers are damp on the screen, clammy. With dread settling in my stomach, I open my calendar for two weeks ago. Pinned to the Wednesday of that week are the words

Junebug due to Erik

It was due two weeks ago.

I have seventeen panels drawn for my next book, and it was due two weeks ago. Now I understand why Erik has emailed, casually "checking in" twice. Now I get why Benny gets nervous whenever he's brought up *Junebug*. I have never in my life missed a deadline—not even for something as small as a math assignment.

I pace outside the building, running late for the meeting with Austin and Langdon already but I can't let this wait, either. Benny doesn't answer when I call, and I leave him a rambling message, hysterically trying to explain what happened, that I put it in my calendar and then somehow immediately made a mental note that it was due in March, not February, and could he call Erik and explain and please tell him that I need an extension and I won't ever ask for this again, this is completely my fault.

My phone lights up with a text from Oliver—Good luck today!—and my panic magnifies. I have no idea how I am supposed to focus on anything today knowing how monumentally I have screwed up.

"Morning, Loles!" Austin calls from somewhere behind me, and when I turn, I see him sauntering out of a parking deck adjacent to the building. He smiles widely and I drop my phone into my purse, still shaken.

"Good morning."

When he approaches and sees my face—no doubt I'm pale and look like I'm completely panicking—he draws his brows low, giving me a playfully grumpy face. "You don't look like a badass ready to kick some ass today!"

"I just realized I missed—"

Austin doesn't care. He's already walking past me and tilting his head for me to follow.

I pinch my shirt over my breastbone, fanning it over my skin as I walk into the building behind him. And *goddamnit*: my blue silk shirt already has wide sweat marks under the arms.

It can only go downhill from here. My first instinct is to call Oliver, to tell him everything and unwind as he calmly explains how this is all normal, and lays out how I'll get it all done.

"Langdon is on his way," Austin tells me. "What were you saying? You missed a what?"

"Oh," I say, tripping to keep up with his fast strides as he enters the elevator. "I had to send something to my editor." My head spins and I pull my phone out of my purse again to see if Benny has returned my call.

"Oop, none of that!" he says, tapping the top of my phone with his index finger. "We've got a lot to do today." Leaning in, he adds, "Nothing's more important than this, is it?"

———

AUSTIN LEADS ME to a conference room and hands me a printed copy of the script—my first glimpse—telling me I have a half hour to look it over while we wait for Langdon to arrive.

"He's stuck in traffic," Austin says, frowning down at his phone.

"I haven't even read through—"

"Don't worry," he says, gently interrupting me. He comes around the table to sit next to me, and his sincere wince tells me he knows how overwhelming this must be for me. I just can never tell whether or not he's on my side. "We have all day to pore through this. I swear, Lola, you'll have so much time with this script you'll want to burn it soon."

By the time Langdon arrives and the three of us sit down, my notes on the first few scenes are shakily written and disorganized. The document in front of me is one of the most exciting things to ever happen in my life, but I can't manage to engage fully. My thoughts vacillate between *Junebug* and Oliver—from anxiety to relief and back again. But Langdon and Austin are already very familiar with the script, and even without the deadline panic and the Oliver obsession hijacking my brain, I feel like I'm chasing a car down the street to keep up with the conversation. I need to focus. I can't look to see if Benny or Erik has called me back. I just need to get through the day.

Just get through the day.

Just get through—

"So, Lola," Austin cuts into my efforts, using the tip of his pen to scratch his scalp. The loud *scritch-scritch-scritch* seems to echo through the room. I run my hands up over my bare arms, wondering why the air-conditioning is cranked so high. "We were thinking in the opening scene," he continues, "Quinn could be coming back from the library rather than waking up in bed."

I scan through the section in question, noting that I hadn't written any comments there. I actually *liked* the opening scene. "Well, it's sort of less scary to first run into Razor outside the library than it is to wake up to him standing in her bedroom," I argue.

"I'm just not sure the audience will be sympathetic to Razor if he's in the bedroom of an eighteen-year-old girl," Langdon says.

I stare at both of them. "Especially since Quinn is fifteen."

Austin glances up at Langdon and I catch his subtle

head shake. "Let's focus first on the library-versus-bedroom issue."

"The audience isn't supposed to be sympathetic to Razor at the beginning." Do I really need to explain this? I feel the other stress melting away as this one begins dumping fuel on the fire in my chest. "He's a deformed man with scales and teeth as sharp as knives. He doesn't look like a hero because at the beginning, he's *not*."

Austin launches into an explanation about audience confidence and first impression and there's so much jargon that after a few minutes of it my brain starts to slowly ebb away, thinking instead of Oliver, in his office.

How he told me to be quiet.

How it felt like he knew I was starting to panic at the idea of leaving for three measly days.

How much he seems to love me already, how much he trusts me to get it right.

How much I need him here right now, eyes centering mine, helping me get through this one minute at a time.

". . . so the issue really is grabbing them up front, curling our fist around their collar, and yelling in their faces that they'll love Razor," Austin continues, "no matter what he does. Right up front, in the first scene. It lets us forgive him when he acts out, later."

I nod, head swimming. What's he saying makes sense.

But it also doesn't, right?

And fuck, I know I missed most of his lecture, but I can't help but fight, just a little longer. "I just think—"

Langdon sighs heavily, looking to Austin in exasperation. "We don't have time for this."

"No, no," Austin says, waving easily to Langdon, and giving me a winning smile. "Let her speak."

The words swim in my head and for several, long, painful seconds I forget what scene we're talking about. "Um . . ."

"The open . . . ?" Austin prompts, with deliberate patience.

Nodding quickly, I say, "I prefer it to happen the way it is in the book."

Under his breath, Langdon sneers, "Now there's a surprise."

I whip my head to him. "Excuse me?" I ask, my heart beating so hard I'm shaking. "Isn't this an adaptation of the book? I edited that scene for *weeks* to get it right."

A sarcastic smile curls Langdon's mouth. "You're how old?" he asks, leaning forward with his elbows planted on the table.

I sit up.

The panel shows a girl with a barrel of propane, holding a match.

"Twenty-three."

"Twenty-three, and you wrote a book, and some people liked it, and now you understand Hollywood." He flicks his fingers in front of him, leaning back in his chair. "I'm not sure why I'm even here, then."

My blood turns to steam. He just said *what*?

"I guess I'm not, either," I finally manage, voice shaking. "You're forty-five with only one screenplay adapted for a major film studio and it grossed less than eleven million. Our budget is ten times that."

Langdon draws a deep breath, and it makes him look like a dragon preparing to exhale fire. "My focus has been indie films, giving me a niche perspective that allows me to—"

Austin tries to laugh, but it comes out as a shrill burst. "Langdon, stop it. Don't be a diva. Lola is just telling us how she feels. This is all new to her." He turns to me, placating. "Some of this—and I know it will be hard—will just have to be you, trusting us. Trusting me. Trusting Langdon. Trusting the *process*. Do you think you can do that?" He's already nodding, already smiling as if I've agreed.

I stare at him, stunned.

"Great," he proclaims. "We'll tweak the opening just a tiny *tiny* bit, and then boom! Your world will unfold on the screen!"

THE REST OF the meeting is equally abysmal. Langdon eventually gets over his tantrum, but my story is hacked apart, reorganized. Dialogue I love is lost, scenes I would never have thought to include in the book somehow make it into the script. It's not that I'm particularly precious about my work, but so many of their changes simply don't make sense. And we have to do it all again tomorrow. And the day after that.

I order room service and get into my pajamas before eight o'clock. Erik called during our brief lunch break and has set up a call for us on Friday afternoon, during my drive home to San Diego. At the very least he didn't sound like he wanted to murder me, but I know when I get home I'm going to have to dive into the writing cave.

My phone rests in the middle of the fluffy bed, black and lifeless. I want to call Oliver, to beg him to ramble and pull me out of this frozen frenzy, but every breath I take only makes it halfway down my windpipe before it seems to push back out.

I want him here. I have a to-do list five miles long but I feel restless in the room alone. It seems crazy, like needing him this way is too much too soon. I spent most of the day wishing I were back in San Diego, rather than at the table working through the script.

But I don't want to talk to Oliver on the phone because I feel inarticulate in my panic about him and me, about the book, about the movie, about everything . . . and I don't want to text him, either, because it's trite to put this enormity in a tiny digital box. I miss him in this weird, frantic way. I want to drive home tonight to be with him. I need him in the hotel room with me and I know, without having to weigh the pros and cons for him, that he would drive up here in a heartbeat if I asked. He would calm me down, make me laugh, tease my insanity into something else. A fluffy toy to prop at the end of a pen. A bright pink plastic slinky. Something disposable and silly.

But if he came up here, he would be on the road alone, late. People are drunk. People are reckless. People text and drive and San Diego is over a hundred and thirty miles away.

My phone vibrates with a text and I look down to see his name on the screen. How did it all go?

Picking up my phone, I start to type about ten different replies but find myself deleting each one. Finally dropping it back on the bed, I turn on the television, get into the shower. I pull out a notepad and spend the next few hours sketching some of the worst things I've ever done and then drop the pad on the bed. Was *Razor Fish* a fluke? I started it when I was fifteen, and it took me three years to finish, two more to edit, and another two to get published. How did I ever expect to write the follow-up in a matter of months while touring, working on the film, falling in love?

The panel shows a monster, eating the furniture.

I'm exhausted but my brain won't stop. I dig into my bag, find a sleeping pill. It stares at me, tiny and white and challenging.

I don't even feel it slide down my throat.

The world narrows from a wide white space to the tiny spot of focus in front of me: my hand holding a pen. The line elongates, dragging off the margin, and my eyelids are heavy trees falling over in the woods.

AUSTIN MEETS ME outside the building again the next morning, handing me a huge cup of coffee. "Figured you might need it, eh?" he asks, sipping his little espresso.

I smile, thanking him as I take it. My thoughts reel: Is he saying today is going to be longer and harder than yesterday?

Or is he saying he thinks I need to be more focused and got me a coffee to help?

I follow him to the elevators, listening to him have a short, bursty conversation on his cell. He hangs up just as we get into the car and press into a cluster of people.

"I want you to know that Langdon really does get the spirit of your story," Austin says, too loud in such a crowded space.

"I'm sure." I want to talk to Austin about this, of course—as well as make sure we'll be able to wrap this up in time for me to get home and back to work—but I really don't want to do it in the middle of a crowded elevator.

"And I get that the age thing is a sticking point to you—"

"It is," I say quietly.

"But Langdon has the film sensibility to know what will work and what won't. We aren't going to draw in the male audience we need with a fifteen-year-old female protagonist."

I can tell everyone around us is listening in, waiting to see how I reply.

"Well, that's a shame," I say, and someone behind me snorts. I can't tell from the sound whether it's supportive or derisive. "Though Natalie Portman was only twelve in *The Professional,* and a lot of Razor and Quinn's relationship dynamics are based on that."

The doors open on our floor.

"Well, there was certainly discussion about the sexual dynamics there, too," he points out.

I open my mouth to give him my opinion—that it's about

damaged people finding connection, and it's never implied to be a sexual relationship between Mathilde and Léon—when the doors open and Austin steps out of the lift.

"Sex sells," he says over his shoulder. "It's not an idiom for nothing."

"Wolverine, too," I call out, loud enough that I know he hears me even if he's charging ahead of me and thumbing through emails on his phone. "He mentors younger girls but never lets it get creepy."

Austin ignores this, and we walk down toward the same conference room we were in yesterday. I see through the glass door that Langdon is already there, sitting and laughing easily with another man—slightly older than Langdon, but fit, with graying hair at his temples and thick tortoise-shell frames.

"Oh, good, they're both here," Austin says, pushing the door open with a flattened palm. "Lola, this is Gregory Saint Jude."

The man stands and turns, looking at me with guarded eyes.

"Our director," Austin adds.

I reach out to shake the man's hand. He's shorter than I am but greets me with a firm handshake, a friendly nod, and then sits back down beside Langdon.

"My dad's name is Greg, too," I say with what I hope is an affable smile.

His answering one is tight around his eyes. "I prefer Gregory, actually."

"Sure. Of course." *Gah.* I'm already unsteady from the

misfire with Austin, and suddenly feel like Razor himself, arriving from a completely different version of this same world. I'm clearly cracking because I have to bite back a laugh at the thought.

Sliding my phone on the table, I'm hit with the need to call Oliver and tell him that. To hear his voice, to get a taste of normalcy.

And just like that, it's as if I've broken the seal and let in the flood of thoughts.

I never texted him back last night, so this morning I sent him a series of heart emojis and a S.O.S. L.A. IS WEIRD text, but his reply—Slept like a rock. Think I've been sleep deprived? Call when you're done today—wasn't nearly enough. I briefly reconsider the idea of him driving up and spending the next two nights with me, but would I be able to focus at all knowing he was within a few miles? And even if I could, when would I work?

"Lola?" Austin says, and I blink over to him, registering that I've been staring at the screen of my phone, and this is probably not the first time he's said my name.

"Sorry. Was just . . ." I turn off the phone completely and smile over at him. "There. Sorry. Where are we starting?"

His smile is wan. "Page sixty."

Chapter TWELVE

OLIVER IS STANDING outside my building on Friday afternoon when the black car pulls up to the curb. The driver opens my door and then unloads my small bag from the trunk, refusing a tip.

"Already covered," he says with a smile.

I wilt. This time I was prepared. I shove the twenty in my pocket and look up.

Mute at night, frantic to contribute meaningfully during the day, I spoke to Oliver only twice in the past two days—for a total of maybe ten minutes—and my reaction to seeing him right now is exactly what I expected. He's wearing dark jeans, a deep red T-shirt, his navy blue Converse. His hair is combed but hangs over his forehead. His lenses don't begin to filter the brilliant blue eyes behind them. When he smiles at me, tucking the corner of his bottom lip between his straight, white teeth, it's like taking ten deep gulps of fresh air.

He takes one step toward me and I move quickly into his arms, pressing into him for more when he squeezes tight, pushing all the air out of me. His mouth is on my temple, my cheek, covering my lips in small bursts of kisses, lips opening, tongue sliding inside to claim me. Out on the sidewalk his hands impatiently move over my waist, my hips, my ass, words sliding across my lips as he tells me he missed me, missed me, missed me.

I want to go upstairs, make love, drown in him. But it's nearly seven, and we have dinner at my dad's. With a groan, Oliver pulls away, nodding to his car at the curb. He links his fingers with mine and walks me to the passenger side.

"Ready?"

I nod. "No."

Laughing, he opens the door for me. "Let's go."

AS IMPOSSIBLE AS it seems, I've never really had an awkward moment with my dad. Even after he came home from the war and we sat across from each other at the breakfast table, both of us unable to think of anything but his nightmare-tortured bellowing in the middle of the night, haunted by the images scorched on his closed lids. Even when Mom left and he lost his mind in a bottle and pills and I would drag him to bed, give him water, listen to his sobs. Even when he came to my room while I was doing homework, and quietly admitted that he needed some help. We've had hard times—brutal even— but it's never been *weird*.

This truth dissolves the moment we pull up at the curb and Dad is waiting on the porch, wearing an enormous grin.

It didn't occur to me until just now that I'm twenty-three and have never brought a boyfriend home.

The second we walk in the door, I know Dad is going to make this as horrible as I expected: his smile reaches both ears, and when he slaps Oliver on the back, the sound cracks through the room.

Oliver smiles easily at him, eyes glinting with humor. "Hey, Greg."

"Son!" Dad crows.

My stomach turns tight and sour. "Dad, don't," I warn.

He laughs. "Don't what, Lorelei?"

"Don't make it weird for the rest of all time."

He's already shaking his head. "Make it weird? Why would I do that? Just saying hi to you and your new *fella*. Your boyfriend. Your—"

I growl at him, cutting him off.

Reaching for something behind the couch, he pulls out a Barry White CD and an ice bucket with a bottle of champagne. "To the happy new couple!"

Oliver laughs, a single short burst of delight—always so easy, never makes it awkward for anyone—and takes the bottle from Greg. "Allow me the pleasure."

"I don't think I had any say in the matter," Dad jokes.

I squeeze my eyes closed. It's both the best and worst thing that the two of them are such good friends.

The panel shows the girl, throwing a frying pan into the air and standing quietly beneath it.

I pat both their shoulders as I walk past them. "If anyone needs me for this self-congratulatory wankfest I'll be in the backyard."

Dad calls after me—"Don't you want a glass of this New Relationship Champagne, Lola?"—but I'm already through the kitchen, pushing out into the crisp open air.

It's gorgeous out. Passion fruit vines crawl heavily up the fence separating our yard from the Blunts', weighing down the ancient wood so that it bows toward our lawn. During the summer days there are so many bees inside the web of leaves that I used to imagine they could work in concert to lift the leaves, the fence, the yard, our house from the earth and take us somewhere else, like pulling a sticker from paper. When the fruit grows ripe, it falls from the vine, making a tiny popping sound against the hard earth below. I close my eyes, remembering the feel of the vibration of the bees above as I would crawl into the vines and feel along the ground for ripe fruit to take inside.

I feel like I haven't breathed in days, but now that I'm away from L.A. I can. I'm aware of the tightness high in my throat and how it eases, a fist unclenching. Tension still knots my stomach. I have so much to do.

The script isn't even finalized; Austin and Langdon compromised by letting me edit the version we came up with, on the condition that I don't revert any of the agreed-upon changes back to the original version. Erik has given me two weeks to finish *Junebug*, which is good because soon after that, I leave on another book tour, and return a week later to the first day of principal filming on set. I've never had to juggle this much before, and every time I have to switch my headspace from movie *Razor Fish* to book *Razor Fish* to

Junebug, it feels like learning how to write all over again. I am a reservoir, slowly draining water.

From the house, I hear Oliver's low voice and then Dad's burst of laughter followed by the pop of a cork. Despite the twisting worry in me, I bite my lip as I smile at the sound of their indistinct words, spoken in happy, easy tones. They're a bit over-the-top when together, but I knew this about Dad already and still brought Oliver to dinner. They're so genuinely fond of each other, and that knowledge is both a relief and terrifying.

The voices inside disappear and then the screen door creaks behind me, slow footsteps make their way down the back stairs, and I feel a long, warm body settle beside me on the lawn.

I lean into his side, closing my eyes and wanting to roll on him, luxuriate in the feel of him.

"Where's Dad?" I ask.

Oliver slides an arm along my back, cupping his fingers into my waist. His mouth finds my neck and he speaks into it: "Putting the finishing touches on our Coming Out dinner."

I laugh, closing my eyes and taking a deep breath.

"You don't like how he's taking all of this?"

"I do. . . ." I hedge. "It's just like having a new haircut. You want everyone to like it but you don't really need everyone to notice it quite so *intensely*."

He bends, kissing the corner of my mouth. "You hate this sort of attention, don't you? You want this, us—*Loliver*," he says with a smirk, "to be a fact. Settled. Old news."

I smile up at him, a million beating wings let loose in my

heart. "Or maybe I want him to smile and be quietly *knowing*, but let me be the one who's giddy over *Loliver*."

"That's rather selfish," he says, teasing. "And for the record, I've never known your dad to be quietly knowing about anything."

I bite my lip, looking up at him. His mouth is skewed by a tiny smile and I can tell he's teasing, but he's also not. "I know."

He turns to me, rubbing the pad of his index finger along my bottom lip. "Greg's happy for you." Pausing, he studies me while I manage several short, shallow breaths under the gentle scrutiny. When he says more, his voice is quiet. "I get the sense you haven't brought many boyfriends home."

"Or *any*," I say and his gaze becomes heavy, dropping to my mouth. "You're the first."

"You've had other long-term boyfriends, though?"

Reaching up, I touch my fingertip to his chin. "I wouldn't call you and me *long-term* yet."

He laughs. "I guess that depends on your definition; we've certainly been building up to this for a long time. I mean someone you've been with long enough to want to bring home."

"Are you asking me how many people I've been with?"

A smile curves his lips. "Not directly."

I laugh, telling him, "You're my fifth." He makes a little grumpy face I've never seen before, and I ask, "Do you want me to ask *you*?"

"You *can*," he challenges, meeting my eyes and maybe

knowing I won't actually ask. I wait, and finally he laughs through a wince, "Though I don't actually know. There were lots of random nights in uni. I'm going to guess around thirty."

I nod, looking back over to the fence and holding my breath until the sting evaporates from my lungs.

"You don't like that answer," he says.

"Did you like *mine*?"

Laughing, he agrees: "Not really. In my ideal world I took your virginity the other night."

I roll my eyes. "Guys are so ridiculous about that."

"Well, clearly not just guys," he argues. "You also don't like that I've been with other women."

"I don't like the idea that you've *loved* other women."

He can't help the cocky flicker of a smile that flashes on his lips. Oliver leans close, mouth sliding up my neck to my ear. "Well, I don't think I've ever loved anyone quite like this. In this sort of giddy, obliterating game-changing way. Where I can see myself with her for the rest of my life."

This feels so new, so bare, so *exposed*. I wonder if Oliver realizes how scary it is for me to bring him here, to admit—even if I can't say the three tiny words myself—that I care that he loves me. As soon as we open our hearts up to love, we show the universe the easiest way to break them in half.

Thirty women. It's not that it's a surprise or particularly jarring, not after the initial sting, anyway. It's that it's new after months of never discussing these things. I can't decide if I love or hate how everything I learn about him makes me feel like I don't really know him at all. I know what art would make his eyes go wide, which movies he hates and which he loves. I know what to order him if he's late to meet us at the Regal Beagle, I know that he's an only child and that he doesn't like ketchup. But I don't know his emotional heart at all: who he's ever imagined he *might* love, how he's been hurt, and what kind of boyfriend he's been to some of those women. What might send him away.

His hand comes up to my back, rubbing in small, slow circles.

"I missed you," he whispers.

God, my heart. "Me, too."

"Why did you not call me more?"

I shrug, leaning into his shoulder. "I didn't know what to say. The meetings were hard. I missed a really important deadline. I went to a weird place."

"What deadline?" he asks, pulling back to look at me.

"Junebug," I say, and feel the now-familiar roll of nausea over it. "It was due two weeks ago."

"It *was?*" he says, eyes wide. "I didn't—"

I nod. "I know. I had the date right in my calendar, but in my head I thought it was next week. Even if it was next week, it would be late."

"How can I help?"

It's weird—but wonderful—to hear him ask this. Weird because it comes out so easily, so readily, and for the first time I really do see what Harlow meant about me being clueless: this sort of question has been second nature to Oliver for as long as I've known him.

"I don't know. I'm going to dive into it all tomorrow morning." I squeeze my eyes closed, wanting to put that aside, just for another couple of hours. "Anyway, I'm sorry I didn't call. I didn't like being away. But then I didn't like not liking being away."

He laughs quietly. "That makes perfect sense."

"I took sleeping pills a couple of the nights."

I feel him turn to look at me. "Yeah? Do you need that usually?"

"No. But work was really stressful and I sort of turned into mute Lola."

"Still a version of the Lola I love," he says, kissing my hair. "I know her well."

Away from him I felt crazy. Next to him, it's easy to just spill it all and it doesn't seem so strange. How *did* I manage to be away for three days?

He slides his hand into the back of my hair. "You'll stay over tonight?"

I should say no but it's not like I'm going to get a lot of work done tonight anyway. Tonight, I need this. I need the Oliver Reboot. Tomorrow, the crackdown begins in earnest.

I nod and turn my face to him just as he leans close, putting his lips on mine. Slightly open. Just barely wet. The tip of his tongue touches the tip of mine and it's a match struck against pavement.

I'm over him, pressing down, needing relief in that aching part of me. Aching *parts:* between my legs. Inside my ribs. I want to believe I can breathe without him but I'm not sure, and I don't know what's more terrifying: thinking I could never be alone again or trying it.

I hear a quiet cry escape my throat. "I missed you."

He kisses me again, whispering, "So did I. Come here, Lola Love."

He draws his tongue across the seam of my mouth, encouraging me to open again. I feel his quiet groan, the urgency behind his touch when he cups my face and tilts his head, getting a better angle. Steam is rushing through my blood, too, urging my hips to fall into the instinctive easy rhythm. Desire flashes hot along my skin when my body remembers sex with him. I want every touch to turn into something deeper and wild. He growls and bites my lip when I grind my hips over him, needing to see if he's hard already, as immediately desperate as I am.

But he shifts me back—reasonably—and I know the backyard of my dad's house isn't the right place for this. I can't take him in small doses yet. I'm not used to kissing him enough to have just a taste.

Pulling away, I lean my forehead against his, catching my breath. It seems like instead of having five senses I now have twenty; *everything* inside me buzzes with sensory overload.

"Sorry," I whisper.

"I still don't really believe you're on my lap like this." He runs his hands up my sides. "Do you know how many times I touched myself to the fantasy of you sitting on my lap, fucking me while I suck your perfect tits?"

I burst out laughing, slapping a hand over my mouth as I glance back at the screen door.

He kisses my chin, his calm smile slowly straightening into a sweetly curved line. He suddenly seems thirty years older than me. He handles this infatuation so well. "We'll finish this later."

When I nod again, he guides me off his lap and we lie down, shoulder to shoulder, staring up at the sky. It feels like an enormous ocean above us, swimming with stars. Oliver's hand finds mine, his long fingers curling around and between.

"Tell me more about L.A.," he says.

I groan, taking a few breaths to collect my thoughts. "I started *Razor* so long ago, I don't think I remember the stumbling at first. But going up to L.A. was like ice water dumped over my head. I felt naïve and useless in these meetings—about my own story—and then when I would go home at night to work on *Junebug*, it was like I couldn't even get started."

He hums sympathetically beside me, lifting our joined hands to his mouth to kiss the back of mine.

"I missed you and was obsessing about us, and couldn't stop worrying about how I was coming off in these meetings." I look over at him. "There were three of them: Gregory— don't call him Greg, by God—Austin, and Langdon."

"Gregory Saint Jude?" he asks, "He did *Metadata* last year, right?" He's obviously more familiar with these names than I am—I had to do some quick IMDb'ing on my phone in the hall the other day—and I have a pang of embarrassment all over again.

"Right. And he's fine. He didn't really engage me much, but Langdon is a total douche. Initially Austin said Langdon really connected to the story, but let me be clear. He *doesn't*. Or, maybe he does, but as a forty-something dude who wants to bang Quinn."

Oliver groans. "So did you finish the edits?" he asks, and I can feel his head turned, the weight of his eyes on me.

"No, we got through it but they're letting me have two weeks with it to 'put my polish on it,' whatever that means," I say. "There are so many things I'm not allowed to change, and the things I am aren't really details I care about. I don't care about Quinn's clothes."

He sighs, turning his face back up to the sky. "I'm sorry it was frustrating, pet. That sucks."

I nod. "It's okay. We'll figure it out. I'm just glad to be back with you tonight."

"Same." He kisses my hand again, and after we have spent several minutes looking up at the stars in silence, the screen door squeaks open and I feel Dad up there, looking down at us. I know what he sees: his daughter lying on the grass, holding hands with a man for the first time in front of him. I can't imagine what he feels, if it's bittersweet or only sweet, or as terrifying for him as it is for me.

"Dinner," he calls quietly.

Inside, he's set the table with placemats and napkins tucked into brass rings. A candle is lit in the middle and when I look up at him to scowl, his eyes are more anxious than teasing. I can tell he knows he's gone a little overboard and I give him a reluctant smile instead.

Oliver sits beside me on the opposite side of the table

from Dad and we serve ourselves in silence. Without me here they'd be laughing and eating unself-consciously. Without Oliver here, Dad and I would be laughing and eating unself-consciously. In this case, two is not better than one.

Dad clears his throat awkwardly and looks up at us. "I am really happy for you two," he says.

I open my mouth to beg for us to change the subject, *for the love of God,* but Oliver senses something I don't, and covers my knee with his hand beneath the table, squeezing.

"Thanks. It's pretty great so far." He smiles at Dad before taking a bite of salad.

"Friends first," Dad says, nodding.

"Friends first," Oliver repeats.

Dad sips his water and then gazes at me, and I see what Oliver must have: Dad usually hides behind teasing humor, but now he's showing rare emotion. "Lola's mom and I met at a bar." He tilts his head, smiling. "Dove straight in. Turns out, we were better at being enemies, but when we were friends, it was awfully nice. I want you to have someone who's better at being a friend."

Raising my eyebrows, I give him a *we're-going-to-talk-about-this-here-and-now?* face and he laughs a little. We don't talk about Mom anymore when it's just the two of us, let alone in front of someone else; there just isn't very much unexplored territory. As of this summer, she's been gone one year longer than they were married. I know the basics any child would know: They had a decent marriage—not a great one—but weren't actually together in one place very often because of his deployments. When he was discharged and returned home, things were too hard for her. As an adult, I've deduced that Dad forgave her long ago and thinks she probably hates herself too much for leaving to ever try to talk to me again.

I think she's a coward who shouldn't bother.

Tom Petty sings about free falling in the other room, and the melody has this way of making me feel like time loops in this slowly expanding arc. We just go around and around and around, and part of me will always be twelve while the rest of me ages, navigating the world with one parent who cared enough for two.

Gratitude for my father swells in me until I feel my breath catch in my throat.

I cover Oliver's hand with mine, grateful for the tiny breath he forced me to take, the step back for perspective, and ask Dad, "Where's Ellen tonight?"

I can tell he's happy that I brought her up: his smile cracks across his face and he launches into a very detailed explanation of her work schedule and late dinner plans with friends. Oliver's hand is a distracting warmth beneath mine: tendons and bones, smooth skin, sparse hair. I want to lift it from the table, press it to my face.

OLIVER DRAWS SMALL circles on my thigh as he drives us home. If I didn't know better, I would think he was doing it absently, but I'm finding that he doesn't do anything without intent. He's quiet but deliberate, relaxed but always observing.

"Where do you want to have sex?" he asks, staring straight ahead.

I turn to grin at him. "Right now?"

Laughing, he says, "No, I mean, some crazy place you want to do it *someday*. Right now I'm driving to my house for the sex."

I hum, thinking. "Small World ride at Disneyland."

He glances at me and then back at the road. "A bit of a cliché, maybe? And illegal, I'm guessing."

"Probably. But every time I'm on it I can't help but think about what it would be like to sneak in there and find a dark corner."

"At night, maybe," he agrees quietly. "Away from everyone. We'd take off just enough for me to be able to get inside you."

I swallow, pushing his hand up my thigh as I imagine his pants hanging low on his hips, the definition of muscles framing the soft hair on his toned stomach, how fast and frantic he would move in me.

"Would you want the ride to be going while I was fucking you in there?" he asks casually, clicking on his right-turn indicator.

Goose bumps erupt along my arms at his crude, growled words. "Only if I knew we were hidden from view and it was just about being quiet."

"That bleeding song plays the whole time anyway." He doesn't look my way, but smiles at this. "I'd want to make just enough noise so that *you* could hear me," he says, turning onto his street. As soon as he says it, I remember the sound of his rhythmic grunts, his hoarse, guttural exhales as he fucks me hard.

He pulls to the curb and shuts off the engine, turning to look at me. The engine ticks through the silent car, and I can feel my heart pounding in my chest and all the way up my throat as he slowly leans in, his focus entirely on my lips.

The house is right there, twenty steps to inside, but we're *here,* kissing like we haven't been alone in a year. Oliver kisses me for minutes, for days, until my mouth is sore from the beard I don't want him to shave; he's tongue and teeth and growl while he presses me into the door. I can feel his hunger in the way he stretches across the center console and cups my head in his hand. I can feel it in the noises that escape every time he gets me at a different angle, every time I pull him in deeper, bite him, suck on his lips.

"Take me inside."

"I will take you. Inside," he says, laughing and opening the door behind me so we half-tumble out together and he has to crawl awkwardly out of my side of the car, practically laying me down on the sidewalk. Anyone walking by would think we were drunk.

Is that what this is?

It's chemistry, I know that for sure, something numbing and piercing at once, something that makes me feel like I'm alive for the first time and dead in other ways—murdered memories of what anyone else felt like before this man. Murdered memories of what it felt like to be over a hundred miles away.

I know the weight of his hands and body, how he tastes just like me after only two deep kisses, the way his laughs turn into moans, and how he watches my hands when I touch him.

Oliver pulls me up so I'm standing and throws me over his shoulder, charging down the walkway and bursting into the house. He lowers me so that I slide down his front, all along him, and feel his chest and stomach and his cock pressing at me from beneath his jeans. His fingers tickle my waist, he gives me a tiny smile and my shirt is up and off, followed by my bra.

The breeze picks up and the open door squeaks on its hinges, Oliver's R2-D2 knocker rattling against the wood. The cool air rolls along my skin, over goose bumps that pebble my arms and stomach. I kick the door closed, blocking out the intrusion of this one additional string left loose and untended. Quiet seals up around us, and then all I can hear is the soft sound of Oliver kissing up my neck.

His hands curve over my breasts, my waist, my hips. My pants are unbuttoned and sweetly coaxed down my legs.

I never want to run out of clothes because every time he peels something away, he kisses me lower, hums against the skin, and bites just the smallest bit. It's like having lust uncorked and poured in bubbly streams across my skin.

"You're soft in all the best places." His voice turns to smoke against my skin as he kneels, pulling my underwear down my legs one tiny inch at a time. "Even sweeter than you are soft."

His mouth finds my breast, nibbling and blowing across

the tips while his hands are busy helping me step out of my underwear. The entryway light is on and he looks up at me, whispering, "You like having your tits sucked?"

I nod, bracing my hands on his shoulders, right there, mere feet from his front door. I push into his mouth and wonder how I'm standing naked and he's fully clothed, and I feel like I can't move because I don't ever want him to stop what he's doing . . . but I want _more_. I grow heavy, desire filling the space beneath my skin until I can't help but beg out loud. He smiles as he kisses me and moves to the other, neglected breast, licking in long draws of his tongue until he gives me what I _really_ want: the closing of his lips around me, the delicious relief of suction.

I stare down at him, at his mess of brown hair brushing against my skin and kiss-swollen lips playing with my breast.

"Is this really happening?

Oliver nods, drawing his tongue across my nipple—like he's licking an ice-cream cone—and then sucks it so deep into his mouth I wonder if he might consume me. My breasts spill from his hands and he licks and bites whatever he can't hold. It's a frenzy; my body has been waiting days for this and has no patience now.

"Fuck." My fingers curl into his hair and he pulls back, looking up at my face as his fingers stroke the inside of my thigh. I make fists in his shirt, pull it over his head, and relish the slide of my palms over his wide shoulders as he kisses my navel, my hip.

I don't want to do this here.

I take a step backward, and then one more, and he's up, following me down the hall with his hands on my hips and his mouth on mine and he's telling me I'm so fucking sweet, he wants me so much.

The world tilts and his bed is soft beneath my back.

The panel shows him looking down at her. She's wide open: the first day with these new eyes. He would take a bite out of her if he could.

Oliver takes his glasses off and sets them on the table near the bed. He braces his hand at my hip, gazing down, letting his gaze move over every part of me. In my peripheral vision, I can see my chest rising and falling but I can't tear my attention from his face.

I remember the time he made me laugh so hard I spit-sprayed Diet Coke all over his Hellraiser T-shirt.

I remember the time he ran up to the loft to show me the *Detective Comics* 31 someone sold him.

I remember when he said "I do," even though he didn't.

I remember leaning on the kitchen counter, sipping coffee, watching him sleep on the couch.

"What's going on in that mind of yours?"

I'm trying not to panic, obsess, fall too fast, too deep.

"I'm feeling things," I whisper.

He bends, speaking against my stomach as he kisses it. "What kind of things?"

"Panicky things."

I can feel his smile. "Let them go."

I close my eyes, threading my hand into his hair. How can such happiness push a sharp spike through my lungs?

"It's good," he promises, kissing down to my hip. "I've wanted this for months. And I know you feel the same. I love you. I feel you thinking it every time *I* say it, in the way your hands find some part of me to hold on to."

His fingers move between my legs, slide down over my clit, barely dipping into me. It's a luxury, doing this, feeling this, being here. It's a luxury to have all night, to have nothing but this thing between us to tend to. He strokes me, soft at first, so slowly, and then he speeds up as my breath catches and my legs open wider, him kissing his way to my mouth, asking quietly if I like it, if his fingers feel good. I nod, arching from the bed, working my body closer, wishing his pants were off so I could feel the thick weight of him in my hand and pushing inside me.

I don't know what he's doing with his fingers but it's fast and slippery and I'm so close, almost there, everything is turning transparent and—

His hand leaves me for a split second and then I feel the stinging bite of his fingers *spanking* me there.

The panel shows the earth, split in two.

He swallows my shocked gasp with a deep kiss, covering my mouth and groaning when heat melts into a fevered need for more and he feels me arch under him, shuddering.

"Oh, God."

He exhales something between a sigh and a "Yeah?" against my lips and strokes me gently again for several soft, slow kisses before he spanks me again three times, fast and sharp.

The next time his fingers circle gently across my clit, I'm crying out, filled with something warm and silver and it bursts out of me, sliding over my skin and filling my blood with smoke. He strokes me satisfyingly hard, eyes wide as he watches me come. When I close my eyes and melt into the mattress below me, he ducks, kissing my neck, hand trailing over to my thigh to spread me even wider.

"You liked that," he says, lips finding my jaw. "I spanked your pussy and you liked it."

I moan, wanting his mouth on mine, the odd reassurance of it.

"You're filthy," he praises, licking my lower lip. "You're *glorious.*"

I sit up, pulling him between my legs and going to work on his belt, his button fly, shoving his pants down his hips with impatient hands. My mouth is watering and his hands brace on my shoulders, ready. His cock juts in front of me, thick to the point of excessive, and I feel the way his torso clenches when I pull his foreskin back, bend and lick around the crown, sucking.

I've only given a few blow jobs in my life and each time it was such a conscious effort filled with so much thought—

is it good,

oh, God, my jaw is sore,

will I have to swallow?

None of that is happening now: all I can think is how

much more I want to take, how the skin is stretched so tight around him, how I can practically feel how it must be for him when I lick him wetly, suck at where he leaks, pull the entire head of his cock into my mouth and as far down as I can take it. My hands find his balls, feeling, *knowing.* This body is *mine* to know, mine to touch, and he helps me move, helps me find a rhythm and his hips shift with me, his voice encourages me with the broken sounds and tiny grunts and I love how hard he gets, harder, harder as I suck and he's close, *oh fuck,* he's so close already and I ache for it. I want him to come in me, on me, over me, and he's there, thrusts wild, hands making fists in my hair, voice growing louder in warning, accent thick and garbled but I don't want to stop, I want him like this: hips flexed as he's coming in my throat, growling as I suck all the way through it. He presses his lips to my hair, groaning as the final spasms of his orgasm shake through him, and the feel of it is like a million tiny lightning bolts dancing across my scalp.

He stares down at me, catching his breath as I kiss up and down his cock.

I have never loved doing that before, but holy fuck, now I'm obsessed. I collapse back on the mattress, biting my lip through an enormous grin.

Oliver shifts forward, bending over me with two fists planted beside my hips. "You just sucked my soul out of me."

I roll to the side, giggling and feeling pretty fucking proud of the head I just gave because just looking at him I can tell it was stellar. He kicks off his pants, rolls me back so he's above me, and kisses my breasts, down my stomach . . .

and in a haze I realize where he's headed, what he's going to do.

"No," I whisper, quickly adding, "It's okay." I slide my fingers under his jaw, guide his face back up to mine.

He's gone quiet. Oliver kisses me once but no more. He stares down at me, studying my face.

Something is wrapped around my heart, growing tighter the longer I look at him—the floppy brown hair and blue eyes still full of satisfaction, but now also mixed with something else, something *knowing*—and I have to close my eyes to ease the ache of it because it was all so perfect until I stopped him.

"Look at me." He waits and then urges, *"Lola."*

I open my eyes, focus on his mouth. The soft bottom lip, dark stubble shadowing his jaw.

"You don't want me to kiss you here." His fingers drift between my legs.

"I do. . . ."

"Then why did you stop me?"

"It's . . ."

"It's what?"

"It's a *thing.*"

" 'A thing'?" He pulls back a little, a jerky movement that tells me he's not sure he likes what I'm saying. "I don't know what you mean."

God, I am so bad at articulating this. "The whole back-story."

"The what?"

Sighing, I throw an arm over my face and am grateful he doesn't immediately pull it away. "You know. About learning from your roommates and her friends. How you became this oral sex legend. It just means you've done it with a lot of women."

When I move my arm, I see that he looks briefly amused. "You just gave me the blow job of my life."

"I'm as surprised as you are," I tell him honestly. "You inspired me. I haven't been *taught*."

He sighs. "I was wondering if it bothered you, or if you were teasing me."

I reach up, trace his mouth with my fingertip. "It doesn't bother me or make me jealous. It makes me feel like I have to *get it*, if that makes sense. I don't like oral sex. But with you, if I don't come it's because of me." He starts to say something but I press my fingers to his mouth so I can finish my thought first: "I'm not very good at relaxing when guys are doing that to me. I never have been; my mind wanders and I start thinking of other things and . . . I realize that makes me weird, but there you go."

He closes his eyes. "Do you feel the same with me as you have with these other men?"

The hilarity of this. "No. Of course not."

"Have you considered that you didn't enjoy it because they weren't very good at it?"

"Yes, but I've also considered that I didn't enjoy it because they didn't, either."

He stares at me, head tilted, expression unreadable, until he whispers, "Or maybe you need to be comfortable with the person in order to be comfortable with the act?"

"No . . . I mean," I whisper, feeling truly naked for the first time tonight, "what if you don't like it with me?"

His gaze softens. "How could that possibly happen?"

When I don't answer he whispers, "Lola. I've already felt you. I've tasted you."

"I know."

"On my fingers. On yours. Do you remember how I responded?"

I close my eyes and nod. I remember the sounds he made, the way he seemed to want more.

He lifts my hand, kisses my palm. "I'd be so careful with you."

"I trust—"

"I'd start slow," he interrupts, kissing me again. "Just kissing you there first."

I bite back a smile but it dissolves when his tongue slips across my palm, tracing in a soft, wide circle. His lips come together and he sucks gently on each of my fingers.

"I wouldn't suck too hard. Wouldn't lick too fast."

Swirling around my palm, his tongue forms smaller and smaller circles until my hand feels wet and warm under his kiss and I ache so intensely for him that I feel a little breathless. "And it's me. It's Oliver. Not some *other* guy."

I smile, pulling my hand back enough to run my finger across his stubbly chin.

"Circles, I think," he muses. "Just around and around and around so steady and gentle until you're soaking wet with legs spread wide and you're clawing at the sheets, begging to come on my lips. I'd want you begging for my mouth every time we're alone."

He looks up at me.

"And I'd give it to you, Lola," he says quietly, earnestly. "I would suck the pleasure straight out of you; I wouldn't toy with you. If I could get you there I would, whenever you want it." He slides his tongue along my index finger to the tip. "I want to be so good you never let me go."

I exhale a hoarse, begging noise. I already can't imagine my life without him.

"But after I'd do that, I'd need to feel you."

"You would?"

He brings my hand between us, circling his cock. "See, even the idea has me hard again and I just came. Already I'm so bloody hard for you."

After studying his face for three deep breaths, I nod, and he shifts back again, this time kneeling between my legs at the side of the bed.

He watches where he touches me and I fight the urge to cover myself, closing my eyes instead. I feel his hair brush my thighs as he bends forward, feel his breath when he exhales against me, and then feel the soft kiss, one more, and then his lips part and cover me, and his tongue is there, touching, stroking so carefully.

"Holy fuck," he growls, and his hands shake as he spreads

my legs, urges me to rest my feet on the mattress. "Holy *fuck,* Lola."

I no longer want careful.

I no longer want gentle.

I want him to pull out every fucking trick he ever learned because if he can make me feel this much with one single kiss, I'm dying to know what I feel when he pulls out all the stops.

Once I'm situated he quickly returns to me, trying to be slow. He's watching me—eyes glued to my face—and my chest twists when I see how anxious he is to please me. Pushing my head into the mattress, I arch into him, whispering, "It's good, it's good, it's *good,*" and it unleashes something in him. I don't know what he's doing; I don't know if I even have the muscles he's using but it's fast and perfect and better than any sex toy I've ever found.

Holy shit . . .

I want to watch but there is too much to *feel.* The wet slide of his tongue, the vibrations of his sounds, how my thighs shake, my stomach grows tight, pleasure crawls up my torso.

But *oh* . . . how his head looks between my legs. How his arms wrap tightly around my thighs, a band of muscle keeping me open for him. The long line of his back, his ass in the mirror across the room, the definition of his thighs as he rocks absently, loving me with his full body but touching me only with his—

Sensation snags me mid-thought; it's felt consuming, nearly surreal, but then it's more than good, it's *everything.*

It's his sounds and his breath against me, and the pleasure growing on the surface of my skin and plunging deep until I can't process anything but the way pleasure rockets through my body.

I get it.

I get it now.

"I'm coming," I cry through a choking exhale.

And—holy shit—I'm coming so hard.

He grunts encouragement, looking up at me as I say it again, and again, with wonder in my voice and it's still true after so many gasping, preparatory breaths. It seems to build forever, growing and never cresting and I'm saying it so many times I can feel him laugh proudly against me, holding his rhythm and giving me more, and better, and *holy fuck* I have time to wonder if this is a completely new thing my body does, whether every other orgasm was some sad bastard cousin of *this* orgasm, the one that seems to never end.

"Okay," I finally manage to say aloud as he climbs up my body, kissing across my skin. He's breathless, and hard. "I admit: you won this round."

He laughs into a kiss to my lips. "I'd say we both won that round."

WE'RE STILL AWAKE when the sun rises on the other side of the sky, slowly brightening Oliver's room. The sheets are mostly on the floor, pillows crushed between the mattress and headboard, but I am centered perfectly on the huge bed, carefully covered by Oliver's endless, smooth naked skin.

"Are you going to be able to work?" I ask, trying to see past him to the clock.

He mumbles into my shoulder: "More importantly, are you going to be able to *walk*?"

It's a good question.

Laughing, I ease out from under him and climb out of bed, walking unsteadily to the bathroom in the hall. I feel tender everywhere; I want to stay in bed all day and sleep curled around him. I don't want to think about everything else. Anything else. I want it to evaporate.

For the first time in my life, I resent work.

He joins me in the shower. After no sleep and hours of sweaty, wild sex, I assume we're both too tired for much more than kissing. But being drenched in steam and pounding water, the sudsy slide of his skin across mine and the suggestion his fingers make when they move over my ass and between, stroking, leaves me begging him for something I never thought I'd want before.

I look up at him. "I want to feel you there."

Water drips down his forehead. Thick lashes, clumped and wet, frame his brilliant blue eyes as he studies me. "You're sure?"

"I'm sure." I push onto my toes to reach his jaw, to scratch it with my teeth.

Oliver turns me to the wall, kissing my neck as his fingers run down my back, over my backside, until he carefully eases one slick finger in and out, then two, slowly stretching me. While he whispers and groans, telling me he'll be careful, telling me how much he loves me, he finally enters me there, inch by inch.

"You okay?"

I nod. I am, and I'm not. I'm overwhelmed and split in two and wishing I could have more of him, and everywhere all at once.

He's bare in me like this, fingers snaking around and touching me from the front but I can feel his fascinated thrill and once he starts moving he doesn't last very long. The satisfaction I feel in his sounds, the way he shakes and moves so arrhythmically, the bouncing echo of his surprised shout when he comes loosens all of the fear I've held on to that I have him but could lose him.

That everything good in my life could vanish and he would leave me.

That we could build a life together and have it yanked out from beneath us.

That I would unravel, that nothing else would matter but this.

Right now, he is everything.

Oliver washes me, eyes heavy and sleepy, lips thanking me with every kiss. "How's my girl?"

I answer the question he's asking, and not the bigger one—the *enormous* one—because existentially, at this moment, I am not okay. I'm drowning in what I feel for him.

But I'm not physically hurt. "I'm good."

His mouth finds mine, desperate and wet.

I realize it's a cliché but everything changes for me after that shower. I don't think I'll ever love anyone the way I love this man.

While we get dressed in silence, he keeps looking at me with this strange mixture of awe and relief.

"You're okay though?" he asks again from across the room, pulling clothes out of his dresser.

I nod, mute.

I *love* him. I love him more than anything and it's obliterating everything else around me.

He comes over and studies me, cupping my face in his hands. "Lola Love, you're *not* okay. Is it me? Is it what we just did?" His face grows tight.

Shaking my head, I stretch, sliding my arms around his neck and pressing my lips to the warm, clean skin there. He bends, holding me tight. I want him to hold me all day long. I want to keep the rest of the world at bay, and just be here, with Oliver, until it's time to climb back into bed again.

———————

I AM DAZED, drunk. I climb the steps to my apartment slowly, exhausted but in the best way.

The loft is quiet—London is most likely surfing—and I grab a cup of coffee before heading to my room to start working on the ever-expanding list of deadlines. I haven't checked my email in over a day, and still don't want to now. I like the bubble.

And I've barely slept. I glance at my computer, the stylus

sitting so innocently on the digital sketchpad, and I know how much I need to get done today but I also know how much a tiny nap will help.

I fall into bed, closing my eyes and trying to focus on *Junebug* unfolding, her story and who she is. But instead my mind keeps bending back to all the points of tenderness on my body, just to remember. I hear Oliver's voice in my ear, remember every one of his kisses.

I wake only when it's dark out and my stomach gnaws with hunger.

I lift my phone, blinking in surprise at the number of notifications on the screen.

I've missed four calls from numbers I don't recognize, and two more from one that I do: my publicist, Samantha. I swipe the screen and immediately call her.

"Sam," I say quickly. "What's up? I fell asleep."

I can hear the smile in her voice, the way she's struggling to stay calm to keep *me* calm. She's never shown me a second of stress until now. "Oh, okay, I'll reschedule the calls. Don't even worry."

"What calls?" I ask, sitting up and pressing my palm to my forehead. "Shit, Sam, what calls?"

"The *Sun*," she says, adding, "the *Post*, and the *Wall Street Journal* were all today. I knew it was tricky on a Saturday, I'm sorry, it just seemed easiest to move them all so they could run Monday. We'll reschedule for next week."

Something breaks inside me, some panic unbottled and poured everywhere.

I apologize, hanging up, and staring at the wall in horror. I spaced three interviews today. I missed a deadline by two weeks. I don't even know who I am anymore, and the one thing I've always known is how to write, how to draw, how to work.

My phone buzzes in my hands, and I glance down at the picture of Oliver on my screen. My first instinct is to answer, to stroll to the bed and lie down and listen to the honey of his voice pour over me.

Instead, my breath gets cut off in my throat and I hate myself so much in the moment I flip my phone over, putting it facedown on the desk before knocking it to the floor. I have to work. I have to dive in, and work, and finish all this. I'm dropping things—not just dropping, *abandoning* them. I just need to draw one line, and then another, and another, and another until I am done.

The only thing I can do right now is build words and images into a story unfolding and then I will be okay.

I will be okay.

Chapter THIRTEEN

Oliver

*T*HE HOURS SEEM to bleed together after Lola leaves, details around me fuzzy enough to ignore. The sun beams directly into my kitchen, into the windscreen as I drive, in through the front windows of the store, washing out everything around me, bleaching away color. I don't want to do anything but be with Lola, in my bed.

As weekends go, it's a slow one; WonderCon up in Anaheim has most of the local geeks out of town. And I'm grateful for it: I've never not felt like working at the store, but this stage of my relationship with her—the hunger, the obsession, the clawing ache all along my skin to be touched, to fuck, to come—brings a delicious distraction. I indulge these daydreams; I hide in my office to avoid conversation with Joe so that I can stare off at the wall and remember waking up, kissing Lola's warm breasts, following her into the shower.

I tried to be slow, gentle. I was shaking, rigid, and nearly out of my mind when I realized what she was letting me do. She came on my fingers, promised me it was good, but I don't think she realizes how it changed everything for me.

It feels settled, as if we've been together years, rather than days. This is it, she is my life; my heart has already decided anyway.

I call her to make sure she is feeling better now that she's home, focusing on work, but it goes to voicemail. I know work is overwhelming her, L.A. went terribly. It's no surprise that she's shutting herself in to focus.

But this understanding grows into unease when Lola doesn't answer for the rest of the day and she doesn't text. Saturday night passes in silence, with me alone at the house watching B movies on mute, trying to read through a stack of new releases from Wednesday.

Trying, and failing, to feel casual about it all, that we don't need to be together every night, that it's all right if she doesn't reciprocate the infatuation I feel.

When I wake on Sunday, I don't even have a text message from her, and I skip breakfast, feeling mildly nauseous. I get about four hours into busywork at the store—packing up overstock, cleaning out the back counter, putting in orders—before I break, heading into the office and calling Finn.

"Let me ask you something," I say. "You're going to have to be my barometer on appropriate reactions today."

"Wow," he says, "let me just . . . *there*. Had to note the time stamp on this conversation."

Normally this would make me laugh but right now I'm wound too tight. "I last saw Lola on Saturday morning, after not having seen her all week. She'd stayed over Friday. But now it's Sunday evening and I haven't spoken to her since then. I've called and texted, and heard nothing." I spin a pen on my desk. "That's weird, right?"

"That's definitely weird." I hear him cup a hand over the phone, mumble something in the background. "Yeah, I mean Harlow says Lola's home and working this weekend." Harlow says something else I can't make out, and Finn repeats it: "For what it's worth, she hasn't answered Harlow's calls, either."

I thank him and hang up, crossed somewhere between confused and hurt. I understand her wanting to disappear into the work cave this weekend—hell, even last week in L.A.—but it's mildly fucked-up that she can't even be bothered to answer my texts, and if it's going to be something that she does a lot on deadline, we're going to need to compromise somewhere, or at least give me a heads-up on the deal. When she left Saturday morning, she was eager to get to work, but *still,* she was nearly boneless in her satisfaction, dizzy smile in place.

I take the stairs to the loft instead of the elevator, trying to work out some of my stress. Outside the stairwell, I walk down the long narrow hall to her door, stopping in front of it to breathe.

Nothing's happened. Nothing's wrong.

The thing is, that's bullshit. I know Lola. I know every one of her expressions. I have a fucking advanced degree in this woman's reactions, her fears, her silent panics. Even if it has nothing to do with me, *something* is going on with her.

London answers a few moments after my knock, with a Red Vine between her teeth and game controller in hand.

"Titanfall," she explains, nodding me in and turning back to the couch. "Wanna play? Lola's holed up in there."

I shake my head, managing a wobbly smile. "Just wanted to stop in and say hi to her. She's down in her room?"

London nods absently. "Hasn't emerged for anything but coffee and cereal in about a day." I turn down the hall, hoping my footsteps on the wood floor warn her to my arrival. I knock quietly at Lola's door before turning the knob and stepping in.

I've seen her room a few times, and it looks much like I remember; it's an organized mess. The floor is pristine, her bed neatly made. But every other surface is covered, nearly chaotic. There's a huge desk in one corner; her computer and digital sketch tablet are crowded at one end. Every other exposed surface is coated with pencils and pots of paint, stacks of drawings and various sketchpads. Scraps of paper and napkins and even gum wrappers litter the top, random ideas she's jotted down while away. The wall just above and adjoining it is practically wallpapered with sketches and panels, some of them nothing more than charcoal while others are filled in with colors so vivid I'm not sure how they're real. A strand of lights runs the length of the ceiling and I imagine how soothing and calm it must be at night. How much of an escape this must be for her. A dresser beneath the window and both the tables opposite the bed are filled with framed photographs.

I take another moment to look around, and realize I'm basically standing inside Lola's brain. Spots of organization surrounded by an unending, overwhelming stream of ideas.

"It's a little cluttered," she mumbles in lieu of a greeting, and I close the door behind me.

"It's fine," I tell her. *I love you,* is what I want to say, but how many times should I say it without her saying it back? Instead, I bend to meet her mouth in a kiss I've been dying to have since the last one she gave me.

But Lola pulls away after only the barest touch, taking off her glasses and looking up at me. She's disheveled, obviously stressed, and now I notice the four empty coffee cups on the floor near her chair, the wild, buzzy look in her eyes.

"I hadn't heard from you," I tell her. "I was getting a little worried."

She nods, rubbing her eyes. "I've been trying to catch up. I sort of get into this panic mode . . . well," she says, looking back at me, "I assume that's what this is since I've never been so late on a project before."

I rub her arm. "It'll be fine, pet. Just give yourself space to think on it."

She winces, turning back to her desk. "Well it isn't fine right now. I don't really have the luxury of letting ideas bubble to the surface. This is me, on a crash deadline."

"If you want a break from your room, you can work on it at my place," I tell her, looking around us and wondering if a more organized workspace wouldn't help with her current state. "I can make you dinner and you can just sit at the table and work."

Lola shakes her head. "I can't move all my stuff over there. I just need to power through."

I nod, and turn to sit on her bed. "Tell me how I can help."

Lola falls silent, staring at the half-completed drawing on her computer screen. She seems to barely blink.

"Lola, tell me how I can help?"

She closes her eyes and takes a quick inhale, as if she's just remembered that I'm here. "It used to be easier," she says quietly. "I could shut things off and never worry that I was missing out on anything."

I lean forward, elbows on my knees. "Missing out? What do you mean?"

She gestures limply to the computer screen. "I've been working on this for hours, and it's not even half-done. I have twenty-six more pages to do, and so far everything I have is crap." She turns, looks over her shoulder at me. "Before, I could just lose myself in it. Now I know you're at the store, or at home, or in bed. It's all I can think about."

I smile and stand, walking closer to kiss the back of her neck. She stiffens and then relaxes, and I kiss a soft trail to her ear. "I'm here now. We'll learn to balance it. It's hard for me to want to work, too."

"I just wish I could push pause," she says, as if she didn't hear me.

"Pause?"

Nodding, she pushes back from the desk, standing and forcing me to take a step back as well. "Just . . . to get this done. I know that we're going to be together. I want it, I do. I just . . ."

In a sickening rush, I feel cold all over. "Lola, it won't always feel this consuming between us."

She shakes her head. "I think . . . to me, it will. But I can't
mess this up, Oliver. This is huge to me. I know enough to
know it doesn't happen every day, and I will be *sick* if I mess
it up."

"I know, love, I—" I stop and my heart trips in embarrassment when I catch up: She's not talking about us. She's
pointing to her screen again.

"I've been working on this dream since I was fifteen,"
she whispers. "I almost don't know what life looks like without it, and yesterday morning I wanted it to just go away so
I could sleep because we'd been up all night. I hate working
with Austin and Langdon. I hate that I'm late on this deadline. But this is what I wanted to do. I *have* it now and I'm
letting it fall apart."

Unease fills my chest. "We don't have to spend every night
together. I would never expect you to slow down the pace. I'm
only here because it was weird for me, after how we left things
Saturday morning, to not hear from you. I was worried."

Lola sits down at the edge of her bed. "I know. I'm
sorry."

I find a place beside her, take her hand. "There's nothing
to apologize for. I'm just sorry about how stressed you are."

She nods, and nods. It's slow, continuous, almost de-
feated. And then she turns her eyes up to me. The rims of her
lids are red, her eyes bloodshot. "*Should* we hit pause?"

My brain stumbles over the words. "What?"

She swallows, trying again: "Should we take a break?"

I, too, have to swallow past a lump in my throat before I can speak, and it takes several tries. "I'm not sure what that means."

"It means I want to be with you, but I don't think I can right now."

I don't understand. "'Right now'?"

She nods.

My brow furrows as I try to catch up. "So . . . you need to work for a week in quiet? I can do that."

Lola stares down at her hands. "I don't know. I think maybe we should just try to go back to where we were a couple of weeks ago, and then see how things are this summer."

I gape at her, feeling like my heart is dissolving in acid. "Lola, it's *March*."

"I know." She's doing the nodding thing again, swallowing back tears. "I know. I just really suck at both. I really suck at it, and I don't want to mess this up, or that"—she points at her computer—"and I think I have to do the book without anything else. Without you so . . . available."

"I understand that L.A. was terrible, and you are stressed about work, but this isn't the way to deal with that. You have feelings for me," I tell her, my voice thick with frustration and urgency. I *know* she does. "*Strong* feelings. I'm not imagining how it is between us, Lola."

"I do have feelings," she admits, looking at me with watery eyes. "I'm crazy about you. But this is more important right now. I wasn't ready. I shouldn't have gone to your house, played poker. I should have waited until I was done with all of this."

I stand, rubbing my face. "Lola, this is a terrible idea. People don't just *take breaks* in relationships to catch up on work."

Her eyes close. "There isn't a good option here." She turns her face up to me. "Would you wait? Just . . ." She shakes her head. "Wait for me to figure it out?"

"For *three months*?" I ask.

"Or less. I don't . . ." She looks away. "I don't even know what I need."

I turn and stare at her chaotic desk, feeling anger and hurt and confusion reach a churning boil in my chest.

"Please don't be mad," she whispers. "I wasn't going to say anything but then you're here, and I'm not disappearing, I'm *not*, I'm just saying that I have to get this done."

I nod, wishing I could turn to stone.

"Oliver, say something."

My voice is low and hurt when I tell her, "You could have simply said to me that you need to really buckle down this week. *That* would have made sense."

She scrubs her face and then looks up at me, pleadingly. "I need to have nothing else going on. I need this to be the only thing on my mind."

I walk to the door and turn to face her, leaning against it. "You're sure this is what you want? To push *pause*? To take a break?"

A panel shows him, breaking the glass, his chest on fucking fire.

She nods. "I just need to know that I don't have anything else I can be doing. That being with you isn't an *option* when I have to work."

"So we're not together anymore," I say flatly, "because it's too good, and too distracting to you."

"We *will* be," she urges.

"Do you even hear yourself? That's not how it works, Lola."

"Let's just—"

"Hit pause," I interrupt. "Got it." My laugh is a short, dry breath. "Lola, I love you. You know that. And you want me to just . . . wait for you, for months, to be ready again?"

She looks at me helplessly. "I have to put this first."

"As my best friend, I sort of feel like you shouldn't want that for me," I tell her. "I think it's bullshit, actually. I think you're stressed about work, but I think you're also just full of shit right now."

She looks sorry, but she also looks *relieved,* as if I've agreed to this flaming piece of shit she's put between us.

"So this is done," I say.

"Maybe we can talk in a couple of days?" she asks when I open the door. Her voice breaks on the last word and I just can't be fucking bothered. I've never felt I'm worthy. I've never been the most important person to anyone. But before Lola, I've never needed to be. Fuck. This.

"Maybe I just need to—"

I shut the door before I hear the end of her sentence.

Chapter FOURTEEN

Lola

"*A*M I GOING to have to drag you out to breakfast to talk about this?"

I startle awake where I've passed out on my desk and find Harlow standing in my bedroom doorway, arms crossed over her chest. There's fire in her eyes, ammunition in the way she stands. When Harlow is in a mood, she spits bullets.

The bright Monday morning light blasts into my room. "I was going to call," I tell her lamely, squinting. Looking around, I try to get my bearings. Other than the horrible ten minutes with Oliver yesterday, I've been working straight since Saturday night. My monitor has gone dark in power-saving mode. I slept with my stylus against my face, and have a stack of Post-it notes stuck to my arm. "So you heard?"

"Yeah," she says sharply. "I heard." She walks over to my closet and begins pulling out clothes. "Let's go."

I lean into my hand. "Harlow, I've got so much to do."

"You can spare an hour. And the body needs to eat. Come on, Lola."

Under normal circumstances I would climb into bed and ignore her. Today I know better. I finished a few panels and the rest of the story yesterday, but my head feels like it's filled with glue, and my heart is just doing the perfunctory contractions. Sending Oliver away like I did turned me from a distracted lovesick airhead into a deadened, productive robot. I honestly don't know which I prefer. Guilt over the hurt on his face plagues me, and I close my eyes for a few deep breaths, struggling with the instinct to call him and apologize.

Harlow drives in silence, jaw tight. We all know what Harlow's silence means. I just don't know if it means she's pissed at me or . . . someone else?

Do you even hear yourself?

I feel like you shouldn't want that for me.

I think you're full of shit right now.

When I remember Oliver saying this, my heart fractures, dropping tiny pieces in the cavern of my stomach.

Yeah, she's most likely pissed at me.

"Are you okay?" she asks as we drive down Washington.

The answer is an easy *no. Junebug* isn't there yet, and I don't know how I'm going to find the heart of the story when I'm frantic like this. Besides, I feel like I made the right call *and* fucked everything up with Oliver at the same time. When are scientists going to invent a wisdom pill? Or implant a chip in our heads to let us know when we've made the right decision in a critical romance-career-balance situation?

Plus, I can't be on this particular street without getting a sick lurch in my stomach, remembering the sight of Mia, broken and bloody, under the truck for over an hour.

I manage a scratchy, "I'm fine."

Harlow throws me a quick glance as she drives and I can feel her questions building like air pressure rising in the car. She pulls into the parking lot at Great Harvest and turns off the engine, looking at me. "Would you rather talk about it out here, or in there, with all of us?"

My laugh is a short, flat cough. "Let's just head in. I really only have an hour."

With a decisive nod, Harlow opens the door and leads us across the parking lot.

Mia and London are already in the booth when we walk in, and they smile perkily at me. I can see from Mia's face that she's trying not to react to my appearance. I got a quick glimpse in the bathroom mirror before leaving, and it's fair to say I look like I just walked on set as a zombie extra in a horror film.

"So, hey," I say, sitting down and putting a napkin in my lap. "What's new?"

London snorts at this, genuinely amused, but her expression straightens obediently when Harlow flashes her a *We Aren't Letting Her Joke Right Now* frown.

"Oliver came over for dinner last night," Mia says, skipping all preamble and leaning in to keep her voice down. "He said you broke up with him."

"I didn't *break up* with him." I smile at the waitress when she pours me some coffee but I'm sure to her it looks like I'm just baring my teeth. I blink, licking my lips and then biting them to keep from asking Mia what he said, how he looked.

How he's doing.

"I'm telling you," Mia says, "that's what he thinks. That you broke up for good."

I take a sip of my coffee, feeling the odd sensation of marble hardening in my chest. He didn't understand what I was saying. To be fair, I'm not even sure *I* understood what I was saying; I hadn't exactly planned for it to come out that way. But it felt right to ask him for some time to make sure my head was turned in the right direction. He's understood everything I've needed up until now, why not this? When Mom left, Dad crumbled and we barely scraped by. Friends would bring groceries and act like it was no big deal, but to us, it was huge. I never want to have to worry about how I can make ends meet. I never want to worry that I can't take care of myself. I never want to feel like I'm simply abandoning something important to me, and if Oliver can't wait for me to feel more grounded then we have bigger problems.

"So you *didn't* break up with him?" Harlow asks. I can tell she's trying to figure out where to fall on this. Is she protecting me and what I need right now, or is she preparing to smack some sense into me?

"I just told him I needed to hit pause."

"*Seriously?*" Harlow asks, and I know she would actually be reaching over and pinching me if she didn't think it would draw attention.

"Look, I don't know why this is such a big deal." I take a deep breath, staring at the pattern on the surface of the wood table. "I'm really late on a deadline because I just spaced it—no other reason. I have all these script edits I need to have done in a week and a half and spent most of the time in L.A. ineffectively arguing with the douche bag screenwriter. I'm also supposed to be coming up with ideas for the book that comes out right after *Junebug,* and they wanted the first few pages of that turned in a week after *Junebug* is due . . . which was two weeks ago. Meaning: the first few pages of the *new*-new book are already a week late. I leave for book tour in two weeks. I just . . ." I pick at a tiny hangnail on my thumb. "Everything was already busy with travel and writing, and as soon as I let the idea of being with Oliver into my head, I really fell hard, and fast. I was really disorganized up in L.A., I flubbed deadlines. I saw how quickly I could lose it all." Finally, I look up at them. "I want to try to get a few things handled and then let myself enjoy . . . it."

I can feel the way they exchange worried glances but they all seem to be unsure how to respond.

"You do have a lot on your plate," London says. "I mean, I get that."

"But it's Oliver," Mia says. "It's not like . . ." She lets the words trail off, and

I know

I know

I *know.*

It's Oliver. It's not like he's pushy. It's not like he gets in the way.

It's that I was getting in my own way.

"Even when you're busy, you still check in with us every

couple of days. Why does it have to be different with him?" Mia asks.

I can't answer that. I can't, because I don't feel like I should have to explain to someone who is madly in love with her new husband that it's different when you're in love, versus checking in with girlfriends. I want to be near Oliver every second. I'm not sure I can do the dance of balance yet; I want every particle of him touching every particle of me.

"How did you deal with it when Ansel was working crazy hours back in Paris?"

She shrugs, poking at the ice in her water with a straw. "I left him alone at night to work."

But—Jesus—how how how? I want to ask. The mystery of it makes me want to rip at my skin. If Oliver was in the room with me, or even down the street at the store but still *mine,* I would never get anything done. I would let *Razor* and *Junebug* and everyone else I love just fall into the cracks. I've proven that.

"I just feel like you're being so hard on yourself," London says quietly. "I feel like maybe you're punishing yourself?"

And yes, she's right. I am. I know we can't stop what we're feeling. I *know* that. I can see my three friends studying me like I'm a fascinating bug in a glass dish, because—at least for Harlow and Mia—they would never worry about how to balance these things. Mia's done it before, and Harlow will just bend the world to fit the palm of her hand.

I'm not so naïve that I think this is a common thing to ask.

I want to scream out loud that I realize I've asked something huge of Oliver, something unreasonable even, but
I'm not sure if I can apologize, either, and I know that—
eventually—he'll understand. I don't want to lose my career. I
don't like the way I so easily let things slide the minute Oliver
became my lover. I feel like I have to scrabble up this little hill
and then I'll be more grounded, more established. I'll be better for him, and better for *me*.

I pull a pen from my bag and a crumpled receipt and start
drawing.

*The panel shows the girl, hunched over her desk. Scraps of
paper litter the floor. The desk is covered in pencil shavings.*

"So you think he's moving on?" I say, head ducked, heart
slowly shredding.

Everyone pauses, and with my pen poised on paper I feel
the protective egg trembling under my ribs, threatening to
roll off the table and shatter. I want Oliver to be my friend. I
need him to be my friend, because I love him. Am I an enormous idiot? I don't feel like what I was asking was extreme,
just some quiet, just a little bit of rewind. I don't know how
I'll deal with it if I hear that things are really done.

"I mean last night he was pretty mad," Mia says with a little
shrug. "He didn't really want to talk about it much. We spent
most of the night walking around the house while Ansel and
Oliver planned what renovations they could do themselves."

Normally, he would have called me afterward to share all
of this. No, *normally*, I would have gone with him. I've been
Oliver's default plus-one for months, and he's been mine.

Now, not only do I not get sex with him, I don't even get phone calls.

"Do people not do that?" I say, cupping my coffee mug. "Do people not ask to put relationships on hold even if things are good?"

"Lola, that is called *breaking up*," Harlow says slowly.

"So it's a stupid question?" I bite out, defensive at her tone.

She tilts her eyes quickly to the ceiling, exasperated with me. "I mean, why not just tell him you're going to have an insane week and you'll call him when you have a free night?"

"Because it's like my creativity shuts off when it's an option," I say. "I don't want to work when I'm with him. I've never *not* wanted to work. And, sorry, but this has to come first. I built this *first*. I can't just drop it because I started seeing someone and juggling the workload got *hard*."

And this, right here, is when I know Harlow wants to smack me again, but she doesn't. She just nods, and reaches across the table for my hand.

———

I TEXT OLIVER a simple, Hey are you okay? after breakfast, but he doesn't reply. By the next morning I just turn off my phone so I'll stop looking. So I'll stop wishing.

I stay holed up in the work cave until Wednesday evening before giving in and walking down to Downtown Graffick. The path between my apartment and the storefront has seen thousands of my footprints, and standing just outside it feels oddly nostalgic. Less than a week ago I was climbing out of a town car and hurling myself into Oliver's arms. Now I feel queasy imagining walking in and acting like everything is normal.

Over the last two days, I've started to feel like maybe I am the biggest idiot on the planet.

Maybe it doesn't help to remove temptation. Maybe it's worse to slowly realize *a pause* means he's not mine anymore.

The bell rings over the door and a few customers look up, smiling vaguely before returning to their browsing. Behind the counter, Not-Joe waves with a smile that slowly flattens.

"Hey," he says, putting down the book he's reading.

"Hey."

And now what do I do? Pretend that I was just here to buy a couple of books?

"Is Oliver around?" I ask, immediately giving up on pretense.

Not-Joe's expression grows uncomfortable, and he looks toward the door. "You just missed him."

Shit.

"Okay, thanks." I turn, walking down the manga aisle, trying to decide whether I call him, or just go to his house and tell him I'm an idiot and I don't really want to break up, or even take a pause, and can we please just pretend that never happened?

I'm flipping absently through a book when I feel someone come up behind me.

"Okay," Not-Joe says quietly. "What the fuck is going on?"

I put the book back on the shelf, turning to face him. "What do you mean?"

He tilts his head, frowning. "Come on."

"With me and Oliver?" I ask. I mean . . . it's not really Not-Joe's business, but when has that ever stopped him from wanting to know? He nods. "I don't know," I tell him. "We had a little fight, and I wanted to try to talk to him."

"The reason I ask," he says, brows furrowed, "the reason I am *confused*," he clarifies, "is that he just left with Hard Rock Allison."

I stare blankly at him.

"They went to get dinner."

———————

I ZOMBIE-WALK HOME, eat some Rice Krispies out of the box, and put on my headphones, working like a maniac until three in the morning. It's like I've hit a switch where I can't even think about what Not-Joe told me, or I will completely unravel.

When I wake around seven, I stumble to my computer and stare at the screen, squeezing my eyes closed and then open, trying to clear them.

Nothing. Nothing comes to me. I need food. I need fresh air.

London is making coffee in the kitchen, and pours me a cup when I walk in, wordlessly handing it to me.

"Thanks," I mumble.

My phone buzzes in my hand and I look down to a message from London in the group text box with me, Harlow, and Mia: She's up.

I glance up at London. "It's . . . seven thirteen. Have you guys been waiting for me to get out of bed?"

"Sort of," London says, smiling gently.

Harlow replies, Lola: we're meeting at the Regal Beagle tonight.

I stare at my phone and then put it down on the coffee table, picking up my mug instead. I can't deal with Harlow quite yet.

London walks around the counter and into the living room. "Are you going to come?"

I sit down. "I don't think so."

"That means yes?"

"It means probably not." I wince apologetically. "I have to work."

She sits down next to me on the couch, and for the first time since I've known her, London's eyes aren't smiling. "You've been out of that room for a grand total of an hour and a half since Saturday night. It's *Thursday*."

I nod, taking a sip of coffee. "I'm getting caught up. It's good."

"Look," she begins, "you don't get to pretend you're just fine and also not talk to anyone. If you're sad, tell me to stay home with you so you can talk my ear off. If you won't talk to us, just keep pretending that being a crazy, work-obsessed hermit is normal, but get your ass to the bar for one fucking evening."

"Is Oliver going?"

"Yes," she says. "Your *friend* Oliver is going."

I lean back against the couch and close my eyes. My heart is already racing two hundred beats per second.

TONIGHT IT TAKES me forever to get ready. Am I furious or guilty? I have no idea.

I do know that I have a closet full of new clothes I've bought for book signings and appearances and who knows what but I hate them all. One dress is too short, another is too long, another is too tight. Do I show off cleavage or keep it all hidden? Do I look grubby to show him I don't give a crap who else he goes out with, or do I put in the effort to look amazing?

Finally I pull on a black V-neck sweater (some cleavage) and my favorite jeans with boots. My hair is longer than it's ever been—halfway down my back—and instead of a ponytail or easy bun, I leave it long and straight. I keep it tucked behind my ears, but at least it gives me something to hide behind if I need it. I've never worn much makeup—never had need for foundation or powder—and tonight all I put on is lip gloss.

I hate kissing with it on; it's the chastity belt for innocent drunk kisses with men I desperately love but who maybe went on a maybe-date with someone else last night.

The gang is situated in the regular booth toward the back

when I arrive. I see Ansel, Mia, Finn, Not-Joe, London, and Oliver, whose back is to me and whose broad shoulders I assume are blocking Harlow from my view, because I can hear her laugh from clear across the bar.

My stomach crawls up my throat. I wave hello to Fred and stand at the side of the booth, waiting for Oliver to notice and let me in. It's a bit like watching dominoes fall as everyone sees me in succession, smiling instinctively before the smiles crumple as they *remember*, and they turn to look at Oliver.

I swear my heart is going to beat its way out of my chest.

For the love of God. His breath catches when he sees me standing there, and he just stares right at my face for what feels like a million, pounding heartbeats.

And, just like that, I feel like I've been slapped across the face. I don't just miss him, I *need* him. I don't want this distance. I don't want it to be over. I don't want to lose him. For fuck's sake, how do I take care of everything?

Finally, he moves over to let me in, smiling a little down at the bench. "Come on in."

He's wearing a dark green *Preacher* T-shirt and the same dark jeans he wore the other night when I undressed him, went down on him for the first time.

I can still feel his skin on my lips, his trembling hands in my hair.

I can still remember the way he sounded in the shower. What we *did*.

The panel shows the girl standing in front of the mirror, the words I AM NOT READY FOR THIS. I AM NOT

EVEN A LITTLE READY FOR THIS corkscrewing around her body.

"Hey," I manage.

"Hey." He swallows, eyes on my mouth for only a breath before he puts his expression in order, poker-facing it as only Oliver can. This is the first time I've seen him since Sunday afternoon, and it feels like my heart was put back together inside out.

God, if this is hard for me, I can't imagine how this must be for him. Terrible. And look at him, calm and poised, always composed. I don't think I've ever admired anyone the way I admire him.

"Hey, Lola," Ansel says, smiling so wide his dimples dip all the way to Mars.

I smile back.

"So, how's the book coming?" Harlow asks a little too loudly.

I give her the Really? We're going to talk about this right here? face, and simply say, "It's fine."

"Everything's fine," she mumbles, and I see Finn elbow her gently.

This is the most awkward moment in the history of time, and I sit there, stabbing at my decision with a fiery poker while tentative conversation starts up around me. I fall back on instinct, pulling a pen out of my purse and bending to doodle on a cocktail napkin. I can sense how Oliver's head is turned toward me, how his eyes watch me draw. That's his instinct, and it melts me how he's always done this: leaned in, wanted to be a part of it.

It's like there was a film between us, some restraint that was peeled away the second we kissed. Before, I had feelings, he had feelings, but we were able to carry on breathing, speaking, joking, drinking. Now, I'm just . . . a bare wire, sitting too close to a spark. I want to punch him for going out with Allison, I want to stroke him and beg him to forgive me. Between us the air warps and simmers. I can almost feel his hand, so warm, on his thigh next to mine. Out of the corner of my eye I can see his finger twitch.

Me, too, I tell him silently.

I thought I was making a hard—but good—decision and now I look back on that Lola from last Sunday and feel like she was the most naïve person alive. I have no idea what to do—whether I should just turn to him and tell him I'm sorry right now . . . and sitting here with him I can't even remember anymore why I thought I could do this. Coming out of the fog of the stress for a night, being this close to him—the scent of his fabric softener, the proximity of his strong hands, legs, his smooth neck, his quiet laugh . . . he's right—it just doesn't work this way. I *love* him. I want to be with him. Asking to hit pause *was* bullshit.

Oh my God I am an idiot.

With a jerky motion, Oliver straightens, inhales, and apparently decides to move the table out of the silence of doom. "Joe. What are you watching?"

Not-Joe pushes his hair out of his face. "Videos of cows being milked."

I look up. Everyone else is staring at Not-Joe, brows drawn, speechless, too.

Harlow holds up a hand, halting all discussion. "I don't even want to know." She waves to Fred at the bar. "Three important updates from me: One, I'm sick of airplanes. Two, I'm sick of *boats*."

I thank the Universe for Harlow's ability to knock down the wall of silence.

"And three," she says, "a trashy she-beast tried to bang my husband today."

We all gasp and look at Finn just as he mumbles, "False," into his mug of beer.

Harlow turns to him, eyes wide in disbelief. "Did she or did she not put her hand on your arm and *giggle like a whore*?"

"She did," he concedes, laughing.

"And did she or did she not squeeze your juicy bicep?"

He nods. "She did."

Leaning in close, she growls, "And did she or did she not then *hand you her room key*?"

"Which I immediately handed back," he reminds her. "That's not trying to bang. That's *failing* to bang."

Finn holds up his hand and high-fives Ansel's offered palm.

"So gross." Harlow takes a sip of wine. "She had the fakest huge boobs I've ever seen," she tells the rest of us, clearly already over it. "Which reminds me." She holds up a finger near his face and he playfully bites the tip. "This shirtless thing they're having you do while filming? Not a fan."

"You're losing it," Mia says.

"You're not a fan of me shirtless?" Finn asks with a knowing grin.

Harlow puts down her wine and some of it sloshes over the lip. "Not when people ogle you!"

"Totally losing it," Oliver agrees, nodding to Mia.

"You knew this would be hard," Ansel reminds Harlow.

"Of course I am losing it!" Harlow yells. "Everyone wants to bang my husband!"

A group of people nearby look over at us, but Harlow just scowls at them until they turn back toward the bar.

"I don't," I tell her.

Finn raises his bottle to me.

Mia swallows a sip of her drink and nods. "Me either."

"I like you, Finn," Oliver says, "but I also don't want to bang you."

Slowly, slowly, the tension dissolves from our table and I nearly want to sing. The sound of Oliver's voice, so deep, so perfectly curled, makes my skin hum.

"I'd bang him." Not-Joe speaks this at his phone screen still playing cow videos.

We all stare for a beat before deciding in unison to move on.

"Harlow," Ansel begins, "you've married one of the three most loyal men alive. I bang Mia. Finn bangs Harlow. Oliver bangs Lola. It is the way of things."

My heart comes to a screeching halt, and beside me, Oliver goes completely still.

"Hey!" London says, feigning insult at this exclusion.

So far, we're the only ones to notice the slip. Oliver begins slowly tearing his napkin apart.

"You can bang Not-Joe," Ansel reasons.

London looks over at Not-Joe and then laughs, shaking her head. "Is it weird to say I'm not sure I could handle him in bed?"

Silence has spread like a slow, awkward game of Telephone around the table, first with Finn looking across at us, then Mia, then Harlow. Ansel's own words finally seem to sink in and he wipes a hand across his mouth. "*Merde*. I didn't mean—"

"It's okay," Oliver interrupts, voice tight. "This is my cue to hit the head."

He apologizes under his breath, wincing because I have to get up to let him out of the booth, and then slips past me. His hand accidentally brushes mine and he jerks away, apologizing again.

I feel like I've been burned.

We watch him leave and once he's out of sight, I bend, resting my forehead in my hands. "Why am I here? I'm ruining his night."

"I'm so stupid," Ansel groans. "I'm sorry, Lola."

"No," I tell him. "I shouldn't have come. He would be having a good time if I wasn't here."

"That's not true," Finn says firmly. "You guys need to figure this out. This is dumb as fuck."

"Says you," Harlow snaps.

"The way he looks at you," Mia whispers. "It's like he's trying to light a fire under your skin."

"He always did that," Harlow says, and then takes a drink of her wine. "Looked at you like if he stared hard enough you could hear each other's thoughts and wouldn't have to say them out loud. Like he wanted to be in your mind, wanted you in *his.*"

"He didn't," I tell her.

"He *did.*"

"Didn't what?" Not-Joe asks, looking up from his phone.

"I was telling Lola that Oliver always looked at her like he wanted to absorb her."

"Not absorb her," Not-Joe corrects gently. "He just wanted to get a piece of her no one else got. And he does, clearly." He lifts his chin to me as proof. I catch it right when I turn back to look at him from where I've been staring, waiting for Oliver to return..

We all fall into contemplative silence, sort of stunned by this.

"I mean he's not Rogue or anything," Not-Joe mumbles, lifting a hand to touch Mia's arm, and dramatically pretending to absorb her strength a la Rogue before absently turning back to his phone. "So tell him that he has a piece of you. Fix whatever broke."

Ansel and Finn are staring at where they fidget with their coasters, but Mia, Harlow, and London are all staring right at me.

"*What?*" I ask.

"I agree with Not-Joe, which is . . . new," Mia says, offering an apologetic wince. "You need to do *something*. You're both miserable. Go talk to him. Tell him how you feel, even if it's messy."

"It's probably not the best time," I say. I cannot imagine anything I'd like less than talking to Oliver at a bar about what I did, and about his dinner with Allison. Just the thought of having that conversation in public turns my stomach into a sour knot.

I look over to the bathrooms, wanting to see Oliver emerge and also dreading the way it will make me feel when he does. But something else snags my attention . . . a face I haven't seen in forever.

It takes my brain several seconds before I realize who I'm seeing. I look over at Harlow: she's smiling at something Finn said. I look more carefully at Mia: she's reading something London has shown her on her phone. But Ansel's attention is moving between my face and the person I've spotted over by the bar. Ansel knows something is up . . . he just doesn't know why my eyes have gone wide. Because he wouldn't necessarily recognize Luke Sutter.

From across the room, Luke sees me first, and his face falls. I can almost feel the way he doesn't want to look at the rest of the table, doesn't want to *know*. But he can't help it:

his eyes slide around the curved booth, tripping unseeing over Not-Joe, London, Harlow, Finn . . . eventually landing on Mia. For a second, the duration of a heartbeat, I see the life being punched out of him.

"Who is that?" Oliver asks as he returns to the table, jealousy making his voice sharp.

I startle at the sound and the vibrating warmth of him so close to me before standing to let him in. At his question, Mia looks up, following his attention to where Luke stands, and she goes pale. I can't remember the last time she saw Luke, but I know it's still hard for her, still weird how much things have changed. He's barely the same person anymore.

"Um . . . it's Luke," I say, and Ansel's body goes rigid at my words. "Mia's ex."

I realize I don't know how much he knows about Luke, whether he knows they were inseparable from the age of eleven, how we all just assumed Luke and Mia were forever. Has Mia told Ansel about the worst fight they had? The one where Luke whispered, in tears, that it felt like Mia died under the truck that had pinned her to the street?

Over the past few years, Luke has been nothing like the guy I used to know, but I'll always adore him even if on the surface he seems like such a cocky douche bag. The accident ruined two dreams—hers of dancing, his of having Mia forever. He got over it the only way he seemed to know how: by sleeping with anyone, and everyone.

I look back to Ansel and Mia, and I've never seen this before—anger on Ansel's face—but I recognize it immediately. His gently ruddy cheeks turn red, his eyes harden. Mia slides her hand down his arm, whispering something in his ear, cupping his face and urging him to look at her. At first he resists, glaring over at Luke, and then he nods, closing his eyes and finally turning to her waiting mouth, claiming it deeply.

"Je t'aime," he whispers. "I love you so wildly I sometimes forget you aren't so fragile."

Finally, I look away, giving them privacy. When I locate Luke across the room, I can see his jaw twitch as he watches them kiss, but then his easy smile is back and he turns away, flirting with a couple of women near the bar.

"So *this* is Luke," Oliver begins, so close to my ear. Goose bumps break out along my arms. "The one who would drive you to concerts."

I nod, nearly wanting to cry over the effort he's making to talk to me. "He and Mia were together in high school, and for a bit . . . after."

"After . . . you mean, after the accident?" he asks quietly.

"Yeah. It wasn't a good time for Mia, and Luke was pretty heartbroken that she never really came back the same as before."

"You liked him, then?"

I look over at Oliver, meeting his eyes full on—and so close—for the first time all night. Whatever I've been keeping enclosed in bubble wrap threatens to break free at the way he's managed to compose himself. I want to launch myself at him and alternately shake and kiss him. I can see the pain as a tiny ripple in his blue eyes, but otherwise he's just Oliver: the same steady, placid Oliver I've known for months now. And I *hate* it, because I knew the other Oliver, too—the one who gave me pleasure so intense I saw stars—and I want some reassurance that I'll see him again. That he'll *let* me see that side again.

"I do like him," I say. "He said some shitty things, and has screwed up more times than I can count, but he's a good guy."

I earn a wry eyebrow twitch for this, but before Oliver can respond aloud, Ansel pipes up: "Well, it has been lovely, friends, but I feel the need to take my wife home and impregnate her with seventeen of my robust male offspring."

Oliver grabs his wallet from the table and his body tilts closer to me as he slips it in his back pocket.

"You're leaving, too?" I ask. "I just got here."

He nods. "I know. Sorry. This has been a great experiment, but I'd rather go home and clean the bathrooms."

I laugh at this, even though I'm really not ready for him to leave yet. "I think I know what you mean."

When I climb out and he follows me, on impulse I keep him from immediately leaving by wrapping my hand around his arm. He looks down in surprise, but follows me without resisting when I lead him a little ways from the table, into the shadows.

I let go of his arm, moving a step back and taking a couple of deep breaths. I didn't plan to talk to him about this tonight. I'm not good on the fly like this, but I can't let him out of my sight without saying something, without giving something more.

"Okay, so," I say, voice a little wobbly as he remains silent. "Tonight sucked."

"A bit," he agrees blandly, and I don't miss the way his eyes briefly slide down my face to my lips.

I want, I want, I want.

"I'm really sorry," I say. "I know this is hard. . . ."

Oliver shrugs, and then nods once. I groan inwardly. *God,* this is painful. I'm trying to find a way to articulate that I don't know how I'll do it, but I want to try to balance being his lover, having him as a sounding board, and keeping pace with everything I have to do. It feels impossible to get this all out, especially when I'm standing so close to him and can't even seem to find words past my need to touch him.

Finally, I manage, "I came to the store to see you last night."

His face grows a little tight. "You did?"

"Did you go out with Allison?"

He rubs his jaw, seeming unsurprised that I've asked this. "Yeah."

The panel shows a girl-shaped puddle on the floor.

Heat burns in my eyes. "Was it . . ." *Goddamnit.* I look to the side, feeling like I'm unraveling, vibrating. "Was it a date?"

When I look back at him, he's just staring blankly at me.

"Or," I start again, "I mean is that what you're doing now?"

"Is Allison *what* I am doing?" he asks with a sharp bend to his words. "Are you serious, Lola?"

"I didn't know if it was a date, and I realize I have no right to ask—"

"You don't."

"I know," I say quickly, "but it kills me to think of you two fooling around."

He doesn't say a word, but his jaw tightens and everything comes to a standstill in my brain.

At my shocked silence, he growls, "Isn't that what I am supposed to be doing? Trying to pass the time until you're ready to hit *play*?"

He still hasn't answered my question. I realize he's hurt—that I've hurt him, and that is where this is coming from—but I've never seen this sharp, sarcastic side of Oliver before. I hate myself so much right now, and I hate him a little, too, because it feels like he cheated . . . even though I'm the one who asked for this.

My chest grows tighter and tighter until I have to take a deep gasping breath, and with it comes the burn of tears in my throat. I nod, trying to smile, but my face breaks and I turn away before he can see.

I hurry down the hall toward the ladies' room, swallowing a sob, but I hear a couple of his quick footsteps and then Oliver's hand comes around my shoulder. "Fuck. No. Lola, don't go. I'm an arse."

I don't turn to face him as I'm madly wiping my cheeks. It's mortifying. I hate to cry alone, hate it even more when someone witnesses it, and right now it's like someone is aiming a hose down my face; I go from dry to sobbing in a blink.

"You're not an ass. I am," I say, and from my voice it's obvious I'm crying. "I am just so afraid of messing things up with the books, and now I've messed things up with us."

He turns me gently and I look up at him, imagine him in my room, peeling away my clothes and my insanity and just making it *us* again.

"I didn't kiss her," he admits. "We had dinner, but in the end I didn't let anything happen."

I nod, swallowing back a relieved sob.

"But are you expecting me to not *try* to move on?" he asks quietly. "You told me I should just wait idly by while you get your life together without me. That's a horrible thing to ask, Lola."

I rest a palm on his chest, my words spilling out in a mess. "I don't think we're thinking it was the same thing," I stumble. "I don't think I meant what you think I meant? Or what I said? I'm so sorry."

He pulls away from me a little. "I don't believe this whole break was just . . . a misunderstanding. I was pretty clear on what you were saying."

"I want to talk about it," I tell him. I'm trying to organize my thoughts into some sort of order, but the music is loud and I can feel our friends watching us. "Not here, like this. But soon?"

He nods, looking at my mouth. But then he starts to shake his head instead, saying, "I don't know, Lola. I don't know. This is just a fucking mess."

Panic starts to climb into my throat. "I don't want this to be over, and—"

Oliver cuts me off with a gentle "Shh," reaching a hand up to tuck my hair behind my ear. He stares at his hand as if it moved there on instinct before he drops it limply to his side.

My heart is a drum, deep in the jungle of my chest, and it bangs and bangs and bangs for him. I know it won't ever diminish. There isn't any clock we can rewind, no way we can stop time.

"I miss you," I tell him.

He smiles toward the floor, blue eyes soft behind his glasses. "I miss you, too, Lola Love."

The mix of heartbreak and relief spills from me. When he calls me "Lola Love," I wonder if there's at least a chance at friendship after all of this, and whether that would be wonderful, or torture. "I thought you were going to tell me you kissed Hard Rock Allison."

Oliver looks up at me with a wince that is both sweet and sad. "Reckon I wouldn't do that. I don't feel that way for her." He runs a hand over his jaw, blinking away. "I was angry and I wanted to be distracted, but I wouldn't betray my own feelings like that." He laughs without humor. "Your love is branded on my brain; yours is still the only kiss I want."

The weight of my feelings flips something over inside me, and before I've even realized it I say: "Do you want to come over tonight?"

Oliver closes his eyes for a beat, trying to smile, but it barely curves his mouth. "I don't think—"

Oh God. My insides have liquefied in horror. "Shit, never mind. Sorry. Of course you don't."

Oliver takes a step back, looking helplessly around before rubbing his face and turning back to me. "Don't play games with me." He looks at me, eyes searching. "Please. I can see in your eyes you're still sort of a mess. I can see you don't really like what you've done, either. It just . . . days later, it feels too late to come to me in this blur of feelings and panic, and I can't help but feel like it's related to you hearing about Allison."

"*No*, Oliver, it's not—"

He continues over me, shaking his head emphatically. "I'm not sure if you were really afraid this relationship would interfere with your career or were hoping to stall it before you loved me. And either way, I'm not sure what to do about it. Both options suck." He bends, kissing me just beneath my ear, and continuing quietly, lips barely an inch from my skin: "I'm in love with you, Lola, but I'm also terrified you'll ruin me."

Chapter FIFTEEN

Oliver

_I_ HAVE ABSOLUTELY NO idea how to behave around Lola. And clearly, neither does Joe.

I hadn't seen her in the store in over a week, and when she finally walks in the morning after our awkward talk at Fred's, immediately making her way back to the Marvel section with only a wave in my direction, Joe doesn't even call out to her or propose in front of the entire store. I can feel him watching me, gauging my reaction.

"Lola's here," he says finally, lifting his chin to where she's disappeared down the aisle.

My heart has swerved to the edge of my chest. "So she is." She'd asked me to come home with her last night—and fuck it was tempting to imagine putting it all aside and falling into bed, relishing the sex—but not in a hundred years could I have said yes. I could practically feel her guilt, her regret last night, but Lola has no idea what she wants right now; she's an emotional land mine, and not one I'm prepared to walk over willingly.

Joe comes around the counter to stand beside me. "You're not going to go over there?"

"Not that it's your business, Joe, but no. Maybe in a little bit, but it looks like she's here to look at books."

"I don't get you two at all," he says under his breath.

"I'm not going to fret over the opinion of a man who spent much of an evening out watching cows being milked before moving on to videos of men pulling trucks using ropes tied to their dicks." It's easier to joke, because what more can I say? Right now I reckon I *don't* understand, either.

There's a part of me—the adoring part that has long felt like Lola can do no wrong—that wants to take responsibility for all of this, sensing that I should have anticipated her panic over work *versus* us, that I should cut her some slack for what she said, that having dinner with Allison looked bad. But the conversation in her bedroom—where she wanted me to simply hang around while she focused on getting her work done—showed me how young she really is. Naïve, even. I knew it, truly I did, but I never really thought how it might slap me in the face.

Naïve myself, I suppose.

I want Lola to have all the success in the world, but am still bewildered over why she thought I would somehow get in the way of any of it.

And maybe more than a little wounded. I'd been Lola's biggest fanboy and loudest cheerleader—hell, I even wear my *Razor Fish* T-shirt whenever it's clean. I was the most devoted lover, too . . . even though it was only for a week. It stung to be so easily set aside.

Still, with her near, I'm aware that I've never needed or

wanted anyone like this. It's a pull, nearly a physical draw to be close to her. Just knowing she's in the store, a swarm of bees has taken over my chest until it feels like I'm shimmering inside. Her hair is down, lips full and bare. I remember the drowsy tilt of her head, watching me kiss my way down her body, the feel of her thighs over my shoulders, the honey of her cunt on my tongue.

Lola looks up from behind her comic, catching me staring, and waves limply. I wave back, then turn and find Joe right behind me, his eyes skipping from me to Lola before he shakes his head.

"Well this fucking sucks," he says.

"It's fine." I crack open a tube of pennies and dump it into the register drawer.

"Fine?" he asks. "A week ago, she walked in and climbed you like a tree, and today she acts like you're the resident librarian."

"Things are . . . complicated," I sigh. I love her, but I don't want to be with her just now. I want her to do better.

"She's still into you, you know."

Shutting the register, I give him an exasperated *this-isn't-your-business* look. "I know, Joe."

But Joe is undeterred. *"And?"*

"And I'm beginning to wonder if she was right to worry that we'd screw everything up," I tell him. "Maybe we were better at being friends."

I greet a customer who walks up to the counter and Joe steps aside while I ring him up. With his purchase paid for and in a bag, I smile and hand it over to him. Joe is still watching me, expression disapproving.

"Maybe you're forgetting the part where you're in love with her," he says.

I lean against the counter and scrub my hands over my face. "I haven't forgotten."

"Then what the fuck are you doing over here when she's back there?"

I shake my head and stare with tired eyes to where she's flipping through a comic, listening to someone on the phone. "Joe, it isn't your business, and it isn't that simple."

"Are you going to go out with Allison again?" he asks.

My stomach recoils. "It was just dinner."

He nods in understanding. "It's like how you grow up eating Hershey's chocolate, and think, 'This is delicious chocolate.' And then you have Sprüngli and are like, "Dude, Hershey's is shit.' "

I glance at him. "Sprüngli?"

"Swiss chocolate place," he says with a vague wave of his hand. "My folks have a place in the Swiss Alps."

Now I turn and fully stare at him. "Who the fuck *are* you?"

Laughing he says, "I'm definitely not a guy named Joe."

"Don't tell me," I say, holding up a hand. "It'll ruin the mystery."

With a little shrug, he walks back toward the office. The bell over the door rings and I see Finn and Ansel walk in.

"G'day, Finnigan," I say. "I didn't know you were sticking around today."

He throws me an aggressively patient look at this nickname while he takes off his jacket. "I've got the rest of the week off."

Ansel cuts into the small talk. "Are we going to lunch? I'm starving." Finn and I exchange amused looks: Hungry Ansel is the only version of our friend who is ever sharp.

"Yeah, just let me—" I start to say, but Lola picks that moment to wander up from the back of the store.

"Hey," she says to each of them, before finally looking to me. Her cheeks grow pink, smile widens. "Hi."

"Hi," I say, heart beating, throat constricting, muscles tight.

I fucking love you.

Finn turns to Lola. "You wouldn't by chance have spoken to my wife in the past hour, would you?"

"It will never stop being strange hearing you call her that," Lola says, shaking her head. "Mia is someone's *wife.* Harlow is someone's *wife.*"

And Lola was mine, for twelve hours. Then she was something else, something even better, for only a matter of days.

Finn stares at her, mouth pressed in a straight line while he waits for her to answer his question.

"And actually yes," she says, reaching up to pat his head. He slides his eyes to me as if I've somehow put her up to this. "She was driving up to Del Mar to get some signatures from . . . someone . . . and you know how bad the reception is up there."

Finn nods, reaching over the counter to grab a snack-size Snickers from my secret stash under the register.

Ansel sees and practically knocks him over to get one for himself.

"Lola," Finn says, tearing into the packet. "Let me ask you something."

Her eyebrows rise expectantly and the expression is so sweet, I have to look away before I step closer.

"I'm planning to take Harlow up to Sequoia for the weekend. Camping, quiet, you know. Do you happen to know if she's working?"

Lola smirks up at Finn at the same time I feel my own eyes widen. "You're driving?" she asks.

He nods.

Lola glances at me and for a moment, the weirdness between us is gone and we're on the same team. "You're driving *six* hours," she says, "to take Harlow *camping* in the *woods* for an entire weekend."

His brow pulls tight as he turns to look at me. "Those are the bullet points."

"Have you *met* your wife?" Lola asks.

Finn's mouth curves into a cocky smile. "She'll get into it."

"If you say so," she says with a wink. *Fuck.* My chest does a tight twist at the playful side of her coming out. "And yes, I think she has the weekend off."

"Lola, you're still here," Joe says, walking out from the back room with a banana, peeling it suggestively. "Ready to run away with me yet?"

"Not quite," she says, grinning.

"What were you doing all the way back there, anyway?" he asks.

She stares at him, before glancing quickly to me. "Browsing. And then Benny called. I have something big due next week. So . . . I'm changing the trip I had scheduled to L.A. for the week after."

I file this away. I didn't even know Lola had a trip coming up, let alone one she needed to postpone. I hate this distance between us—the pointlessness of it all, the *absurdity*—the way things seem to be moving forward in both of our worlds and we aren't compulsively sharing any of it. I miss her.

Fuck. I need to get over it.

"Well, I'm glad you're here," Joe says, "because I wanted to show you something." He walks to where he was just a moment ago, pointing Lola's attention to a shelf. "Look what came in."

"Oh my God," she says, and moves to get a closer look. From where I stand, I can't see what they're looking at, but Lola adds excitedly, "Can you get it?"

Joe smiles over at me. "Oliver? Can you reach the new consignment item?"

"I got it," Finn volunteers, taking a step toward the ladder, but Joe stops him with a hand to the chest.

"I think Oliver knows what I need."

I give him a warning look, sensing he's up to something. But as soon as I get on the ladder and glance up, I know immediately what they're talking about. Joe has somehow managed to find a set of the action figures based on Lola's book, and placed it up on the shelf for her. I start to tell her that I haven't even been able to get these new yet, but when I turn to hand it to her, I realize that her eyes aren't on the box at all, but on my bare stomach, where my shirt is riding up.

I clear my throat and Lola blinks back up to my face, before turning about six different shades of pink. Joe is already laughing, and wearing the smuggest *I told you so* face I've ever seen.

"You are such an asshole," she says under her breath to Joe, laughing and punching him in the shoulder before taking the box from my hands. I'm half-irritated with him, half-amused at his persistence.

"Where did you get this?" she asks, avoiding my eyes.

I shake my head, having never actually seen one in person before. They're not even available online yet. "I didn't know we had one."

"I bought it today," Joe says proudly. "It's the first one I've seen."

"Someone was selling this?" I ask, and notice that even Finn—a guy who looks like Superman but probably couldn't differentiate Catwoman from Batgirl—has moved in for a closer look. Even Ansel is interested.

Joe shrugs as if it was no big deal, and takes a bite of banana. "Yeah."

"They made this for the *book*?" Ansel asks, peeking over Lola's shoulder to get a better look.

Nodding, Lola says, "It's part of the promo for the paperback release in a few months. *I* don't even have one of these. I've been waiting to hold one for weeks now."

I love that she feels this way, and love even more that I'm here for this moment because work has been shit for her lately, and she needed this little victory. I reach over and take it from her, before dropping it into a fabric shopping bag with the store's logo on it. "It's yours now."

Her mouth drops open. "I can't take this."

Joe shakes his head. "The guy brought in a bunch of stuff. I get the sense he swiped it from a random assortment of promotional goodies sent to his work, and had no idea that it hasn't been released yet. I didn't pay much for it."

"I could *kiss* you guys," she says, looking down into the bag, and then quickly realizes what she's said. Her bottom lip is pulled between her teeth and she stares at the floor.

Despite the mess she's made of things, something primal comes to life in me, and I have to look away.

"I would totally let you do that," Joe says, "but I have a date. Oliver can have my share, though."

It's like an elephant has been dropped in the center of the room, and everyone suddenly finds something to study, intensely.

Joe groans. *"Please,"* he says. "I don't know why you two are fighting this. You're never going to be just friends."

And with that, he reaches for his Greenpeace key chain from behind the register and walks out the door.

Nobody says anything for what has to be the most awkward ten seconds in history.

Finally, Ansel clears his throat. "So . . . lunch. Lola, would you like to join us?" he says, smiling sweetly at her.

Her eyes go wide and she looks at me as if for guidance. I smile, hoping it looks better than it feels because inside I am a giant ball of uncertainty. I want her near me, but I want her to figure her shit out first.

Lola's phone chimes in her hand and she glances down, reading. We all watch as her shoulders slump and she exhales a quiet *"Fuck."*

"What?" I ask, the whiplash instinctive protectiveness roaring to life.

"It's Greg," she says, turning off the screen with a sigh. "Ellen broke up with him." Looking at Ansel, she says, "Thanks for the invite, but I've got a couple of calls to make then I need to go over to my dad's."

"I hope everything is okay," I say, and Finn and Oliver quietly echo the sentiment.

She throws me a tiny, shy smile, holding up the bag. "Thanks again, Oliver. This means so much to me."

The bell over the door rings again as she leaves and the three of us watch her make her way down the footpath.

I'm a tangle inside, hating to see her walk away, wanting to be close to her even when I'm angry, but still feeling the need to build a cage around my heart.

Turning back to my friends, I say, "Remind me to fire Joe the next time I see him," I say, scratching the side of my neck.

The store is empty, the afternoon is dead. I reach for my

keys and turn the sign to read CLOSED, and motion for them to lead the way.

———————

WE WALK THE few blocks to Bub's near Petco Park and are led to a table near the patio.

"How *are* things with Lola?" Finn asks, looking at me over the top of his drink. "You guys seemed . . ."

"Tentative," Ansel finishes for him. "Which, I'll tell you, is really strange to watch."

"It's about the same." I stab at my ice water with the straw. I haven't really felt like talking about it much since the conversation went down, but I've told them both enough to know things with Lola aren't great. "We're still 'on pause.'" I hesitate. "I think she wanted to unpause, though. She asked me to come over, last night at Fred's."

The waitress stops at the table and we each order a burger and rings. When she steps away, they're both looking at me expectantly.

"I mean, of course I said *no*," I tell them.

Silence rings around the table.

"Because obviously she needs to figure her shit out," I say.

"She can't do that with your penis in her mouth?" Ansel asks, and Finn punches his shoulder. "What? That was a serious question."

Finn lifts his chin, asking, "Has the thought occurred to Lola that she might be even busier in four months? They aren't even filming yet. I mean, I go a week at a time without seeing Harlow, and it sucks, but I know it won't always be this way."

"I don't know," I say. "I can't pretend to know what's going on in her brain right now."

"I always felt like you two had a secret language," Ansel says.

"Me, too," I admit. Our server sets the giant basket of onion rings down in the center of the table. "And because I'm a total asshole, I made things worse by going out with Allison Wednesday night."

Ansel's eyes widen. "Hard Rock Allison?" I nod and he lets out a burst of air and reaches for his beer. "Why the hell did you do that?"

Shrugging, I admit, "It was just an impulsive thing. She came by and asked if I wanted to grab dinner. I was pissed at Lola and said yes."

"Did she think it was a date?" Finn asks.

"Yeah. She did."

Finn studies me. "You didn't fuck her."

"No," I say quickly, "I clarified where I stood as soon as we sat down. But I still feel like I cheated because I knew it would make Lola jealous if she knew. I wanted to rip my skin off by the time I got home."

"And if Lola had done the same thing?" Finn asks.

My skin flushes hot again at the idea of Lola with anyone else. "I'd want to rip *his* skin off."

"*Does* Lola know?" Ansel asks, wincing.

"Yeah, she came here looking for me. Fucking Joe the brain surgeon told her."

"You would have told her, though," Ansel says, and then furrows his brows. "Right?"

"Of *course*," I tell him, giving him an exasperated look. "I nearly called her in the middle of it because I felt so guilty. But then I didn't, because I thought, *What if she's working and actually gets pissed off at me for calling her to confess that I'm having a platonic dinner with another woman?*" I run my hand over my mouth. "It's a mess. Clearly I am more concerned about all of this than she is. I don't know how to interact with Lola anymore, and that just feels . . . wrong."

"You're both idiots," Finn says. "Lola is a mess, too, for what it's worth."

"But that's what falling in love does to you, okay?" Ansel says, grinning. "I'm a happy idiot because of Mia."

"I . . ." I start to say, and feel laughter bubble up inside me. Despite everything, being around Ansel is infectiously uplifting. "Lola is hands down one of the smartest people I know and I fear she is, to borrow a phrase from Harlow, extremely relationship-dumb."

"Mia mentioned that Lola tends to always put her comic stuff first," Ansel says, folding his arms in front of him. "That she's been that way even when they were teens."

Protectiveness tightens my chest, and I defend her: "She had a rough time. It wasn't easy for her, that's all."

"Well, shit, Oliver, maybe that's the point," Finn says.

"Maybe she needs to know that this . . . *thing* between you isn't all-or-nothing. That you're not cutting her off completely just because she's still figuring it all out."

I grab an onion ring and give him an amused smile. "It's nice to hear you sounding so wise on the topic, Finn."

He lifts his chin to me, grinning back. "It's nice to see you guys fucking up, too, *Oliver.*"

THE SKY IS getting dark by the time I manage to wrap up at the store and get to the loft. I'm relieved to spot Lola's car almost immediately—she hasn't left for her dad's yet—and I pull into the first guest spot I see before I get out and make my way to the main door.

Their lobby is usually busy by now, the elevators full of people getting off work or headed out for the evening, but it's strangely quiet tonight. I'm alone in the lift as the floors tick up on the illuminated dial overhead, alone with my thoughts as I try to figure out exactly how to have this conversation.

I'm still not really sure what I'm going to say. I just want to see her. Maybe simply apologize again about Allison; that was shitty, especially since I was pretty sure Lola would hear about it somehow. Maybe just tell her, now that I'm calmer, how—even though it wasn't what she intended—it was brutal to be so immediately shuffled aside, a distraction, an obstacle.

I don't think we're ready to jump back in to where we were before everything melted down. I just need her to *talk* to me. As terrible as it sounds, it was good to see her so upset at Fred's because at least I could tell it was hard for her, too. I used to feel completely safe with Lola; even without talking about our feelings, I knew where I stood with her by how she sought my company, my opinion, or even just eye contact. She was the first American woman I'd never had difficulty reading. Lola's always been deliberate in her decision making, and it was no different when it came to us. So I was blindsided when she ended it sort of hysterically right after I felt things click for us.

I know I hadn't been the only one deeply in love that last night at my house.

I know I didn't imagine how profound it was in bed, all night, in the shower.

My steps are light as I move along the concrete hallway and I stop when I hear Lola's voice through the sliding steel door. I pull out my phone to check the time. I didn't see London's car outside and it's definitely late enough that she'd be at work. Harlow is supposed to be in Del Mar all day, and I might be wrong but I think Mia teaches around this time. So who could she be talking to? Her dad? Benny?

I stop just outside the door and am trying to decide if I should knock and run the risk of possibly interrupting her with someone, or whether I should come back all together, when she gets louder.

"I know," she says, with a definite edge to her voice. "And we talked about this last week. Like I told you then, I've got deadlines of my own to meet. I'm sorry you feel like this is going to cut into your schedule. But if you and Langdon would have actually engaged in this conversation every time

I attempted it in the meeting I took an entire week off to attend, you'd have heard me telling you the same thing I'm telling you now."

I feel frozen in place. I've never heard Lola talk this way to . . . well, anyone. The logical part of my brain is telling me to turn around and call her later, and that nobody ever heard *anything* they liked while eavesdropping. But a larger part of me is intrigued, dying to know who she's talking to and fascinated by this side of her.

There's a rhythmic thump on the other side of the door, the sound of her boots as she paces back and forth across the wooden kitchen floor. I'm just about to leave when the sound comes to an abrupt stop.

"No, I absolutely understand what you're saying. But what *I'm* saying is that Razor wouldn't do that. I know there's a certain feel you're going for, but it's in direct contrast to anything the main character would do."

My eyes widen and my stomach evaporates into nothing. She's talking to Austin. Holy shit. There's a minute of silence punctuated by "Uh-huh" and "Yeah," and "I see," and I'm holding my breath, wondering if she'll stick to her guns or let him turn the conversation around and manipulate her into getting what he wants. My heart is pounding so hard in my chest I briefly worry she'll be able to hear me from inside.

I didn't realize until right now how badly I needed to see her take charge of her career again. It was eating her alive. It was changing her.

"Listen," she says, and I can hear the forced calm in her

voice, "I feel like I've been really accommodating about a lot of the changes you've asked for, and like I told you, I understand where you're coming from, I do. You make movies. I don't. But what I *do* do is write stories and create characters and build worlds, and the two characters in this world are not in love with each other. There's no romance angle to play up, no sexual tension. Change that and Razor's motives and every one of his actions can be called into question. He does the things he does because he sees what she can become, not because he's in love with her."

I press my hand to the doorframe and feel my chest unwind. And despite everything that's happened between us the last few days, I'm smiling, knowing Lola is fighting for the things she loves. She can take care of herself. If Lola can handle a studio full of film executives, she can fight her way back to me.

Finn's words replay in my head and although he made a few good points, I know Lola. She might be inexperienced when it comes to relationships but when she wants something, she knows how to fight for it. She doesn't need saving. If I went in there now and tried to walk her through everything between us, I'd always wonder if she'd have come back to me on her own.

I have to believe she'll fight for us, that I'm not wrong about her. I have to believe that I want to be there for her, always, but that she doesn't need me to be.

I move away from the door and turn back toward the elevator, the sound of her voice growing fainter and fainter with each step.

Chapter SIXTEEN

Lola

IT'S BEEN SO long since I've slept in my childhood bed that it takes me a full five seconds to figure out where I am when I wake up.

It's the glass knob on my closet door that clues me in. Every single door in this house has these giant, crystal knobs. Mom bought them on a whim during one of Dad's deployments, and spent an entire weekend furiously swapping out the generic brass ones for these. They're heavy, and seem to glow like an eye at the perimeter of each door. It's one of the things I've always loved about this old Craftsman house: everything feels so sturdy, even when the human contents seem to fall apart with the slightest breeze.

A small knock sounds on my door. "Lorelei?"

"Yeah, Dad."

He pauses and then the knob turns and he pokes his head in. "I didn't hear you come in last night."

"I came to check on you but you were already sawing some pretty serious logs. I'm not surprised you didn't hear me."

He laughs stepping into the room and I see he's holding

two mugs of coffee in one hand. "I don't remember the last time you slept here."

"Me, either." I sit up and pull my hair back from my face. A glance at the clock tells me it's only six. Dad has always been an early riser from his days in the Marines; he considers this letting me sleep in.

"You didn't have to come all the way over here."

Taking the coffee from him, I say, "I wanted to. It's been a while since you liked someone as much as you liked Ellen. I want to see you happy."

Dad looks at me skeptically. "You hated her."

"Okay, maybe I didn't *like* her, but maybe I also wanted to be here for you, jerkface."

"I'm okay." He grins. "Maybe you needed a change of scenery."

I inhale the steam, and let it help wake up my brain. "Maybe."

Dad sits on the corner of my bed near my feet and sips from his mug, staring at the wall. I can sense the looming start of a conversation, the moment when he talks about Ellen, or asks me more about what's going on with work, with me. I feel restless in my skin, like I'm not sure I want to be here, but I don't really want to go home, either.

To be honest, it's how I feel about every single thing in my life right now: I want this career I've created but I want it to be smaller, simpler, more manageable. I want Oliver, but I don't want to *need* him so much. I want to be able to breathe without feeling like my chest is bound with rope but everything is dialed up to eleven right now. And most of all, I want to know how to fix what I've done. The prospect feels overwhelming.

Dad's eyes flicker to my duffel, obviously hastily packed and sitting open in the corner. "You know, we talk, but we don't *talk*," Dad starts. His voice is weak, sort of reedy, and this is always what happens when we get emotional. Neither of us knows how to do it. It's like putting a kid on a bike for the first time. They'll stare at the pedals and then look up like, *What am I supposed to do?*

That's us, talking about feelings.

"We talk almost every day," I remind him.

"I know everything you do, but not much of what you *feel*."

I groan into my coffee. "I thought we were here to talk about you and Ellen."

He ignores this. "You've been on a work bender," he guesses, turning to look at me. "I'm serious. I want to talk to you. You're a mess."

My dad knows every one of my best and worst choices. He knows every part of my story and so I always assumed he knew what I felt, too, simply because he knows *me*. But he's right: we don't dive deep into our feelings. We never have. We crack jokes and use sarcasm to make each other laugh, but we don't label emotions. I'm not sure if it makes me feel better or worse that I do the same thing with Oliver.

"Come out in the kitchen and let's have breakfast. Let's talk."

I look around the room to see where I'd strewn my things as I crashed into bed last night. "Actually, if you're sure you're fine, I should head home. I have a mountain of work." I close my eyes, swallowing down the bubble of panic already working its way up my windpipe.

"No," Dad says, and he has a sharp, level tone that I'm not sure I've heard since I was a little kid getting into trouble. It makes my brain itch, makes me long for open air and more physical distance.

I put my mug down on my bedside table and get out of bed.

"Kitchen," he says. "Ten minutes."

"YOU LOOK LIKE hell, kid."

"You said that already." I walk past him to start another pot of coffee. "I just have a lot going on with work. Tell me what happened with Ellen."

He settles on a barstool and spins in small arcs as he speaks. "Apparently she started seeing some guy she works with."

"Are you using the term *seeing* loosely?" I ask, leaning back against the counter, facing him.

"Out of respect for my daughter's delicate sensibilities, yes. More accurately, she was fucking some guy at the bar."

I wince. "Did she tell you?"

He laughs, drawing out the single word with a twist in his voice: "Nope. I saw her with him when I went to surprise her after her shift. She was leaning across the bar with her tongue halfway down his throat. They looked pretty familiar."

"Want me to punch her?"

Laughing again, he shakes his head. "I want you to make me your special eggs and tell me something good."

I turn toward the fridge, pulling out a carton of eggs and a stick of butter. "I've got nothing."

"Nothing?" he laughs. "How's Oliver?"

I shrug, grateful that I've got my back to him as I grab the bread. "We're doing about the same as you and Ellen."

"Oliver *cheated*?" he croaks.

"No," I hurry to say, immediately defensive. "Nothing like that, it's . . . it's just a long story."

"You may have noticed I'm currently minus one girl-friend. I've got time." He watches me pull two slices of bread out of the bag and rip little circles out of the middle for Eggs in a Basket, his favorite breakfast. He always watches me make this with a look of wonder on his face like there's some voodoo involved. It's adorable; the *secret* is bread and eggs cooked together in a pan. Sometimes I'm amazed he's survived living here alone.

"What's going on?" he presses. "You were here with him the other night and the two of you could barely keep your hands off each other. Now you're here, sleeping in your old bed for the first time in ages. Talk to me."

I set the eggs and bread on the counter and pull out a frying pan.

"I don't want to talk about Oliver," I tell him, and am

blindsided by the sting of tears rising up out of *nowhere*. I know Dad sees me brush them away, so I mumble, "Sorry, I'm just wiped. I'm messing everything up. The movie, the new series. Oliver. All of it."

"That doesn't sound like you, especially not with Oliver."

I laugh, lighting the burner. "Doesn't sound like me? Do you remember the first time Oliver came over? You looked at him like he was an endangered species."

"It was new," he says in his defense. "You'd never brought a guy home before."

"I panicked about work and told him I wanted some space. So, he went out with someone else," I say, and brush at my eyes. "He's mad and I guess he thought that would help." I place a pat of butter in the pan and watch it melt. "I regret saying what I did, and now I'm not sure how to fix it."

"But you just . . ." He pauses and shakes his head. "I'll admit, Lola, I may be more upset about this than about Ellen."

And now, relief. There had been a tiny piece of my brain that was stuck on the image of Dad after Mom left, and worrying he would go to that terrible place again if Ellen ever left him. Thank God he won't.

"Now, back up," he says. "What happened with work?"

"I missed a deadline. Not to mention three interviews I slept through."

Dad's eyebrows rise to the ceiling.

"I've never missed a deadline in my life and now I'm so distracted I'm turning books in late and unable to focus. . . ."

I drag the bread through the melted butter, flipping to coat both sides.

"But—and don't get upset with me here," he says, holding up his hands, "I'm just trying to understand—what does that have to do with Oliver?"

My stomach twists with the discomfort of talking this out with my dad, but I'm already sort of all-in here. "Lately I sit down to work and find myself drifting off, wondering what he's doing, or thinking about something he's said. I've been so preoccupied I thought I had another week to finish *Junebug*."

"I'm guessing you didn't."

"It's three weeks late now. I think I blamed it on what was happening with Oliver, instead of . . . I don't know . . ."

He takes a few moments to let me finish before he says gently, "Instead of you just being completely, and understandably *overwhelmed*?" in a way that suggests the root to my freak-out is really obvious to him. "Lola, baby, your life had been turned upside down—even before all of this stuff with Oliver."

I crack two eggs into the pan, adjusting the flame so they don't pop and sizzle. His easy understanding makes my eyes grow shimmery again with tears. "I know."

"You've been on more planes in the past few months than that United pilot who lives down the street."

"I know."

"Do you remember when you first started drawing?" he asks.

I think about it for a beat, wiping my eyes, and then say, "No."

"See, that's because you always have. Little doodles here and there, those coloring contests we'd get at the grocery store. But when your mom left, it changed. Instead of being something you did for fun, it was *all* you did. A compulsion. I wasn't sleeping much and I'd walk by your room in the middle of the night to find you hunched over your desk, working. It was your safe place. I wasn't always the most communicative person back then, and you put all those thoughts and things you felt or wanted to say down on the paper."

I don't say anything, watching the eggs cook as I wait for him to continue. The yolks are this brilliant, sunshine yellow. The whites so starkly bright and slowly settling into the bread. I can practically see the heat in the pan, the way the air weaves and warps over the surface.

"You needed *Razor Fish*. You needed that world you controlled, where you didn't have to say anything or risk messing it up because the characters were yours. They said the things you couldn't. They didn't care if you got something wrong. Razor wouldn't ever leave. He's your family." He pauses. "I'm sure it's scary to want someone the way you want Oliver."

I give him a blank look. "Dad."

He returns my stare, but his is softer, more knowing. Wiser. "I'm sure it's scary how overwhelming it all is. I'm sure it's scary to feel like you have to split your attention between two things you love. You don't want to lose either of them.

You don't want to leave either of them. And you've known Razor longer."

I look back to the pan, flipping the bread and egg over neatly.

"You did something dumb, and instead of Oliver being the strong, steady rock you're used to, he did what you suggested and gave you a break. He went out on a date to prove a point."

I can feel him lean closer, elbows on the counter. "Do I have the situation figured out?"

I poke at the food with the tip of the spatula, ignoring what I'm sure will be a smug smile on his face and hating the way this conversation brushes over the raw little edges left from my fight with Oliver at the bar. "Yeah."

He stands, walking to the cabinet to grab a plate. "But at least he did it when you told him to, so you weren't surprised."

I cough out an incredulous laugh. "Are you implying that I intentionally sabotaged this thing with Oliver?"

Dad shakes his head. "I'm just saying you're complicated. You've got relationship baggage and no matter how much you think you've got it all together, you don't. I always worried you'd have abandonment issues—and you do." I look up at him, mouth agape while I mentally compile a tirade for the centuries, but he continues: "Thing is, it occurs to me you're not afraid of being abandoned, Lola, you're afraid *you're* going to abandon the things you love."

Something rattles loose inside me. "Dad—"

"So you're preemptively abandoning them. Or, if I know you as well as I think I do, you don't let things get too deep in the first place."

I work to swallow past the heavy swell in my throat, easing the spatula under his breakfast and sliding the food on the plate he's holding in front of me.

A quick glance up, and my eyes snag with his.

"You aren't your mother, baby," he whispers.

My throat grows tight. "I know."

"*No,*" he says, holding the plate with one hand so he can reach forward, cup my cheek. He forces me to meet his eyes again. "Listen to me. *You aren't your mother.*"

I nod—quickly, wordlessly—blinking back tears.

"Figure out how to balance Oliver with a career you've wanted your whole life," he tells me. "Because you'll end up with neither if you think you have to choose."

———

I STEP OUT of the elevator and see London at the other end of the hall. She's in shorts and a tank top, and I can make out the ties of her bikini where they're knotted behind her neck.

With the door locked she straightens, and sees me over her shoulder. "Hey, stranger. I tried to call but you didn't answer."

"Sorry," I say. "I was at Greg's."

She nods and drops her keys into her small bag. "I figured. Your toothbrush was missing and you weren't with Oliver."

I nod, hitching my bag up my shoulder. "Ellen broke up with him so I went over to see how he was doing."

She makes a face that perfectly captures my own ambivalence; she knows I wasn't a fan. "Is he okay?"

"He's okay." I chew my lip, trying to make sure I don't sound crazy or jealous or . . . anything when I ask, "How did you know I wasn't with Oliver?"

London's dimples are the cutest dimples in the world, and when she smiles at me in easy reassurance, I want to hug her. "Oh, I ran into him at the Regal Beagle."

Oliver without me at Fred's? My heart immediately sags. "You did?"

"I went to talk to Fred about a job," London says, "and when I came out of his office, Oliver was sitting at the bar."

I avoid meeting her eyes by searching for my own keys. "Was he . . . with Finn or Ansel or anyone?"

London gives me a knowing smile as she crosses her arms and leans back against the wall. "Nope. Just sitting there by himself, all sad sack and pathetic. We hung out for a few minutes, and when I said you were out for the night, he asked if I wanted to hang out."

"Oh." The image of Oliver needing company makes me sad. I'm immediately grateful London was there, with her easy humor and ability to deflect drama. London is Drama Teflon.

Her hair is pulled back from her face and piled high on her head. She nods and the little wispy ends that have come loose move with her. "I think he just needed some company and didn't want to drink alone. Which was fine, because we all know I didn't have any plans anyway." She laughs, and then tilts her head to our apartment. "He's still here, by the way."

My skin grows hot, my eyes moving to the door. "He's *what?*"

"That boy is a lightweight, too. A couple beers and three episodes into a *Walking Dead* marathon and he was out. Still is." She points over her shoulder toward the loft. "On the couch."

I look down to the keys in my hand. I'd planned on calling Oliver when I got home, or maybe even stopping by the store, but thought I'd have a little more time to think first. "Thanks for keeping him company."

"No problem. He's a lot of fun. If he wasn't yours and I hadn't sworn off men until menopause . . ." she says, giggling as she pushes off the wall. "Anyway, I'm off."

"Beach?"

"High tide in forty-five minutes. I'll be back around dinner, though, if you want to hang out?"

I nod and turn to watch her go. "Yeah, I'll have to work tonight but I'll be here."

London takes the stairs and I wait until she's gone before I turn back to the door, finally fitting my key into the lock.

It's quiet inside, still early enough that with the curtains closed the apartment is cool and dark. I slide the door shut as quietly as I can and wait, letting my eyes adjust to the dim light. There's the soft, rhythmic sound of breathing from the couch, and I set down my things before stepping into the kitchen for a glass of water, and maybe a shot of vodka.

The recycling bin is full of empty beer bottles, and my stomach warms with a familiar longing: tipsy Oliver is too adorable, all goofy smiles and happy blue eyes. I'm actually sad I missed it. But then I remember why he was here—because he needed company—and any warm fuzzies evaporate immediately, replaced by the same twisty sensation I've had for days.

I reach for a glass and fill it with water, swallowing it down in a few icy gulps.

It's strange how familiar this feels. Oliver is on the couch again, one foot hanging off the edge, the other bent at an odd angle and tucked beneath his opposite leg. He's on his back, one arm stretched high above his head, the other resting on his chest. His shirt is askew, the thin blue fabric twisted up around his torso, leaving the majority of his lower stomach and hip bones uncovered. His glasses are on the table next to his phone, and there's a discarded blanket on the floor.

A night on the couch means he'll definitely be sore when he wakes up, and I'm not sure if I should wake him or keep staring at him. Staring is definitely easier and my eyes are hungry after days without him.

I miss his hands, how strong and greedy they are. I miss his stomach, the firm skin, soft hair. I miss his forever-long legs, his hips, his—

"Lola?" he says, and I jump, quickly blinking back up to his face.

"Hi."

He pushes a hand through his hair and looks around the

apartment. "Hey . . . sorry, I crashed here. I didn't even hear you come in."

"I'm a ninja," I say, and he gives me a wan smile. "You know you can stay over anytime."

The offer ticks between us heavily, meaning something different the longer we're silent. He rubs his eyes before bending to pick up his glasses and slide them on. Things have never been so awkward with me and Oliver until recently. It hurts. I mean, it twists something inside my ribs to have it be this stilted.

"London saw me at Fred's," he explains, bending to pull the blanket off the floor. "She asked if I wanted to hang out— just hanging out, drinks and whatnot—she was sort of insistent, actually—"

"It's okay," I cut in, fighting a smile. The sensation is like warm water in my veins: relief from hearing him needing to explain why he went home with another woman, even if it was with my roommate. "I caught her on her way to the beach. She told me that she ran into you."

He nods slowly. "You didn't come home last night."

Oh. Did he forget . . . ?

"I was at Greg's."

He winces, pinching his forehead. "Fuck, that's right."

The relief in his voice is *everything* to me. "He and Ellen split."

Looking up at me, he asks, "Is he okay?"

I nod. "He seems fine, actually. I think she was just a very available pair of fake boobs."

He laughs and scratches the back of his head, asking with more care, "Are *you* okay?"

God, that is a huge question. "Yes and no."

The silence stretches between us and I wonder if he's done holding my hand, if this is his way of forcing me to talk. "I told Austin yesterday that there were some things he couldn't change, and the romance angle was one of them."

Oliver leans forward, resting his elbows on his thighs. "And how did he take that?"

"Not very well. He said we'd talk about it more, but I have no intention of changing my mind. If they want my input, that's where I stand."

He nods. "That's good, I'm proud of you. And for what it's worth, I think you're right."

"I've also been thinking a lot. About us."

The quiet that follows is a terrifying abyss, but I just wait, needing him to show me that we can talk about this again.

"Okay," he says, finally. "What have you been thinking?"

"That I'm so, so sorry about the other night," I say. "I got scared."

He narrows his eyes and tilts his head as he studies me. He's tired and unshaven, and it doesn't look like the last few days have been very easy on him, either. "You don't have to apologize for being scared, Lola."

I shake my head. "I messed up."

Oliver stands, reaches for his jacket on the arm of the chair, and slips it on. He puts on his shoes and picks up his phone. "You've worked your entire life for this; it's understandable that you'd be protective of it. It's understandable that you wouldn't want to let it crumble."

He takes a few steps toward me, close enough that I have to tilt my chin to look up at him. "What *hurt*," he continues quietly, "was how you thought it would be easier to drop *me*. How easy it seemed for you to make that decision right there, on the spot."

Tears prick at the surface of my eyes. "It's not easier. It's awful."

He nods. "And I messed up, too," he says, eyes holding mine. "I hate that I went out with someone else, even if I had no intention of touching her."

My heart rips. "I want to go back to the way it was," I whisper, trying not to break out in a full-on sob.

"I don't think we can do that," he says, looking down at where his fingers absently reach for a strand of my hair, letting them slide down to the ends. I feel more tears burning in my throat, behind my eyes, and my chest goes tight. "I don't know that we *should*."

"Oliver, *don't*." I reach to wipe my face, but he grabs my hand, slipping his fingers between mine.

"No," he says with sweet urgency. "I *mean* I think we need to come from a more open place next time." He rubs his fingers over my palm, massaging. "I think we need to come from a place where you talk to me instead of letting me be the one to pull everything out of you."

I swallow, and then swallow again, trying to process what I think he's telling me. "You're saying we can try again?"

He looks up, stark blue eyes flicking back and forth between mine. "You want to be with me still?"

A tiny smile pulls at his mouth. "I never stopped wanting to be with you. I just needed you to figure your shit out."

I let out a snorting laugh through my tears, relief making me feel a little shaky and hysterical. I nod quickly, wiping my face, trying to get my shit together *now*, in front of him.

"Stop," he says quietly. "This isn't what I mean. I don't mean you should hide when you're emotional. I mean you should recognize that I'm the guy who wants to see how you're feeling. To hear about it."

I hiccup, managing a hoarse, "I'm feeling relieved. Very, very relieved."

He chews on his lip, watching where his thumb rubs my cheek. "Look, Lola, I meant it when I told you I don't need easy or perfect. But I do need to know . . ." He trails off, his brows pulling down as he frowns a little. "I just need to hear that you're not going to do that again. It really wrecked me."

"I won't." Even the thought makes something grow tight and brittle inside me. I reach forward to put my free hand on his chest, for grounding. I can feel the firm, steady *duh-dum-duh-dum-duh-dum* of his heart under my palm. "I couldn't."

Silence fills the space between us, and I know there's so much more to say, but I sense we aren't doing this now. Still, I know we're going to be okay because the weight of the quiet isn't suffocating. It's just Oliver + Lola again, quietly putting words together in their heads.

"How are things going with *Junebug*?" he asks, reaching

with the hand that isn't holding mine to tuck my hair behind my ear.

I sniff, looking over his shoulder. "I'm about three-quarters done."

"Do you like it?"

Wincing a little, I admit, "Not yet. But I will."

"That's a start." Oliver squeezes my hand and then lets it go. "You can text me whenever you want, or call if you need to talk something out."

I blink, not wanting him to leave yet. "Where will you be? You can hang out here if y—"

"I'll be home or at the store," he says gently.

"And me?"

I don't know what I mean.

Or I do, but I don't know how he can possibly answer that.

But as much work as I have to get done, I need *him*, too. I realize at the same time he seems to that the admission is in the question, and he leans forward with a smile.

"You'll call me every day. You'll answer my texts." He brushes his lips across mine, only once and I chase him a little when he pulls away. "If you need lunch, I'll bring it to you. If you need anything else," he says, eyes searching, "well. Call me."

"If *you* need anything, too . . ." I say, feeling like I'm tripping over every emotion rioting in my chest.

Oliver smiles. "Okay. To the writing cave you go." He gently sweeps both thumbs under my eyes, cleaning me up.

"This isn't a pause for us, it's just you needing to buckle down and finish. Managing this will be a part of our life. Sometimes I get you every night," he says, eyes moving over my face. "Sometimes I have to share you for a week or two."

He has to clean me up again because more tears fall when he says this.

Laughing, he kisses my nose, telling me, "So *go work*, Lola Love. I want my nights back."

Chapter SEVENTEEN

Lola

I HATE EVERY WORD, every panel.

The folder on my desktop labeled "Crap" has four times as many illustration files as the one labeled "Keep," but I get it. The lesson—coming at me from all angles these days—permeates my brain with the subtlety of a pickax: sometimes you need to do it all wrong before you know how to do it right.

I don't see Oliver for a day, then two, then a week goes by, and I miss him with this pitted ache. But we're talking every night, and he sees every line, every word I put down—sees the good and the bad, and the truly hideous—because I send it all to him, needing another set of eyes.

His eyes are the salve to the burn of my panic. Behind them is a man who is measured and fair, who can step outside his instinct to soothe and realize that what I really need right now is honest criticism.

The panel shows the girl, hands cupped, waiting for rain. He blocks her from the fever of the sun.

"WHAT ARE YOU doing?" he asks.

It's a bland Tuesday night, my newly negotiated deadline is two days from now, and Oliver's called to check in after having dinner with Harlow and Finn. His voice sounds gravelly, like he's lying down in bed. I picture him home alone, with his hand resting over his chest, staring up at the smooth white ceiling.

Is he dressed?

Or is he wearing nothing but his boxers?

How often does he imagine kissing me, touching me, moving into me?

"Sitting at my desk," I tell him. "Staring at a mess."

He goes quiet, and some instinct trips inside me, telling me he's running through the same list of questions.

"Did you finish the last fight scene?" he asks, at length.

I shake my head, swallowing a sip of tea before saying aloud, "Not yet. But it's getting there. Other than that one scene, I'm done." I rub my face. "Just finishing up the panels."

"I liked the ones you sent with the green backdrop." His voice is slow, lazy, feels like warm syrup poured across my skin. "Made Junebug seem more triumphant somehow, like she was surrounded by trees."

I smile. "I think so, too. I'll go back to those. My brain just feels like it needs a rest."

"Right," he says, and I hear the small grunt he makes when he sits up. "Let's see what's on."

In the background, his feet pad down the hall and I hear the rustling of the phone against his shoulder before he returns. "Your choices are *Die Hard* . . . um, *Paul Blart: Mall Cop*, or *The Matrix*."

I dunk my tea bag back into the hot water a few times. "Is that a serious question?"

He goes quiet for a beat, before his voice returns with uncertainty. "Yes?"

"*Matrix*."

I can hear his smile when he says, "It's on FX. Now: go get a beer, turn off the computer, and take two hours to watch a movie."

I hear what he's telling me: creativity needs to breathe.

"Why don't you come over and watch it with me?" I whine quietly. I haven't seen him in an eternity.

"Because I'd fuck you as soon as I set foot in the door, and you're in the cave."

My heart erupts and I imagine a sunbeam blasting from my chest. "Oh."

He laughs. "G'night, Lola Love."

I want him to tell me he loves me. I need the way his voice coils around the words, but it's my prize at the end. I know it is.

When the movie is done, I put my empty beer bottle in the recycling bin and head back to my room, finishing the scene in an hour.

I'VE ONLY PRINTED out two full copies of *Junebug*, but I can't stop touching them. I splurged on the glossy cover with black matte title font, the thick pages bursting with color in between. Color explodes from the front, too; I'm not sure whether Erik will want to keep this cover or not, but I'll fight for it: iridescent blues, greens, reds, yellows swirling around my winged June and her beloved Trip. Chaos fades behind them, promising that, no matter what story opens these pages, there is triumph inside.

I'm proud of it, and giddy to show it to Oliver.

I pull up to the curb and listen to my old car tick in the silence. Oliver's house is a small blue rambler on a tiny, square lot. His lawn is making a desperate attempt to grow, but Oliver refuses to water as much as it needs, because of the drought. The paint is faded, the walkway cracked in places. It is at once unremarkable and perfect. I can see myself here. I can see *us* here.

My heart seems to inch its way up my throat at the thought of being with him in casual, daily ways. I miss the everyday chatter. I miss, even more, the time alone with him, loving, being loved, *making* it.

Reaching for the books, I pick them up, holding them in the sun. One copy is for me. The other is for Oliver. I don't need him to tell me it's good; I know it is. But I want him to be the first to read it in full, because it's our story, too. He's seen it in pieces, but I wonder if it will sink in once he reads it from cover to cover. I recognize that's how I create, at least for now: I unload my life on pages, transporting myself to a different world and seeing how I might react, survive, thrive.

I lift the R2-D2 knocker and let it drop against the heavy wooden door. There's something reassuring about how Oliver looks when he answers: dressed in a T-shirt and jeans, hair mussed, half-eaten apple in hand. Despite everything that's happened between us in the past few weeks, he's still the only man I've ever loved.

He smiles happily when he sees me, pulling the door open wider and I wonder in a pulsing heartbeat if I could ever have been with anyone *but* him, Oliver Lore: now transparent to me, always up front and on the level.

"Hey," he says. "This is a nice surprise."

"Hi." I nearly choke on the single word.

"I didn't think I'd get you until Friday."

His gaze drifts to what I'm holding, and I hand him his copy of the book. "My ticket inside, I believe?"

His laugh is cut off halfway past his lips when he gets a good look at the cover art. My heart soars as his eyes go wide, his mouth releasing a slow "Holy shit."

The panel shows the girl, drops of rain spilling from her hands.

"I love you," I say in a quiet, desperate burst. His attention breaks from the cover, and he looks up at me, eyes round with surprise.

Oliver steps out onto the small porch, absently dropping the apple at his feet and tucking the book under his arm. His hands come up to my face, cupping my jaw, eyes searching mine.

"Yeah?" he whispers.

I nod, saying it again. "I love you."

His eyes are blue, but spotted with little swirls of green: an ocean contained in an iris. With a little smile, his lips come over mine, a sweet sweep from one side to the other as he hums, and my entire world shifts back into focus. "She loves me."

"She does." I can't take in a deep enough breath. I want more; I need him closer. I've spent the last week and a half working for this exact moment, motivated by the prospect of forgiveness delivered in a kiss.

But he only gives me one more, this one a little longer, lips parted, just the hint of his tongue.

"Take me inside," I beg, stretching to taste his neck, his jaw.

"I'll take you all night," he promises before planting one last kiss on my mouth. "But first, we talk."

Ducking inside, he grabs his coat and then takes my hand, shutting the front door behind him. In the past few days, we've talked about such surface things—the store, my book, Not-Joe, Harlow and Finn, the parade of new releases I don't have time to keep up with—but nothing heavier yet. We've wrapped up our hearts like presents, placed carefully beneath the tree.

It's three blocks to the beach, and at this odd hour there aren't any surfers dotting the water's surface. Only the occasional solitary figure walking down the beach, a dog forging the path ahead of them.

We find a quiet section of the beach, broken by only a few sets of footprints, and stand a few yards away from the ocean's edge. It's windy, and still a little cold, but I'm warm in a long-sleeved shirt and with Oliver standing only a few feet away from me. We watch the waves crash for a few cycles and then I hear him clear his throat, as if he wants to say something.

He comes at me slowly, with a smile, and it's like watching a form moving through water. Behind him the sky is a pristine cornflower; it's still getting dark so early, down the coast, toward downtown, it looks like liquid blue sky with city lights bleeding everywhere.

"This is where we talk?" I ask with a smile, and I force some bravado in my eyes; I honestly have no idea why we're at the beach and not on the couch in his living room, facing each other.

Me on his lap.

His hands beneath my shirt.

His mouth on my throat.

"I don't reckon I know what else we need to say," he says, shrugging sweetly. "But I know if we were at my place, we would have sex. And I just want to be with you for a little while first."

When I look back up at him, the way he watches me is more intimate than any kiss could be, any sex, anything. I have this wild vision of climbing him, clawing at him, trying to get inside him somehow. I just need to *connect*.

"Are you still mad at me?" I ask him, chest aching. "A little, I mean?"

He shakes his head, and I see it past a shiver of tears through my eyelashes. I don't know where they're coming from. Relief, maybe. Probably exhaustion. More than a little triumph.

He reaches across the space, brushing away the first to fall. "I'm not mad."

I nod, hoping if I keep swallowing, I won't start crying harder.

"I'm not going to leave you," he says. "You know that, right?"

A river of tears follows: the dam bursting. "It's not that."

But it is. My fear the past two weeks is at least *partly* that—that I changed his love, broke it somehow in the same way Mom broke mine—and now three feet between us isn't nearly enough to dilute my need to touch him.

"Lola," he says, stronger now. "I don't want to be without you. I'm not leaving you. Even if you're busy. Even if you're scared. Even if you're unreasonable or crazy, I won't leave."

"It's not—"

"But I need to know that *you're* not going to leave, either. I can't feel like I come second. You will always come first to me," he says. "I will never take you away from your art, but I don't ever want to feel like a *distraction* to you." He watches where his fingers brush more tears off my cheeks. "I've realized . . . I've never needed to matter to someone as much as I need to matter to you."

He steps closer, his coat pressing against my chest, and I lean into him, wrapping my arms around his waist and pressing my face into the hollow of his throat. He smells so good. Familiar, clean. He smells like books and fabric softener and the ocean. His arms come up around my shoulders, one hand on my back, the other in my hair.

"Okay?" he whispers.

"You matter," I tell him urgently. "You matter so much, Oliver. In fact, you became *everything* and it scared me. I think the idea of messing up with the books felt a little like losing someone in my family."

Oliver studies me. "I know."

"I went to a crazy place when I let it all get so bad. I guess I need to figure out how to manage that." I shrug in his arms. "I think I can. Okay? Asking for space only made it worse. So much worse."

He kisses the top of my head, nodding.

"You said you knew it would be intense like that," I remind him. "But you were right: I didn't. I haven't felt that before."

"I'm glad, though," he says. "I want to be the love of your life." Tilting his head, he reconsiders, adding, "At least, I want to be the *human* one. I can share you with Razor."

I try to laugh but my throat is tight with emotion, making my voice come out a little strangled when I ask: "Have you seen Allison again?"

"No," he says in a burst, pulling back to look at me. "*Lola*. I love you. I told you already, I don't want to be with anyone else."

An enormous knot loosens in me. "Okay. Okay." I don't know why I had to ask this, but I did. Allison *likes* him. She's an option for him.

He exhales, his chest slumping against me, and I can practically *feel* his guilt. "I know it feels like a betrayal that I did that. It feels that way to me, too."

I nod, swallowing back another sob. "Such a small one in comparison. Oliver, I'm an idiot."

He laughs. "It feels good to finally talk about this stuff, though," he says. "Feelings and things about us. And not just when we're having sex. I mean out here, on the beach."

"Okay," I say laughing, "I guess I agree it's good we didn't go inside."

"We would be making a lot of noise, but nothing intelligible," he says, bending to press his forehead to mine. Desperate need for him explodes in my blood and I feel the ache spread like a vine inside my chest.

"Oliver . . ."

But he pulls back, eyes heavy with desire, determined to keep talking. "I've wanted you for so long," he says. "Sometimes it grew so enormous it left me feeling faintly nauseous. I went on a date shortly after we met and I moved to San Diego, and was miserable. I came home and listened over and over to a voicemail you'd left me. It was this rambling monologue about how much you hate Pringles but it was really a love letter to Pringles."

I laugh; I know exactly what message he's talking about.

"I got myself off to the sound of your voice that night," he admits, then looks at me darkly.

My heart hiccups; heat spreads from my chest down down down between my legs.

"I've done very, very crude things to you in my head."

"Like what?" I ask.

"Licking, biting, fucking," he says quietly. "Coming inside you. On you. Just after you or, sometimes *before* you, making you play with me until I was hard again."

I can't catch my breath, can't remember how to swallow.

His eyes darken again when he says, "And that thing we did in the shower."

I suddenly feel very, very aware of the fact that he hasn't kissed me again since we left his house. That it's been over two weeks since he had his hands on me, and far longer since I let myself be completely lost in the feel of them.

His head angles down, lips skirting across my jaw. "Your turn for a recap."

"I had a crush on you in Vegas but sort of got over it when I thought you weren't interested," I tell him. "And then I was buried in the launch of *Razor* and just . . . mainly . . . fantasized about you."

"Yeah?"

"Yeah," I tell him. "Licking, biting, fucking. And that thing we did in the shower." He laughs without sound: a gentle rumble in his chest against me. "But then I drew you nearly naked and the fantasy wasn't enough anymore. I mean, I have approximately twenty drawings just of your dick."

"Must have been hard to find places for all that poster board," he says, smiling.

"I mean, obviously. Go life-size or go home." His hands slip into my coat, ducking under the hem of my shirt. Cool fingertips meet the warm skin of my waist, my ribs, the top swell of my breast above my bra, and our eyes meet for a few seconds until he bends, kissing me once.

"Hi, girlfriend."

I feel my smile all the way to my knees. "Hi."

"You're okay?"

I nod. "I'm so, *so* good."

Silent communication isn't new to us, but the message in his eyes is. There aren't words for what he's saying, at least not in any language we know. He's desperate but elated; his body is amped up, but it isn't about fucking for the sake of orgasm, or ironing out some twist between us with pleasure. It's this intense, perfect *connection* he feels. I know because the same thing is thrumming in me.

I slip the top button of his jeans free while his eyes hold mine, granting silent permission. The three beneath it open with only gentle coaxing. Oliver's breath comes out fast and warm on my cheek.

"What are you up to, Lorelei?"

"Touching you."

I look down, watching my hand dig into his boxers, but I can feel when he looks up and behind me at the beach, making sure we really are alone out here.

I tilt my face to his, silently asking for a kiss.

"This massive, *massive* love . . ." he murmurs into my lips, trailing off when my fingers slide over the swollen, slick head of him.

Oliver wraps his coat around us both, obscuring my bent arm, my hand when I pull him free of his boxers. His mouth opens against mine, tongue sweeping over me for tiny strokes, hands clasped together at my back to keep our cover intact. There are so many ways to declare love, to *make* love. I swallow his sounds, stroking him in this slow, nearly lazy way until he's shifting against me, until he's shaking, until his kisses stop and he's too focused on the pleasure of it. His lips go slack, simply pressed against mine, and I'm greedy for the little grunts that begin when he's close, swollen to bursting, knuckles pressed into my spine, begging. We've been nearly silent: a couple embracing, kissing on the beach in the darkness, but when something splits open in me—relief, thrill, tension unloaded—it pulls a paradoxical sob from my throat, and Oliver leans forward, coming with a low groan.

He's warm in my hand, wet and slippery, urging me with a tiny retreat of his hips to not move my fingers anymore. But I don't want to let go; I like the way it feels to share these languid kisses, hold the satisfied weight of him in my hand, cocooned in his circle of body heat with the enormous ocean crashing beside us.

Finally, I move my hand away as he buttons his pants back up, laughing at the mess. Once he's situated, he kisses my nose, unwilling to let me out of the shelter of his jacket. And with the water lapping near our feet, it feels like Oliver and I have been together for years; the quiet between us is simply too easy for this to be a fickle fling.

When I look up at him, he's staring out at the water but feels my eyes on him and turns to gaze at me, smiling. "I like it out here," he says.

"I do, too."

"I was thinking . . . you shouldn't buy a house," he says. "I've got a good one."

Excitement and unease boil together in my stomach. "I was thinking the same thing while I worked up the nerve to come to your door. But then I figured . . . one thing at a time."

His eyes smile first and it spreads down to his mouth. "One thing at a time," he repeats. "But just don't buy a house. It'll be a huge waste of money."

Stretching to kiss his chin, I suppose now is as good a time as any to tell him I honestly don't know if I ever want to be married again, I don't know how to do any of this and am pretty sure I'm going to fail . . . a lot. "But I don't—"

His fingertips come over my lips and he covers them with a small kiss. "Shh. We are not our friends. We have our own path, okay? I'm just being optimistic here."

With a smile, I pull him down with me onto the sand and we sit and watch the moonlit foam of the curling surf. Oliver tells me stories about his first year in the States. I tell him stories about the year my mother left. We grow quiet and nearly fall asleep on the beach before we wrestle each other awake and halfheartedly argue over what to get for dinner.

I'm so lucky.

I'm so lucky.

The panel shows the girl, and her boy, raised hands dusted in sand as they try to count the stars.

Acknowledgments

$\mathcal{L}$OLA'S LESSON WAS also ours: sometimes you need to do it all wrong before you know how to do it right.

We hope you had no idea that we wrote this book twice. The first time, it took us three months. It was a good book, but it wasn't Oliver and Lola's story. The second time, it took only five weeks, and we knew as we put the words on the page

this

this

this is Loliver.

Thank you to Adam Wilson for seeing it. You didn't tell us how it should be, but you knew how it shouldn't be, and—as always—you were right. Did you have to do a couple of shots before that phone call? We certainly had to do a couple shots after. But we're so glad you know these characters as well as we do, and that these books matter as much to you as they do to us.

And thank you, Holly. You called it a barnburner, you wore Ansel's corsage, and you're available and present for all of the tiny and enormous moments. It means a whole, *whole* lot, but you get that, because you're Holly.

Erin, you're there at the drop of a hat with some of the most astute and detailed feedback. It's amazing the things you find that we miss after twenty reads, but your brain is magical, and your enthusiasm is *kiiiiind* of everything to us. Thank you, thank you, thank you.

This job is an obscene amount of fun, and partly that's because we get to write about hot people doin' it, but mostly it's because we have Kristin Dwyer, Kresley Cole, Alice Clayton, and Nina Bocci keeping inappropriate humor alive. What would we do without you guys? Let us not imagine it.

Thank you to our prereaders Erin Service, Tonya Irving, Sarah J. Maas, and Alex Bracken. Yours are the opinions we need to hear, and you're *never* wrong. Marion Archer, thank you for taking the time to read it so carefully. Your feedback was not only what helped us finish this polish, but what also tied so many tiny pieces together. Thank you, Lauren Suero, for the tremendous amount of work you do every day, Jen Grant for being Team CLo since day -365, Heather Carrier for the graphics that still make us react audibly, alone, in our offices. Thank you, Caroline Layne, for the unbelievable illustrations that brought Loliver to life.

We love everyone in our Gallery family: Jen Bergstrom, Louise Burke, Carolyn Reidy, Adam Wilson, Kristin Dwyer,

Theresa Dooley, Jen Robinson, Sarah Lieberman, Liz Psaltis, Diana Velasquez, Melanie Mitzman, Paul O'Halloran, Lisa Litwack, John Vairo, Ed Schlesinger, Abby Zidle, Stephanie DeLuca, Lauren McKenna, and Trey (later, skater).

This book is dedicated to Eddie Ibrahim, the original Oliver who pushed us to embrace our fandom side, gave Lo all the gateway comics so long ago, and has long been the bedrock beneath our wiggly foundation. We adore you, Superman, we really do.

To Blondie, Dr. Mr. Shoes, Carebear, Cutest, and Ninja: best families ever.

The truth is we would be nowhere without our readers, and we would simply be two gals writing stories on our computers without bloggers. Because of all of you, we have bestselling books on shelves. We are so grateful for everything you do to support us, whether it's writing up a review or simply telling a friend to buy our book. We hope we've done right by you again, and we trust you to let us know. Thank you for being here with us.

Beautiful
SECRET

NEW YORK TIMES BESTSELLING AUTHOR
OF *BEAUTIFUL BASTARD*

A NOVEL

CHRISTINA LAUREN

NEW YORK TIMES BESTSELLING AUTHOR

GALLERY BOOKS
A Division of Simon & Schuster
A CBS COMPANY

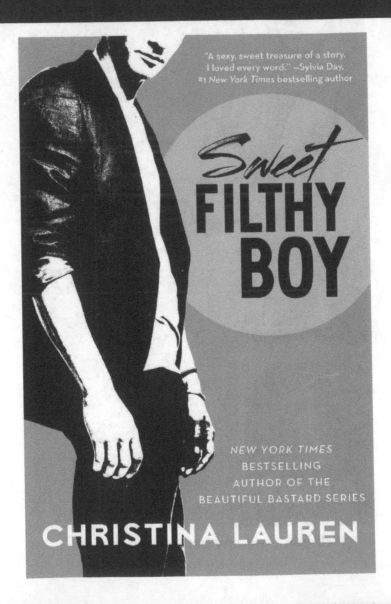